ELIZABETH LANDRY

Call Me Stewardess

A Novel

Originally published in Quebec, Canada by Libre-Expression. This book is the English translation of the first volume of a trilogy called L'Hôtesse de l'air that was previously published in French.

First edition

ISBN: 978-1-9991245-0-2

Translation by Jessica Nadeau
Editing by Courtney Vincento
Cover art by Mary Ann Smith

This book was professionally typeset on Reedsy.
Find out more at reedsy.com

For Marie-Pier,
Flight attendants don't die, they just fly higher.

Once you have tasted flight, you will forever walk the earth with your eyes turned skyward, for there you have been, and there you will always long to return.

LEONARDO DA VINCI

Chapter 1

Boston (BOS)

"Ladies and gentlemen, this is a general boarding announcement for Americair flight 762 to Rome. We now invite all passengers to please make their way to gate C14."

I must have walked through this airport a thousand times, yet it feels like I'm hearing this announcement for the very first time. It's a strange feeling. I guess I have gotten used to the sounds. It's as if they have morphed into a soft, barely noticeable hum. Today, though, is slightly different; I hear everything. From the soft-spoken whispers to the high-pitched screams.

In less than half an hour, I'll be on my way to Rome. And I am nervous, too nervous.

When I'm working, I don't notice the announcements. I'm already on board, waiting for the passengers to arrive, and I'm definitely not sitting on one of these uncomfortable seats in the waiting area.

By the way, I'm a flight attendant. But I prefer saying that I'm a stewardess. It's a lot sexier. A flight attendant could be a man or a woman. It sounds a little too masculine to me. The word

1

stewardess is just so much prettier.

Back in the day, being a stewardess was all about not getting pregnant, never gaining weight, and serving cans of Pepsi with a smile. It used to be about being the "perfect" hostess, but good news! Things have changed. Nowadays, a stewardess, aka a flight attendant, can have babies, gain weight, and will definitely turn you down if you request a free upgrade to first class. Because now, she's the boss! Obviously.

Our job has definitely changed over time, but its mysteries surely remain. I suppose it is intriguing to passengers. Our office is about 36,000 feet up in the air, it flies at over 500 miles per hour, and is driven by two men in black who sport yellow stripes on their sleeves. Usually strangers. They talk about women and speak in technical terms that I don't understand. But the yellow stripes command respect.

On the other side of their armored cockpit door live a crew of busy bees. There are junior, senior, and veteran little bees in every crew. Depending on their seniority, they gossip, they sometimes argue, sometimes confide in one another, or they might even despise each other. Some are pretty, some not so much. Among them are licensed massage therapists, athletes, part-time businesswomen, and great cooks too. Together, they fly around in a gigantic metal tube accompanied by all kinds of people: men, women, children, seniors, deportees, prisoners, thieves. Some of them are kind and polite, while others can be grumpy, ill, nervous, or even drunk. And then there are those who seem to have checked their brain in along with their bags back at the check-in counter.

There are passengers who like to chat, among themselves of course, but with us as well. I get peppered with questions about my job. They ask, "So what's your favorite country?" and "What's the worst thing that's ever happened to you in the air?" Or they wonder, "What are the pilots like?" Then, they add an inevitable comment such as, "It must be complicated to start a family." Fascinating, isn't it?

I entertain them with tales about my work. I fill their heads with dreams. I answer their numerous questions with a smile and, sometimes, with inexplicable enthusiasm. I'll even surprise myself by lying and replying, "Wow, nobody's ever asked me this question before!" But to be honest, I rarely feel like participating in their exhaustive interviews. I already have a lot on my plate.

People seem to observe my every move as I walk up and down the aisle, which sometimes makes me feel like a circus animal. I have to hide to eat a sandwich in peace between services and I always feel like I'm under a microscope at takeoff. Some passengers pull on my skirt to get my attention, others steal the magazines from my unattended seat. So, I could certainly do without their endless questions about my work! It's about time I get a few days off and away from it all.

* * *

Tonight, I get to be a passenger. I'm accompanying John, the man I love, on a three-day layover in Italy. While I sit here waiting, he's already on board. John is a pilot. Strangely, when I accepted his invitation, I was convinced that the upcoming seventy-two hours would be the most amazing days of my life. Now, I'm not so sure anymore. Instead, I'm lost in thought; I don't want to move. Once I set foot on the aircraft, will my whole universe change?

I'd rather wait a little longer before boarding. I still have time anyway. Passengers are still lining up with their passports and boarding passes.

* * *

Working as a stewardess is so much more than what it seems. We save lives! Well, I guess I haven't saved a life yet. But that's what I'm trained for, so it would be my first task if we ended up in a plane crash, right?

Of course, I wouldn't want this to happen but, in a way, I like the idea of being the one who could make a difference between life and death. I would open the door and scream at the top of my lungs, "Jump! Slide! Move away!"

My ideal scenario? In the blink of an eye, I'd save everyone. But the truth is, nobody can predict how they would react if faced with such a stressful situation. I'd just hope for the best in myself.

There could possibly be another scenario: I'd open the door, verify that the slide has inflated, look outside, look inside the cabin, then look outside again. With a slight hesitation—one last time—I'd look at the commotion through the flames and the smoke inside. Then I'd yell: "This way! Follow me!" The perfect hero, right?

You have to admit that you've probably wanted to save the world at some point. To help the helpless or stop the bad guys. Little boys want to become firemen or police officers. Little girls dream of becoming veterinarians or teachers. I'm no exception. I want to contribute to the well-being of my fellow men and women.

In the event of an emergency, I hope with all my heart that I'd be able to participate in an evacuation. I'd love to save the day, of course. But there's another reason too. During an emergency, if a passenger doesn't quickly jump on the slide, we must push them. This is the one and only time cabin crew is authorized to push a passenger . . . how convenient!

Being a flight attendant is about caring for the passengers' safety (police officer). Then, we must make them want to come back (seductress). We serve coffee and tea (server), but also provide first-aid care (nurse) and let passengers confide in us (psychologist). And then, we might as well add to the list the containment of infectious diseases (bacteriologist). Why not!

We keep the peace (babysitter), force a smile or two (actress), and reply, "Yes sir, I understand; you are absolutely right," even if he is not. All of this to prevent incidents that could potentially put us in danger. So, just like I was saying earlier: We save lives!

Other than that?

In the winter, I fly to exotic destinations such as Jamaica, Mexico, and the Dominican Republic, and I serve Pepsi or 7UP to people named Susan, Linda, and Donald. But I spend most of my time on board the aircraft, far away from the picturesque beaches. I call those the "teaser flights." We fly three hours to Cancun, Mexico, deplane passengers, and then stay on board. I don't get to disembark with them and go work on my tan. Nope. The next step is bringing home all the burn victims who have just spent a week under the hot Mexican sun.

For a short break, while the cleaning crew gives the aircraft a quick makeover, I step outside to soak up the sun. Then it's *hasta luego*, Cancun!

Of course, some lucky ones do get to stay in the sun. The lucky ones are those with seniority. They disembark to enjoy the warmth and are immediately replaced by the other lucky ones from the week before. Just adding to the tease!

In summertime though, I can finally treat myself. I work transatlantic flights to Paris, Madrid, London, and the likes, and I always stay the night. I buy my duck confit in France and my shoes in Spain. I return from Italy with tons of Parmesan cheese, pasta, and truffle oil, and I serve red wine and fruit juice to passengers named Arnaud, Fabrizio, and Agatha.

On a side note, I must mention the universal phenomenon I have noticed when it comes to juice consumption. Every time—anytime—across the world and in every culture, the said phenomenon lives on. It drives me crazy. I'm not talking about orange or apple juice (I don't really mind serving those). In fact, I actually enjoy serving apple juice. But pouring a glass of tomato juice? Now, that's the worst. I *hate* serving tomato juice. Actually, I loathe tomato juice. And here is why:

Who drinks tomato juice at home? It's not a particularly thirst-quenching drink. We drink tomato juice when we're hungry or we order it when we don't like the soup selection in the table d'hôte. Tomato juice is not the ideal drink. It just isn't. Yet, it somehow becomes the drink of choice for air travelers. Tomato juice is like the plague. When someone orders a glass, every other passenger suddenly wants one.

I'll give you an example. If Mr. A dares to order one from his window seat, inevitably, Mr. B and Mr. C will also request one. Then, their fellow Mrs. D and Mrs. E in the next row will also want one. The ladies behind all the tomato juice drinkers will order one, just because they heard we had it on board. The word spreads like wildfire and we'll run out of tomato juice for the return flight! Thanks a lot, Mr. A.

* * *

All right. It is obvious that my hesitation about boarding this aircraft is totally stressing me out. I've been at the airport for more than an hour waiting for my flight to Rome, but I still can't decide. Should I stay or should I go?

What's wrong with me? I am a thirty-year-old woman going to Italy with the man I love. What's the problem? I should be standing right now, lining up with the other passengers, impatiently waiting to board the plane, but I can't make up my mind. I'm usually impulsive and a bit impatient, but now I'm just sitting here, waiting. I don't get it.

For days now, the anticipation of leaving for Italy has been dictating my every move. Suddenly, that feeling of eagerness has evaporated. For once, I'm actually taking the time to make a well-thought-out decision. I do not feel my usual exasperation toward passengers who walk too slowly to their seats. I am still on the fence about boarding the airplane, knowing that they might close the door any minute now. Arms crossed, I look at the passengers boarding one by one. But I give myself time to clear my head and make the right decision.

I'm obviously lost in my own little world. I've been watching so many men and women handing over their boarding passes to the gate agent. I've even counted them! I need more time but the last thing I want to hear is my name called on the public announcement system: "Attention, please. Final call. Ms. Scarlett Lambert, please make your way to gate C14 immediately. Final call." I wouldn't want to be that indecisive and the line is getting shorter now, so I have to make up my mind: to board or not to board.

I may be impatient by nature, yet I still enjoy being the last one to board. The best way for me to calm my nerves is to stay put. Besides, I hate waiting in line, or what actually feels like we're standing still. I know that people are moving ahead, but it's never fast enough for me.

What is my ideal boarding speed? It's hard to tell, but it rarely happens. Probably due to the many factors to be considered. For example, on a scale of one to ten, boarding speed will vary depending on the type of aircraft, the number of passengers, children and elderly, and, ultimately, on their nationality. The perfect score is always awarded to the Japanese. They consistently score a ten. If I were a passenger on that flight, I'd line up behind them without hesitation. However, replace the Japanese with Italians and the score plummets. Big time.

When I work on a flight to Italy, I have time to redo my makeup, enjoy a cup of coffee in the back galley with a colleague, and read the last chapter of a super thick *New York Times* bestseller, all during boarding.

A flight full of Italians would rarely score higher than five out of ten. Going faster is impossible. They've got the entire *famiglia* on board! They probably just ran into so-and-so's *padrino* in the waiting area, or so-and-so's *mamma* in the duty-free boutique. They just can't help it; they need the gossip. Until the very last moment, they have to catch up. And that very last moment is when they finally reach their seat.

I could intervene to try and speed up the boarding process, but even if I tried my best, I'd risk an intervention from another member of the family, who would reply something completely incomprehensible while dramatically expressing themselves with their arms. All hell would break loose. I prefer working impatiently on my patience instead. One more reason to wait here on this bench and continue to think.

I won't budge until the gate agent makes the final boarding call. That's when I'll have to make a decision, which I believe is pretty soon. When I was packing my bags this morning, I was so sure of myself. Now I feel the complete opposite.

One step at a time, I finally make my way to the boarding gate. "Thank you," says the gate agent. "Have a nice flight!" for the hundredth time.

Wow, she's in a good mood. She must be new to the job. I give her two months, tops. Maybe more like two weeks. Once November comes around and people start flocking to warmer destinations, she'll hand out their boarding passes, flash her brightest smile, wish them a lovely vacation, and suddenly a paunchy man who's clearly had too much to drink will say: "Hey, missy! I said I wanted a window seat and you gave me a middle seat! Me and my girlfriend aren't even sitting together!" Smacking her bubble gum, his girlfriend will say, "Never again, Americair. Never again, man." Little Miss Sunshine will lose that smile pretty quickly. I guarantee it.

* * *

Instead of stalling for time here in the waiting room, I should be thinking about the choice I'm about to make. Why am I hesitating? The man I love wants to spend a few days together in Rome. I should just go along with it, but I still have my doubts. If I board this plane, my life will never be the same. Haven't I desired this man since the day I first laid eyes on him, though?

A day I'll never forget . . .

Chapter 2

Boston (BOS) – San José (SJO)

Eighteen months earlier

There is nothing more satisfying than being tucked under warm flannel sheets on a cold February night. It's an undeniably cozy feeling, but one that can quickly evaporate when the phone rings at four a.m. Epic dreams quickly become living nightmares!

I was on call that morning. In aviation lingo, we say "being on reserve." My role was similar to that of a spare tire: You replace the flat tire to allow the car to go on and reach its destination. Each type of aircraft requires a minimum number of cabin crew on board. Therefore, if a flight attendant scheduled to operate a flight suddenly becomes ill, it is I, the low-seniority flight attendant, who is called to the rescue. I get called on short notice and must rush to the airport. No time to lounge in my big comfy bed. And this is precisely why I wasn't too happy when I heard my phone's ringtone reverberate around the cold silence of my room.

Funny how life can change in a split second. I had been

a flight attendant for over two and a half years and to tell you the truth, every cold winter morning the phone rings, the initial excitement I used to feel on my first flights completely disappears.

I had been so excited for my very first flight; my good friend Becky had also been hired as a flight attendant and we had just moved in together in Boston. To save money, after our initial training we had decided to move in together and had even taken in another colleague of ours, Rupert, who is now a great friend. A new apartment, new roommates, a new job! I was stoked! To top it all off, I had flown off to London on a warm summer afternoon. It had nothing to do with what I was about to go through that morning, picking up that damned phone.

I must admit that things had not changed much for me since my first day as a flight attendant. I was still single and still living with Rupert and Becky, in the same apartment. I was still with Americair, except now was winter and I had just been woken up from a nice deep sleep. I knew it was them, *crew sked*. My frenemy, who would most likely send me off to Mexico and back, as opposed to an overnight in London.

On that day, crew sked could be my worst enemy. Simply put, the Crew Scheduling Department—crew sked— is the department looking after crews. And they had the power to send me to either Paris or Fort Lauderdale, so I was better off trying to be their friend. But who's friend exactly, you might ask?

When flight attendants call in sick, crew sked is in charge of replacing them with another flight attendant. Crew sked also books our hotel rooms when we must spend the night overseas. They call us in Paris to inform us that our aircraft is arriving late, or that they've found my wallet at the airport and are kindly sending it to my hotel. Crew sked has the final say on whether I get to fly to Athens on a four-day layover or to Orlando for a return trip on a plane full of rowdy kids.

Before picking up the phone, I crossed my fingers and quickly wished for the best. Anything was possible seeing as I had just turned twenty-nine; maybe they knew my birthday had just gone by and would assign me to a flight down south, where I would sleep under the tropical sun. The best gift ever! But no matter the destination or the time it was, I had to pick up; I was on duty after all. Still in between dreams, I reached an arm out from under the covers, through the air that had gotten significantly colder in my room, and picked up the phone.

"Hello?

I tried to make myself sound a little less sleepy than I actually was.

"Good morning, may I speak with Scarlett Lambert, please?"

Crew scheduling had to, first and foremost, make sure they were talking to the right person.

"Yes, speaking," I answered.

"Hello, Scarlett, this is Nancy from Crew Scheduling."

Nancy spoke softly, as if not wanting to surge me out of my sleep too abruptly. Or maybe she felt bad about waking me up so early. Regardless, the damage was done, and I hoped she would quickly let me know where I was headed.

"I'm going to need you this morning for a return flight to San José. Takeoff is at seven o'clock, landing tonight at six forty-five. You're working the flight there, and deadheading back."

"Okay, thanks. Bye."

That was the extent of the conversation. I'm not one to ask people to repeat themselves and I had all the information I needed anyway. I knew I had to be at the aircraft by six o'clock, exactly one hour before takeoff, and that I'd be back home tonight. Therefore, I would only bring my small suitcase (carry-on), with a packed lunch to avoid the airplane meals, which are full of sodium, a great source of cellulite. Since I was only working the flight from Boston to San José, Costa Rica, I would wear my uniform and bring a change of comfortable clothes for the return flight; I was *deadheading* back.

The flight I had been assigned to was far from a nice twenty-four hours in Punta Cana, but deadheading back wasn't so bad at all. Crew sked must assign two different crews to operate return flights to Costa Rica as otherwise the workday would be way too long for one single crew to handle. So, there is one team operating outbound and another one operating inbound. While the first crew is hard at work, the second crew can sit back and relax. They'll only work on the way back, which is when the first crew, who looked after the aircraft on the way to San José, can in turn get changed and become simple passengers.

Anyhow, whether we fly as passengers on the outbound or the inbound flight, or even to another destination for work, we call it a "deadhead." Literally, I guess, I'm coming back from Costa Rica with a "dead head." My brain will be switched off so that I can enjoy a movie or a glass of wine, seeing as I won't be operating. I will become a simple passenger. In my opinion, it's much better to come back as a passenger than to leave as passenger on a five-hour flight and have to operate the return portion. I silently thanked crew sked.

* * *

After answering the call, I had to get up if I wanted to have enough time to get ready properly, without rushing. Normally, when I am alone in the apartment, I like to put some music on to wake up, even if it's only four a.m. That day, however, I had no choice but to remain silent. Rupert and Becky were asleep in their bedrooms, right next to the main room. Becky had a couple of days off since she had just come back from a series of flights the night before. As for Rupert, he was also on reserve but they hadn't called him yet. And I thought it was better that way . . .

I jumped out of my bed as fast as I could and picked up my bathrobe. It was so cold in the apartment; my body was about to suffer a drastic temperature drop. I had to get into the shower right away or I'd be frozen for the rest of the day. Why was it so cold! I thought I had turned up the heat before going to bed. Rupert must have messed with the thermostat again. Even after living together for so long, he kept telling me the heat was on too high and our electricity bill was too expensive. Right then, while I was uselessly pondering on the heating situation, Rupert appeared in the living room. I was surprised to see him get up at this time.

"Aren't you sleeping, Rupert?" I asked him, still half asleep myself.

"Crew sked just called me," he answered, scratching his head. "They gave me a flight."

His hair was a mess and his eyes were still half shut. Bare chested, without a hint of a shiver, he pulled up his boxers and watched me enter the bathroom. I couldn't wait to get in the shower but I was also curious to know where he was headed.

"Where are you going?" I whispered.

"I'm just going to San José and back, but at least I'm deadheading back" he answered, without a trace of excitement.

14

He was disappointed and I could relate. Just like me, he would have preferred to be sent off to Punta Cana and dance the night away at the hotel club. Obviously, I would have enjoyed going out dancing with him, but I know Rupert would have preferred to sleep in the Dominican Republic not to have a blast with his roommate, but to meet up with the handsome flight attendants recently arrived from Europe and settling in at the resort. Rupert does like to fool around, but he's always discreet about it. He prefers spending time with men from other airlines instead of conquering Americair flight attendants. At least rumors of his adventures don't go around the company, but around the world instead. Nothing less. Rupert seemed even less thrilled than me about going to San José. In seeing him, I took it upon myself to cheer him up.

"Hey, don't be so disappointed! I'm coming with you and we'll get to chill together on the way back."

I tried to sound happy about flying with my friend but to be honest, I was a little nervous about being on his crew. Everything happens to Rupert at work; he has the worst luck. Either the plane is delayed, his luggage lost, or a passenger falls seriously ill and the aircraft is diverted for a medical emergency landing. And much more. Of all the flight attendants at Americair, none has had half as many misadventures as Rupert has had in two and half years.

A few months before, he was called on a flight to Frankfurt, Germany. He wasn't originally part of the crew but a flight attendant called in sick at the last minute, so crew sked called Rupert-the-Jinx. The flight was due to take off at around nine p.m. They had just finished boarding and were ready to leave when the man filling up the water tanks hit the plane's fuselage with his truck. This created a little bump, which could not be ignored. The captain was made aware and he had no choice but to delay the flight in order to get the bump repaired. The part was easily replaceable so the delay was only an hour, but I am certain that if Rupert hadn't been on board, the truck would never have gotten so close to the fuselage.

But that's not all, there's more to the story. The aircraft took off for Germany and landed without incident. Rupert spent twenty-four hours there, just enough time for a nap and a walk through the city. He went out for dinner with the crew to a small restaurant near the hotel and went to bed early to make up for the night before.

The next day, the crew got on the aircraft that had just landed in Frankfurt. The passengers boarded and they all took off for the US. About an hour after passing the Irish coast, some 36,000 feet in the air, right over the middle of the Atlantic Ocean, a woman came to the back of the aircraft where Rupert was busy setting up the meal carts. She fell into his arms, unconscious. After lying her down on the floor, he raised her legs to help her regain consciousness. When someone faints, this technique usually works 99 percent of the time, but that day, the lady did not regain consciousness. The situation made Rupert quite uncomfortable. He asked another flight attendant for help and immediately called the head flight attendant, known as the chief purser. In a matter of minutes, the situation deteriorated and the woman stopped breathing. There was no doctor on board. The closest airport was now way too far and so there was no point in heading that way. They had to act fast. One flight attendant began performing CPR. The oxygen and defibrillator were taken out. But they were unsuccessful; the woman passed away. As there was nothing else the crew could do, the aircraft continued on its trajectory to the US. The woman was carefully placed on one of the crew seats with an oxygen mask covering her face, looking like an ill lady. The crew resumed the cabin service for the six remaining hours, as if nothing had happened. Thankfully, none of the passengers noticed a thing.

When they landed in Boston, the emergency personnel came in to retrieve the woman's body. Since she had been in a seated position for many hours, her arms and legs had stiffened. The paramedics had to break the articulations in her legs in order to fit her body onto the stretcher. Rupert came back traumatized. Even I was in shock. The jinx had struck hard.

* * *

I wasn't so thrilled to fly with Rupert, and that was the main reason why. Nevertheless, I couldn't do anything about it, so I tried the best I could not to worry and jumped in the shower.

When the hot water finally hit my skin, I started day-dreaming, per usual. When I'm half asleep and have a shower, I start thinking too much or, should I say, I start speculating. I start questioning myself. If I only listened to thoughts then I would turn my life around. I would leave for faraway adventures, far from my responsibilities. But then an hour later, once I'm at the airport, I always find peace and realize that I love my job and that it suits me in every way. That morning, the same thoughts were running through my mind.

Scarlett, is this really what you want in life, to get up at four a.m. and feel sick to your stomach for hours?

Scarlett, you're twenty-nine and still single! You live with a twenty-five-year-old gay guy who skips from one guy to the next and a twenty-six-year-old girl who isn't ready to settle down either. Surely, they won't be the ones helping you find Mr. Right. What are you doing here?

Scarlett, come on, stop overthinking. You know you'll be all right once you set foot on the aircraft. You'll be happy again, like a fish in water.

I was better off keeping my imagination quiet. Anyway, after braving the winter cold in my car and the black of the night on the road, I'd smile again as soon as I got to the airport. I chased the bad thoughts away and focused on getting ready instead, which was much more productive.

I freed the bathroom for Rupert to use and headed back to my room to get dressed. I was never the kind of girl who would take hours to do her hair and makeup. I kept my routine simple to save time, especially when it was four a.m. and we had to get out of the apartment as quickly as possible.

I pulled my long, brown hair up in a bun with the help of the "donut" I had purchased in England the summer before. This little item called a "donut" is absolutely wonderful and has become THE accessory in every stewardess's beauty kit. To use it, you put your ponytail through the middle and pin your hair around it. Your bun then looks fuller and perfectly sleek.

Next step, I proceeded to apply black eyeliner on my eyelids and used the mascara I purchased at the airport's duty-free boutique. I slipped into my favorite piece of uniform: my black jumper. Since my white shirt was hidden underneath, it could survive damage from potential spillage or incidents. There's another reason I love this piece of uniform: It makes my backside look *really* good.

Come on! I'm no fool. I know uniforms ignite people's fantasies. I would challenge anyone to say otherwise. I'll always remember Becky's answer when I asked her what her thoughts were on our future uniform during our initial training: "I don't care what it looks like, a flight attendant uniform is always sexy and I'll certainly take advantage of it. Pilots aren't afraid to use that privilege, and I won't be either!"

She was right, girls fall head over heels when they come across pilots proudly walking around, showing off the stripes on their shoulders. Why couldn't we do the same to men with our smile and attractive behind? Either way, Becky makes the most of it. She's always arm in arm with rich men who are taking her around yachts in Nice or fancy four-Michelin-star restaurants.

Becky is a professional enchantress with or without her uniform, but not me. I only know that the uniform looks good on me and that morning I put it on thinking of nothing more than to make it to the aircraft on time. In fact, we had to go. I carefully tied my scarf around my neck and applied the final touch, one that would turn me into a compelling flight attendant: a pink lipstick called *Enchanted*. Who would I be hypnotizing today? Only the upcoming events could tell.

Chapter 3

San José (SJO), Costa Rica

We had just landed in Costa Rica. The flight had gone relatively well, apart from a rough landing in San José and our late arrival at the aircraft that morning. As Rupert and I were called in for work at the last minute, we arrived late at the airport and missed the captain's briefing. Justin, our chief purser, dutifully proceeded to give us a summary of the flight conditions when we finally made it to the gate. That is also where we were informed that there was possible turbulence in the first hour or so of the flight, which was due to last a total of five hours and fifteen minutes. And since we were the last ones to arrive, we did not get to choose our work positions on the plane in the usual order of seniority. So, we had to put up with what was left.

Rupert was to take care of boarding, an unfortunate position due to all the "hellos" and "goodbyes" it implied. And I was to look after the back galley, the kitchen area where the meal and drinks service carts are located.

During the flight, Rupert and I still had some time to chat a little and he was more than happy to provide me with juicy details on the couple crew members I didn't know. I must say that even though Rupert always brings bad luck on a flight, he is the best gossiper in the company. A quick catch-up with him before a flight allows me to always know who I am about to deal with.

"All right, Rupert, give me the gossip."

"Hm, all these pretty flight attendants have a good reputation, apart maybe from Suzie, who slept with half the company," he casually said.

"Suzie? Which one is that?"

"She's the one who was complaining at the beginning of the flight because it was too hot in the cabin, and then again when we took off, and again when we started the drinks service."

"Ah right, I see the one. She slept with everyone? Pilots, I imagine?"

"What do you think? The worst part is they all had girlfriends."

"I can't believe it! How can a girl do that again and again without having the slightest thought for the poor girlfriends? If us girls had each other's backs and only slept with single guys, no one would ever get cheated on!"

"Come on, Scarlett, don't try to convince me that you've never slept with a pilot even though he was in a relationship? Suzie probably isn't the first, nor the last. You girls find them all attractive even when they're ugly."

"Rupert! We've lived together for almost three years, you should know by now that I've never done such a thing," I said, insulted by his assumption.

"Actually, didn't you kiss two or three of them when we first started?"

"Yeah but I just kissed them because I was drunk and only found out after the fact that they had girlfriends. Anyway, today

I know the drill so there's no chance I'll sleep with one of these pretentious pilots."

Rupert seemed proud of my answer. He was probably happy that I wasn't like that Suzie-Flirt-With-Every-Pilot girl. He could have contented himself with just a smile but instead asked me one more question.

"And if you were to fall in love with one of them, would you still think they're so pretentious?"

"Well, there's absolutely no chance of that happening!" I stated, absolutely convinced of my answer.

* * *

After our quick chat, I immediately returned to work. The closer we were getting to our destination the more I was starting to think that maybe Rupert-the-Jinx would contain his bad omen on our plane. I was already delighted at the thought. Perhaps my own energy had neutralized the spell?

Once on our descent, the captain advised us that the winds in Costa Rica were slight crosswinds and that chances were the landing would be rough. We put all the carts away and proceeded to our final cabin checks in order to take a seat as quickly as possible.

I must admit that never in my short flying experience had I ever felt an aircraft tail sway so much. In fact, I was pretty sure the swaying was unusual since the supposedly experienced colleague sitting next to me seemed very stressed out. I would have thought that after some fifteen years of flying she'd be calmer than I, but turns out she was the anxious one between the two of us.

Well, we can never really know how we'll react in an emergency situation until we actually go through one. But I imagine that with experience, we at least understand the consequences that a sway like today's can cause. To me, this rocking in the sky was nothing more than strong winds pushing sideways on my cabin. It didn't freak me out. I even enjoyed it . . . for the time being, anyway.

Nevertheless, my attitude drastically changed when we made our final approach and got closer to the ground. I was getting increasingly scared as I realized the sway was turning out to be rather extreme. Having seen various Internet videos of very difficult landings in similar crosswinds, I could easily picture the position of the plane. The nose of the aircraft would not be facing the landing strip at all, but only partially, facing the wind instead. From my tiny window, the tail also appeared to be off the runway. I knew that at the last minute, the pilot would straighten everything up and would land this big bird properly. Still, the constant rocking was starting to make me feel nauseous. I didn't dare imagine the passengers' state: definitely nausea and probably a bit of vomiting too.

I focused on remaining calm and latched on to my jump seat, the folding seat reserved for flight attendants. My colleague, on her end, was quite comical with the "Ohs" and "Ahs" she let out between each gust of wind. It is worth noting that we were sitting at the back, in the tail, and therefore it was normal to feel the impact of the winds more strongly. When the wheels finally touched the ground abruptly, or violently, to say the least, we were speechless. Silence reigned over the cabin. There was none of the usual handclapping. From my window, I could see the edges of the runway getting farther then closer then farther again; I even caught a glimpse of the neighboring grass. I did not like what was going on. Would we slip off the runway? The tail moved way too much to my liking. A second passed. Then two. Then three. Maybe more, who knows, it felt like an eternity. At last, the swaying stopped. The plane was straight again. My colleague caught her breath, and so did I. Was it Rupert's curse that had shaken us up? Most likely. And I hoped it would end there.

* * *

Once all the passengers had disembarked, I could finally take off my uniform, get changed, and sit peacefully like any other passenger on the plane. I was going to relax and watch a movie. Now that my work day was, to some extent, over, I was going to make the most of this deadhead and have a nice glass of wine. I proceeded to the first class lavatories to get changed. I hurriedly made my way to the front as I never use the toilets at the back of the plane, especially not after a flight over five hours long. I'd rather do my business in cleaner lavatories and unfortunately for the economy class, the first class ones most often meet my criteria. To be honest, they are in better shape solely because they've been used by only fifteen people or so, not because the people who have access to them are any cleaner.

Once at the front, I caught a glimpse of the first officer by the steps. He was getting some fresh air. He must have been, with his thick-soled shoes, a mere five feet four inches tall, and he stood up straight, chest lifted. I estimated him to be about twenty-five years old, at most. As he seemed quite young and not very experienced, I assumed he must have been the one landing, seeing as the plane swayed much more than usual. I got closer to inquire.

"Wow! We were really shaken up earlier. Who landed?" I asked, as sympathetic as possible.

If it was him, I was hoping he would tell me and admit it had been a rough landing.

"What kind of question is this! You can't ask that!" he barked arrogantly. "Didn't you see the winds outside?"

"Exactly. I did feel the winds, which is why I'm asking you. I would have liked to know what happened."

I had no need to talk to him any further. It was obvious he was the one who had landed the plane. Otherwise, he wouldn't have overreacted. Once again, I had proof of the pilots' big egos. Insulted by my comment, he turned his back to show our conversation was over. I turned around as well. I couldn't care less about his attitude and so I went and got changed in the lavatories.

When I came out, the captain, who I had not met due to my late arrival that morning, asked the whole crew to come to the front so that he could provide some explanation for the rocky landing. I sat on one of the passenger seats and listened.

"First of all, I'd like to apologize to those in the back who got shaken up. The winds were extremely strong and unfortunately we couldn't land any differently," he kindly explained.

I admit that I was surprised by his humility. Pilots who had the courage to apologize this way were very scarce. Perhaps I had been too quick to judge. This captain made me have second thoughts about what I had previously said of pretentious pilots. Obviously, today, there was an exception.

After he explained the technicalities of crosswinds, he wished us a nice flight and returned to his cockpit. I had never see him before. To my own astonishment, he intrigued me and I had

25

no idea why. Of course, he had been kind enough to provide us with some explanations, but there was something else that kept me guessing. He seemed a bit shy and discreet. Actually, he appeared inaccessible, and that was intriguing.

* * *

During the return flight, Rupert chatted away for an hour drinking a glass of red wine. To avoid getting drunk too quickly, he was casually sipping the delicious liquid. It was always the same. If he drank just two glasses of wine he got wobbly. So, I was happy to let him slowly sip away.

As I was exhausted and knew that after just one glass of wine I'd quickly fall asleep, I immediately took the opportunity to ask Rupert if he knew the captain we were flying with.

"No, curiously, I've never heard of him."

His answer surprised me because my loyal friend knew everything about everyone, even if that "everyone" was nobody.

"What's his name?" I asked.

"John Ross. Anyway, that's what's written on the summary of our flight itinerary. Why? What do you see in him? He's got nothing very impressive apart from a nice smile."

"I don't see anything special in him," I answered, trying to hide my agenda. "I was just wondering."

I refused to admit my attraction for the man. He was handsome, of course, but something else intrigued me. Was it his inaccessible man attitude, or maybe his shy smile? I couldn't quite put my finger on it. Either way, I was not going to admit it to Rupert, especially after our earlier discussion about pilots. Our gossiping ended there. I didn't mind. I wanted to keep to myself the fact that, to my astonishment, I was interested in today's flight's captain. Me! Oh dear! I had to get some rest.

* * *

Upon arrival at the airport, Rupert and I quickly went through customs and made our way to the bus that would take us to the employee parking lot. I was glad that we had made it home relatively smoothly. *Flying with Rupert isn't that bad after all!* I thought.

While we were waiting outside, I took the opportunity to listen to my voicemails.

The first message was from Becky, telling me that Rachel had invited us and our friend Paige over for dinner. Becky, aware that I'd be exhausted after a flight, suggested they come over to our place instead. However, what she made sure not to tell Rachel is that I would have refused to drive all the way to her house knowing I'd hear her baby cry all night. After a flight, I am bound to need a minimum of silence.

Let's face it, babies on a plane cry. They're unable to move around, they feel their parents' nervousness, and their ears hurt. Their cries resonate throughout the cabin like little roaring lions and anyone wishing to run away must face the fact that there is nowhere to go. The golden rule is to patiently, impatiently, put up with it. At the end of the day, babies are babies. We can't get upset if they roar a bit during the descent because of the pressure on their eardrums. Still, after a flight, I much prefer silence. Becky, being a flight attendant as well, completely understands the after-flight-state and therefore had the great idea to invite the girls over to our apartment instead.

It was pointless to confirm that I agreed with the plan since it was already six p.m. Rachel and Paige would already be at the apartment. I warned Rupert that there would be women at his place tonight. He simply nodded, not bothered with me since he had other plans for the night, with his ex. I listened to the second voicemail.

Per usual, my mother had had a very quick encounter with my answering machine. As she didn't like "talking to a machine," she refused to leave proper messages. She either didn't leave any at all and called again and again until I answered or, if she was having a good day, she left a short, bone-chilling message. The sort that sounded like: "Someone is dead, call me!"

My mom probably doesn't realize that leaving for work and not being able to be there if something happens to a close family member is one of my biggest fears. But if she knew, would she be more careful? Once again, her tone was ambiguous:

"Scarlett! (no "Hi, love," or "Hello, Scarlett; just "Scarlett"). It's your mother. Call me when you get this!"

It wasn't the right time to return her call but, once again, she had me worried. Since the bus wasn't there yet, I called her back.

"Hello?"

"Hi, Mom, it's me."

"Where were you?" she asked, totally freaked out, as if she didn't know I was a flight attendant and would often leave at the last minute.

"I was in Costa Rica today mom."

"Oh, lucky you!" she squealed.

"Mom, I didn't stay there. It was a return flight. I didn't see anything."

"Ah, still, lucky!"

Obviously, she didn't care to understand the reality of my job, so I simply agreed.

"Mom, was there something urgent you needed to tell me? Because I just arrived and I have to hang up soon."

"Oh no, I just wanted to chat."

"All right, then, I'll call you back tomorrow, okay?"

"By the way, your uncle Albert left your aunt Patricia for another woman," she continued, totally ignoring my attempt to end the conversation. "Your father and I can't get over it. After everything she's done for him. Their kids had just left home. She was just getting a breather when he decided to leave her for another one. How cold-hearted!"

Mom passionately continued her monologue about Uncle Albert and Aunty Patricia. She was furious. She didn't need to go on as I already knew what she thought of divorce. At that moment, I didn't have the energy to spend on trying to understand the reason for the sad split-up, nor for listening to my mom's negative opinion of my uncle. Again, I tried to end the conversation.

"You're right, Mom, it's a horrible story. But as I said, I don't have time to chat right now. I'll call you again tomorrow."

"Okay, kiddo, talk to you tomorrow, then."

Mom, probably disappointed not to be able to talk to me any longer, put on her sheepish voice. But at least she no longer sounded freaked out, and I lost all trace of my previous anxiety. I hung up and took the opportunity to look through emails on my iPhone. All of a sudden, as I was pressing the app icon, I glanced at the rest of the crew walking toward the bus stop. Among them was my captain. Seeing him, I instinctively repeated his name in my head: "John Ross." He intrigued me and I couldn't believe I was attracted to him. A pilot! It was impossible! I got ahold of myself and we all boarded the bus.

My handsome captain sat at the back, alone and lost in his thoughts. Rupert was talking to a colleague so I took advantage of the situation and discreetly observed, from the corner of my eye, what I was so strangely attracted to. I hoped our eyes would meet, even though I wasn't able to hold that dark and deep gaze of his. He was truly making me uneasy without even realizing it. He was definitely unaware, and I went completely unnoticed. All through the ride, he did not look at me once. Nothing. Nada. *Rien.* How frustrating!

I, who just a few hours before had sworn to never date a pilot, was now trying to get a pilot's attention, and he didn't even notice. I was offended.

When we arrived at the parking lot, he got up to get off at the first stop. He turned to face the crew, me included, and wished us a safe trip home. I would have liked him to personally tell me, "Good-bye, Scarlett," but I had to keep it real: His good-byes were not directed at me. Apparently, my *Enchanted* lipstick did not work its magic today. Although, it had faded long ago . . .

Chapter 4

Boston (BOS) – Arrival from San José (SJO)

When I get home after a flight, even if I have guests over, I have to jump in the shower right away. A shower is essential well before my friends' welcome hugs and my precious glass of wine. Rupert doesn't have a choice, he must wait his turn and get out of my way.

Therefore, when I got home, I quickly said hi to my friends and mentioned that proper greetings would have to wait. They probably didn't mind as airplane smell soaks into the skin and is nothing short of disgusting. Throughout the years, it has become one of the smells I despise the most in the whole wide world. And I'm barely exaggerating. More than just one word is necessary to explain the stench. In fact, my hair, my clothes, and my skin reek of old dust that has been soaking up the smells of burnt meals, vomit, and sweaty feet, mixed with a few of the many farts that the passengers let out throughout the flight. Far from appetizing! So, quick, in the shower!

A few minutes later, fresh and squeaky clean, I put on some comfy clothes and met up with my friends. Becky walked up to me with a glass of wine. She looked, as always, very pretty and stylish, with her short hair nicely fashioned. She was wearing the long earrings made by the Maasais she had met during an African safari that she went on with one of her wealthy conquests.

"Here ,Scarlett. Take a big sip. It'll help you unwind. How was your day?"

"It went well. I'll tell you all about it, but first I'll greet the girls," I said, then looked at Paige and Rachel. "It's so nice of you to have come all the way here tonight."

It was important to show my appreciation because ever since Paige had a little girl, who was nearly two years old now, and Rachel had a newborn who was now almost ten months old, it was always up to us to make the journey. As a matter of fact, I was quite surprised they had even accepted the invitation.

"Who's looking after the kids tonight?" I asked.

"Well, the guys. They went out together last week and owed us one," Paige explained with a smile.

"That's good, then! Let's make the most of it while we can!"

Paige and Rachel had become very close since they both had families of their own. Becky and I were also closer since we had started working in aviation. Our realities were different so it only made sense that we got along according to our respective interests. However, I never suspected our paths would go in such different ways after the birth of their children. I was under the impression that Paige looked down on me ever since she had become a mom. And as for Rachel, she hadn't changed too much but still, she often made little judgmental comments about my lifestyle and my single life. Becky, even though she was single and a flight attendant just like me, seemed completely removed from their equation. I knew that in some way I was different, but I didn't feel like changing and Rachel would often try and reason with me. That evening, once again, the conversation was heading that way.

"Scarlett, where did you go again today?" she asked.

"Rupert and I went to Costa Rica," I answered, feigning a bit of disgust to imply that it had not been pleasant to fly, even though I had no reason to do so.

"Ah! Costa Rica is so cool! Was the temperature warm?" Paige asked enthusiastically.

"It looked very humid but I didn't stay long. Just long enough to peek my head out the door for two minutes and then close it again, back to breathing dry pressured air," I added, somewhat sheepishly.

I had gotten used to talking this way to the girls because I always felt some sort of envy from them when it came to my work. By belittling my career, I got the impression that they didn't envy me as much and that they thought that looking after diapers and baby bottles was better than traveling all around the world. In fact, I had a strange feeling that's exactly what they were trying to prove to me.

"So, Scarlett, have you met anyone lately?" asked Paige.

"Girls, you know that if I meet someone, you'll be the first to know."

"Yeah, for sure, but don't you think that if you keep being so demanding when it comes to men you won't find anyone?" said Rachel, putting her problem-solver hat on.

"First of all, I am not looking, I let things happen on their own. And second of all, how am I being demanding, Rachel? Does not sleeping with everyone make me too demanding? Becky is also single and as far as I can see you don't blame *her* for it," I exclaimed, getting a bit agitated.

With my after-flight fatigue and my friends' long-accumulated criticism, I had the intention to finally set the record straight, tonight, right here. Right now!

"Becky is not like you, Scarlett. She meets plenty of people and always has a new date. At least she tries. You, you don't even do anything," added Rachel.

Becky, now involved in the whole story, no longer had a choice but to intervene.

"Woah, girls, I do not *try*, I'm just having fun. It's my choice to lower my standards for my own pleasure. If I was looking for the love of my life I'd probably follow some criteria as well, but it's just not the case right now. I don't understand how Scarlett looking for a minimum of chivalry or something is an issue.

"You're just twenty-six, Becky, you're younger than Scarlett and you're far from being as demanding as her. You dated a few guys who didn't open doors and they weren't idiots. We met them and they were actually quite nice," added Paige.

"And it didn't work out, did it!" Becky exclaimed, cutting off Paige.

"Calm down, Becky. We're just trying to figure out what's wrong with Scarlett," snapped Rachel.

The latter then turned toward me to continue her interrogation.

"If all you want is a gentleman, why do you still refuse to meet my handsome cousin? He opens doors and has been single for over a year," she said, clearly trying to play matchmaker.

"Because he left his wife even though they had a kid together! That's why!"

Did I really just say that? I had never expressed my opinion on the matter whenever Rachel had talked about her cousin Mark. I would simply try to avoid the subject altogether. I knew the story and didn't adhere to it. He had cheated on his wife many times with many different women. She had never had a doubt.

And then one day, he left her. And that's the reason I could never date that Mark guy. I would be the most jealous woman ever. Why would a man be faithful to a girl he barely knows when he couldn't even be faithful to the mother of his child? I had decided to keep my thoughts to myself, but Rachel was on a mission.

"Okay. For me, that's being demanding. You just turned twenty-nine, soon you'll be thirty. Men our age have a past, Scarlett. Anyway, even if you were to keep all of your mysterious criteria, how do you intend on meeting someone when you're always on the go? Is that what life is about, traveling?"

Rachel had never put me down as much as she was putting me down that night. Why was she so adamant about having me date someone, anyone? Was being single so pitiful? It must have been, because Paige settled on simply nodding along to this confrontation. Becky was beside herself, sitting straight up, her eyes ready to pop out, and her cheeks on fire. She was angry, and was probably hoping I'd end this annoying discussion once and for all.

"Okay, girls, that's enough! Mind your own business, won't you? I'm demanding! I was in a relationship for five years in case you forgot! I do not turn away good guys. I just need to meet one of them at the right time. I'm ready to wait. At least I found MY dream job and it makes me perfectly happy. At the very least I love my job. If your perfect lives filled with diapers suit you, good for you. But I don't try to lecture you, so don't you lecture me!"

I couldn't believe what my friends thought of me. They had known me for so long. They should have known that I had always loved to travel and that my life was much more fulfilling since I had become a flight attendant. How could they suggest that I was better off finding a boring job just to allow a new lover in my life?

"Chill out, Scarlett, that's not what we meant. Anyway, as far as I'm concerned, I just wanted to say that I don't believe in one great love and that sometimes it's worth giving someone a chance," Paige softly advised.

But how could I follow Paige's advice? She who had never really given anyone a chance and had met her husband eighteen years ago. They had loved each other, had become good friends, and through time had become comfortable so had simply settled. Unfortunately, love didn't seem to be part of their relationship anymore. So, I still preferred to dream of my one Great Love. I thought that, if worse came to worst, the Great Love that my future lover and I would share might become just love, normal love.

I didn't feel like trying to bring them to their senses. Paige and Rachel lived in another dimension from Becky and me. However, I still wanted to clarify the matter.

"Girls, I understand the way you see things. Rachel, you met your boyfriend online. It's one way of doing things and I admire you for it, but for me, choosing a boyfriend from a menu doesn't suit me. I don't believe in it. I found a job that I love. The man of my dreams will appear one day but I do not intend on going hunting for him just for fear of ending up alone. I remain persistent with my requirements. Sorry."

All of a sudden, they were very interested. They asked what the said requirements were. They finally seemed open] to knowing and understanding my point of view. Becky, who already knew my secret list, raised her eyebrows, urging me to unveil my big mystery. If I wanted my friends to stop judging me, maybe I had to reveal some of the selection criteria I held dear, so I continued.

"To be honest, even though you believe that being single at my age is shameful, I still believe I'm better off alone than in bad company. Since we've started working on a plane, you have no idea how much individualistic behavior Becky and I have witnessed among couples. Frankly, I wouldn't like to have to carry my baby along with all the luggage while my boyfriend easily makes his way to his seat. Just like I wouldn't like him to carry it all by himself either. A couple is a team and we should always help and be considerate of each other. On the surface, Rachel, maybe your cousin Mark is incredibly charming and opens doors, but that kind of courteousness can be learned. Just because a guy opens a door doesn't mean he's less of an individualist. What I notice are the small gestures that betray us, the ones we make unconsciously and show our true colors, such as disrespect and inconsideration for our loved one. I wonder if your cousin Mark would hand over the glass of Pepsi to his girlfriend?"

"What are you talking about?" wondered Paige.

The fact is the girls didn't know the games Becky and I sometimes put our passengers through for a bit of fun. It all began subtly, without us realizing, but then we started noticing some of the actions continuously made by the male passengers and we wanted to test to see if other men would act the same. I asked Becky to explain the simple test, assuming that if she supported the theory, Rachel and Paige might finally be open to understanding my point of view. Becky took over.

"All right, it's a test we call "The Pepsi Test for the Gentleman." Like Scarlett nicely said, we had never thought about testing our passengers but they were the ones signing up for the experiment and we took a liking to it. Now, when we both work on the same cart and a passenger meets the prerequisite, we start the observation. The theory rarely fails."

"So far, I quite like the name of your revolutionary theory, but what is it exactly?" interrupted Rachel impatiently.

"It's simple. We state that men from our generation, future candidates in Scarlett's love life, are generally less considerate toward their ladylove than older men or than Spanish, Italian, and French men, for example," stated Becky.

"It's a bit harsh for a theory but I must admit that guys our age are less likely to pick up the bill at the restaurant," mentioned Paige, who suddenly seemed to be leaning on our side.

"And how do you test your guinea pigs? I don't think Americair would be pleased to know you are making little experiments in the air," joked Rachel, who was also amused by our simple theory.

"Well first of all, we test them without them knowing. The only way to do so is while we serve them. In order to perform the experiment, we need to choose the right candidates. First, the candidate must be a man and he must be accompanied by a woman, whether she's his girlfriend, wife, or even his mistress; it doesn't matter. Then, the candidate must be seated next to that woman. He must be the one seated closer to the aisle, making his friend the one farthest away from the cabin crew. Finally, the couple must order the same drink."

"I understand all those requirements but what does Pepsi have to do with courteousness?" asked Rachel, who couldn't get her head around the whole story.

We had to clarify, so I developed further.

"Imagine you and your boyfriend are on the plane. And I'm your flight attendant. I approach with my cart and stop at your row. Your boyfriend's name is Jonathan, just like in real life. He is obviously a man, so officially meets the first criterion which states that the candidate must be a man. CRITERION #1 MET! Then, you are together on the plane. Whether you are married or common law, I don't care. He is traveling with you, that's all that matters. CRITERION #2 MET! You, Rachel, have the window seat and Jonathan is next to you, closer to the aisle. CRITERION #3 MET! When I approach with my cart to offer you a drink, I look at the both of you and ask what you'd like. You unanimously answer: two glasses of Pepsi. CRITERION #4 MET! There you go, Jonathan is eligible! Therefore, the test may occur," I proudly explained.

"What if I only drink water?" Rachel joked with a mischievous grin.

"Whether you drink water, coffee, or whatever, the point is Jonathan and you drink the same thing. Otherwise, it's disappointing but the experiment doesn't work," I rectified.

"Okay, okay, I was kidding. Go on! What horrible act will my boyfriend do?"

"This is when he will prove his true nature," I added, matter-of-factly. "After you've asked me for two glasses of Pepsi, I pour the first glass. As I am standing in the aisle, it is much easier to hand it to the person seated closest to me. Therefore, the person seated close to the aisle inevitably gets the first Pepsi, seeing as he is more accessible. Moreover, in doing so, I avoid spilling liquid on passengers. To me, it obviously makes sense, so I assume that, instinctively, everyone will understand and distribute the drinks accordingly.

"Unfortunately, it doesn't seem to be the case for everyone, and especially not for your Jonathan. I give him the first glass of Pepsi. I give it to him because he is sitting close to the aisle but also to test him. I evaluate the consideration he shows for his lovely Rachel. He undoubtedly loves you but does he really know you exist?

"Well, looks like he doesn't! Your boyfriend takes the first glass of Pepsi in his hands but doesn't pass it on to you. He keeps it for himself. That glass was meant for you, the lovely far-away lady. While Jonathan dips his lips in the ice-cold Pepsi, you still don't have anything to drink. At last, at the risk of hitting your dear lover's head, I spread my arm toward you to serve you the second Pepsi. And so there you go, your boyfriend just failed the Pepsi Test for the Gentleman. So, tell me, Rachel, would you like to be with the Jonathan I just portrayed?"

"Of course not! But my boyfriend is not like that. I find it harsh to think that if a man doesn't hand over a glass of Pepsi you won't give him a chance in love," answered Rachel, who, once again, couldn't see the big picture behind the experiment.

"Did I say that? I'm just sharing the observations that Becky and I have made. It's a silly example to show you how much men today seem to be self-centered and that is why I do not wish to waste my time on some of them. On a small scale, it's just a glass of Pepsi and it doesn't really affect anybody, but in society or in a relationship, to only think about yourself can cause big damages. I keep clear of that type of man because I am looking for love, I'm not looking to fool around with the first guy I see seated on an aisle seat."

"That test is ridiculous, Scarlett. Anyway, I love my Jonathan the way he is," she threw back.

Obviously, she didn't get it. I had just told her I chose her boyfriend as an example to help picture the situation. I suddenly no longer felt like talking. Becky noticed my withdrawal so took the opportunity to steal the show and entertained the girls with stories of her dates with millionaires.

She started by explaining how she met Damien, her wealthy

French magnate. On a layover in the City of Light, she quietly sat with a book at a Parisian café and he had simply come and sat next to her. Becky had that mischievous look about her that attracted men. Her piercing gaze and full lips had people naturally drawn to her. Damien was forty-five and very handsome. He treated her to champagne all night. They talked about anything and everything. It was pleasant, and before they parted he had offered to take her on his yacht anchored in Cannes. For Becky, this was a golden opportunity. She accepted the invitation and a few weeks later was living the dream, for a few days at least, with a stranger who happened to own a huge yacht by the Mediterranean. I admired Becky's boldness and I wasn't the only one. Paige and Rachel were totally engrossed in her story.

"Wow, Becky, I can't believe how open you are. What a story! To be open in life, that's what's important," confirmed Rachel, who was obviously giving me a hint.

"How did you know that man was nice?" asked Paige, terrorized. "You could have been raped or killed!"

"You're right, but from the second we started talking, I knew he was a good man. He was as gentle as a dove. My instincts don't lie and, so far, I've always had a reliable intuition."

Becky was convinced by her statement, and she wasn't wrong. The week she spent in France has been amazing; nothing went wrong. Listening to her explain the unexplainable trust she felt toward Damien from the very beginning, I let my thoughts drift a bit. I was also convinced that today I had felt the same toward the handsome pilot. I couldn't explain how I knew, but I was persuaded. My instincts told me that John, my handsome captain, had a good heart. I didn't know if he was a gentleman and I didn't mind. I was attracted to his energy and I couldn't explain why. At that moment, lost in my thoughts, I sincerely hoped that I'd soon get the opportunity to confirm my theory.

Chapter 5

Zürich deadhead Paris (ZRH dh CDG)

I spent the following days hanging out at home. As a flight attendant *on reserve*, even though I was getting paid for a minimum number of hours of flying, I did not get called for the rest of the month. I was ecstatic as I didn't have to work the hours and still got paid for them. However, in a way, I still would have liked to fly some more in case I ran into my mysterious pilot. Actually, I was starting to twiddle my thumbs by staying put, as being on call meant I had to remain available and ready to go. I couldn't stray too far from the apartment because if I got called, I had to be able to make it to the airport within three hours or less. February went by pretty quickly and I ended up flying a bit more in March. I even got called to operate flights from New Orleans for a whole week.

I like that city and its people. Maybe it's the musical vibe, or even the French influence, but I feel better there than I do in many other places around the world. Some places are just charming to some people. For example, a few colleagues of mine hate Madrid. They prefer Barcelona, and I can easily understand why: It's by the sea and thanks to Gaudí, the architecture is incredible. I like that city too but I prefer Madrid for its eternal day- and nightlife, its smell of cured ham, and all sorts of reasons I can't even explain. It's simply indescribable. The city's aura rocks my world, without a doubt. Just like Madrid, falling in love cannot be explained, it just happens.

* * *

Just like that, after a winter filled with same-day flying back and forth, summer and its long-haul flights abroad finally arrived. For the first time in three years I got a schedule with fixed flights. I would finally know in advance where I'd be going. I could make plans and have a life! It was far from the typical Monday to Friday, 9-to-5 routine, but I could still plan activities in advance, knowing what days I'd be away. By having a schedule, I could even exchange flights with colleagues. For example, if I was only assigned flights to London and a colleague wanted a London and I a different destination, I had the opportunity to slightly tweak my schedule to my liking.

That's precisely what Becky had done in May in order to fly with me. We had never flown together, so to celebrate the arrival of our first fixed schedules, she had swapped a flight to come along with me to Paris, via Zürich. Simply put, we were operating a flight from Boston to Zürich, Switzerland, then we had to hop on a TGV train to the City of Light. Just like flying as a simple passenger, this is also called a "deadhead." We would sleep in Paris, France, the following night and operate a flight back to Boston.

It was a series of flights spread over three days but in reality, we were only going away for some forty hours or so. We were due to leave at six p.m. on the Thursday, would arrive in Zürich just before seven a.m., and had to immediately hop on a train. Our arrival in Paris was meant to be around eleven a.m., the perfect time for a satisfying nap before enjoying a good meal, without the need to rush. All was well.

In order to be able to work together on the plane, Becky had chosen to fulfill the tasks assigned to the back, right-hand-side position of the aircraft. Therefore, in the event of an emergency, she was in charge of opening the back door, on the right-hand side. She also had to sit on the jump seat accordingly at takeoff, landing, and during any turbulence. As for me, I had chosen to look after another door on the right-hand side, the one just above the wings. That way, I could work with Becky but would also watch over the whole cabin during boarding. Only I, with the help of my counterpart on the left side, was in the main cabin, readily available to help the passengers. Becky would look after the passengers seated at the very back, in the aircraft's tail. What bothered me about all this wasn't that I was surrounded by passengers but rather what the position required of me. I must admit that I wasn't delighted about some of the assigned tasks.

During boarding that morning, I was standing in the middle of the cabin with my counterpart. I didn't know her and was hesitant to chat. I didn't really know what to say apart from asking some basic questions.

"I'm sorry, I don't remember your name," I said to break the ice. I had sincerely forgotten, a mere ten minutes after being introduced. I always had the embarrassing habit of forgetting the name of people I was speaking to when meeting them for the first time. Thankfully, my colleague didn't seem to mind.

"Ah, don't worry about it! My name's Nicole, and you?"

"Scarlett," I answered, happy to see she didn't remember my

name either. "Have you been with the company long?"

"Eleven years."

"Wow! Eleven years! I guess you really love it after that long."

"The work itself is okay, but the lifestyle is amazing. When I leave for a flight, once on the plane, time literally flies. I don't even realize I'm at the office. So, it must mean I still like it. Especially now that I can work all of my hours very quickly and end up having the end of the month off. I challenge you to find another job that'll give you two weeks off per month; you won't find one!"

She was right. Since I had started progressing in aviation, time had flown by. I, too, had fallen in love with the trade. I was far from having fallen for my passengers, or for the intolerable foot aches caused by long hours of standing, yet I still loved my job. Whenever I left for a flight, curiously, it felt like I came straight back. In reality, I barely ever had long eight-day *pairings*[1], but even when I did, if the crew was pleasant, time went by very quickly. Not constantly glancing at my watch while at the office was worth more than gold.

"That's encouraging! I hope I'll still enjoy my job as much as you do ten years from now," I added, smiling before swiftly slipping away to offer a passenger help with his luggage.

* * *

I didn't mind the task of playing Tetris and helping passengers fit their carry-on luggage in the overhead bins. Actually, I preferred lifting many of their suitcases as I could quickly assess where to

---

[1] A *pairing* is any set of flights scheduled over more than one day, meaning I don't come home after a work day but sleep in another city instead.

put them in order to avoid clutter. The faster a piece of luggage was safely put away, the faster the passenger was seated, the faster the aisle was cleared, the faster other passengers could reach their seats, and we could be on our way. It was better to be proactive.

Time came to close the overhead bins and make sure everything was ready for takeoff. During my last round, I couldn't ignore any of my assigned tasks, even the ones I didn't hold dear, such as briefing moms on their babies!

Many flight attendants love babies. They cherish them, cuddle them, and even smooch them. I, Scarlett Lambert, have no interest in the passengers' babies. Sure, I find them cute, but I'm not drawn to them. I'm ready to put up with their cries, out of obligation, but I will not pretend to be the life-saving flight attendant who holds *the* remedy that will calm Mr. Baby. No, thanks!

However, seeing as I'm responsible for everyone's safety, I dutifully make sure that Mr. Baby is ready for takeoff in mommy's or daddy's arms.

That day, per usual, I approached one of the families getting settled on the plane. I looked the mom and dad right in the eyes and asked, without making a fuss, if they had already received the instructions on how to hold their baby while in flight.

"Good morning, have you received your briefing about holding your child during takeoff and landing?"

"No," they answered, rather dismissively.

"All right, I'll explain," I said, ready to deliver my speech as quickly as possible.

I bent down to meet the mother's height to avoid having to talk too loud. I started my speech looking at her since she was the one holding the baby. I also made sure to talk about the CHILD, avoiding any mention of gender. As far as I'm concerned, unless a little girl is showing off cute earrings or is covered in pink, I am hopeless at guessing the baby's gender. As I had been way out of line in the past, I no longer took any chances. A little girl was now a CHILD. A little boy was now a CHILD. No gender. No sex. Everyone was happy.

"First of all, you must not put the seatbelt around your baby. You are the one who has to hold your CHILD."

The woman was calmly looking at me. The baby was also calm, barely drooling, not even crying. So far, so good.

"You must hold it in your arms, against your body, facing you, with legs on either side, just like in the burp position."

At that moment, without any warning, the woman opened her blouse and pulled out her big, spongy, milk-filled breast. As I was bending down at exactly chest height, I perfectly caught sight of the brown nipple ready to greet the baby's mouth. Strangely, said baby had not let out any sound hinting that it was hungry. All the while, the woman continued to look me in the eye, absentmindedly fondling with her massive booby, directing it into her child's mouth. I continued my speech as if it wasn't a big deal. I cheered myself on internally, *I'm almost done.*

"In the unlikely event of loss of cabin pressure, oxygen masks will drop from above your head . . . "

The baby started sucking, making a loud suction sound. I could hear the flow of milk enter his tiny red infant mouth. It was hard at work and I found it surprisingly difficult not to glance at the woman's breast. The baby was getting a perfectly fine feeding but the mom did not seem satisfied. She pulled her boob off the child's mouth and I then had a clear view of a very moist nipple. I continued my speech and this time I hurried, as I was eager to finish.

"... and if there is a loss of cabin pressure, you must put your mask on first, before assisting your CHILD."

I was almost done. Just one more instruction and I could run away forever. As I prepared my closing, my eyes came across, once again, the moist human mammary bit. My eyes went back and forth between the woman's face and the breast she was fondling with. I was hoping she'd understand that a wet breast was bothering me and that she very well could have waited before having it spring out in my face. I continued my instructions with accelerated delivery.

"Lastly, the baby-changing table is in the lavatory at the back. We kindly ask that you dispose of diapers in the bin next to the sink, not in the toilet. Thank you!"

What a relief! I could now leave and never come back. I stood up to indicate the end of my speech. I was under the impression that the mom really wanted to make me uncomfortable. I had become a bit paranoid but still, as I was getting back up, she didn't hesitate to re-plug her baby onto her nipple, now dripping with fresh milk. That was enough. *Next time*, I thought, knowing I'd never dare to, *I'll tell them to hold off for just one little minute, out of respect for my eyes!* I had never really been insulted by breastfeeding before but it would take days for my eyeballs to get over this one . . .

I made my way to my jump seat. I was still in shock when I finally heard the captain's passenger announcement.

"Ladies and gentlemen, my name is John Ross and I will be your captain today. On my right, I will be assisted by First Officer Philip Burns. On behalf of the entire crew, welcome on board Americair flight 322 with service to Zürich. Our flight time today will be six hours, ten minutes, with a cruising altitude of 36,000 feet. I will get back to you with the weather conditions shortly before our final approach into Zürich. Until then, sit back, relax, and enjoy the great in-flight service. Thank you and have a nice flight!"

Had I heard correctly? The captain I had been obsessed with just a few months earlier was flying the aircraft I was on today? How had I not noticed? I then remembered that the pilots that day had not introduced themselves to the crew. It was quite common. Often, in order to be more efficient, the captain's briefing was only provided to the purser, who would then share the information with the rest of the crew. I didn't appreciate the procedure as I still wanted to see the face of the one holding my life in his hands, but I accepted it as I knew how important taking off on time was, and how it could avoid many troubles.

Suddenly, my unfortunate adventure with the woman with the big nipple was forgotten. My attention was now directed at someone else: my mysterious captain. Ready for takeoff, I sat on my jump seat smiling, eager to see him again. He, who had made my heart skip a beat without even realizing it. *Maybe this time he'll finally notice me?* To my own surprise, I really hoped he would.

Chapter 6

Paris (CDG)

Whuen we got off the aircraft, the whole crew boarded the private bus taking us to the train station, where we could hop on a TGV to Paris. For the second time in my life, I was able to catch a glimpse of the object of my desire, of my obsession. I hadn't seen him throughout the night as he had only come out of the cockpit once, to use the lavatories. At that time, I was at the back with Becky, putting carts away. When I heard the bell reserved for the use of calls from the flight deck, I suspected that one of the pilots would be coming out into the cabin. I couldn't imagine myself leaving all my tasks behind in order to run to the front just to find out whether or not it was my pilot coming out for a little chat with the crew. Especially since Becky had no clue that I found one of the pretentious pilots potentially interesting. She probably would have laughed at the irony and would have made me swallow my pride. Therefore, I had chosen to remain at the back, continuing with my tasks. Anyway, I would see John after the flight; I just had to be patient.

We were now all calmly seated on the bus. Strangely, the pilots were coming to Paris with us. Often, once at our destination, they get separated from the rest of the crew. My captain, for example, could very well have spent the night in Zürich and continued on to another destination in the morning. That day, though, it wasn't the case and I was thrilled to see that John and his first officer would follow us to Paris. However, the next day, they weren't operating the same flight as me back to Boston. They were flying to New York instead, with a different crew. Still, I was pretty happy at the thought of maybe having the chance to talk to him a little.

Once at the train station, we all made our way to our designated compartment. I sat across the aisle from John, to his right. Becky had spoken with the first officer for a few minutes and then had fallen asleep. She appeared to know him. Perhaps I had an alibi. Other crew members were chatting away while I was discreetly observing my neighbor from the corner of my eye. He was watching the green countryside passing by the window. I thought it strange that I was attracted to him as he was far from my usual ideal. None of it made sense. Where had my attraction for tall, dark, nicely built, and outgoing men gone? Out the window I guess, since John was mostly quiet, keeping to himself. His hair was a light brown and he wasn't very tall, nor muscly, although he still emitted a strong virility. His hands were massive. Surely strong, powerful even. My imagination was already running wild. His gaze was dark and deep, yet seemed as gentle as a lamb. I was captivated by his charisma, his presence that maybe only I could perceive. He must have been in his late thirties. I was fantasizing about a man. A real one.

He looked exhausted and hadn't even noticed me. In reality, we hadn't exchanged a smile, nor even a look, since the very first time I had seen him in Costa Rica. I really felt like I didn't stand a chance to even talk to him. It was about time I got some sleep.

I thought, *Once in Paris, I won't let any chance pass me by.*

* * *

As planned, a driver was waiting for us at our arrival at the Gare du Nord. We got on yet another bus, impatient to finally get to the crew hotel. I abruptly woke up when the bus stopped at our destination, off a street by the Seine river. Exhaustion had won me over without me even realizing it. I had remained seated up straight but my head had fallen to the side and had rested on the windowsill. My relaxed jaw had dropped, allowing my mouth to open slightly. As for my cheek, it had happily taken the shape of the corner of the window it had rested on. Waking up, I could feel a large and deep dent on my cheekbone. *Being a flight attendant is very glamourous. Oh, so glamourous!* I thought.

I must admit that before working in aviation, I had never known utter exhaustion. Of course, I had spent a few sleepless nights partying with friends before, but that hadn't been extreme fatigue, not even close. After a flight, and especially after a night flight, aka a *red-eye*, I can fall asleep in the blink of an eye. I don't even need a pillow, let alone a bed. Just some sort of headrest.

Being a flight attendant is accepting the fact that we can be so tired that even when someone shakes us up we don't wake up. Often, the crew plans to meet up for dinner but unsurprisingly, some crew members don't even turn up to the meeting point. Not that they don't want to see us, nor that they don't want to eat, they just sleep through, unable to wake from their deep sleep.

As I was trying my best to erase the deep mark from my cheek, I started thinking about a plan to get closer to my pilot. John was at the hotel front desk with the chief purser, helping him get the room keys. That's when I noticed Becky was still chatting with Philip, the first officer. I moved closer, listening in to their conversation, still rubbing my cheek. All of a sudden, the perfect opportunity came up.

"Are you guys planning on eating out tonight?" the first officer asked my charming friend Becky.

"Well, I don't know," she said, unsure as to what she should answer; knowing that she and I would be eating dinner together but assuming I'd probably not be interested in sharing a meal with a pretentious pilot.

Therefore, she quickly glanced in my direction, hoping to read an answer from my facial expression. I slowly nodded in agreement. As I suspected, Becky was quite surprised at my open-mindedness and my welcoming of Philip among us, so she asked me directly:

"Scarlett, what are our plans tonight?" She said this with the sort of smile that meant, *It's up to you, but I'm interested and would really like him to come with us.*

"Well yes, we could have dinner together. I suppose the captain would come too?" I swiftly and innocently asked.

"Yes, of course. We had already agreed to meet in the lobby at six p.m. Would that suit you?"

"That's perfect with us! See you at six, then. Have a good nap!"

I looked at Becky to make sure she was okay with this. She seemed very happy that I had accepted the offer but I also saw in her eyes the many questions I'd have to answer about my sudden open-mindedness.

We each got our respective room key and made our way to the elevators. Becky waited for me and got on the same elevator.

"So, what was that all about, Scarlett?" she asked, all secretive, hoping I'd confide in her.

"You're gonna laugh at me if I tell you," I said, laughing myself.

"No, I won't! I'm no fool. I know you don't normally like to eat with pilots but today it didn't take much convincing at all. What's going on?"

I remained silent, which started to frighten her.

"Are you interested in Philip by any chance?"

"No, not at all! He's all yours. I'm more interested in the other one," I finally admitted.

"Whoa! What's happening with you? Are you going mad? You, a pilot? Are you turning into a Suzie!?" she said, obviously kidding.

She couldn't believe it. There was no way I, Scarlett Lambert, could be interested in a pilot. Was I suddenly possessed by Suzie, our Suzie-Flirt-With-Every-Pilot colleague? Becky was cracking up in the elevator. At the very least, she was amused by my confession. The elevator doors opened on my floor and I quickly ended the conversation before the anticipated evening.

"Listen, Becky, I don't even know him and have never even spoken to him. I'm interested and I don't really know why, so please, I'm asking you to not mention anything about this tonight. We're gonna have a nice evening and then we'll see how things go. Maybe after he says a few words I'll no longer find him attractive anyway. Okay?"

"Of course, Scarlett, you can rest assured I won't say a word. I'm definitely not going to spoil one of the rare times you're actually attracted to a man. Go have a nap. Everything will be all right. I'll see you in a bit!"

I thanked her and went straight to my room.

When I entered, the air conditioning was on maximum. As I was already frozen from fatigue and the cold air on the aircraft, I quickly turned it down. Then, I proceeded to the most important after-flight task of all: having a shower. I threw my suitcases onto the desk and luggage rack by the wall. I made sure not to put anything on the floor apart from my heels. The carpet might have appeared to be clean but it probably wasn't. I then hurriedly took my uniform off and hung it up to avoid creasing.

I jumped in the shower. The hot water made me feel better and, once again, with the little energy I had left, thoughts came flowing. I thought about the evening that was about to happen. I was looking forward to talking to John and finding out more about him. I kept thinking about the upcoming evening until I got into bed. I shut the curtains to keep the bright Parisian daylight from entering the room and adjusted the alarm on my phone for four p.m. Sleeping for four hours seemed reasonable as the longer I stayed in bed, the harder it'd be to fall asleep again at night. Comfortably wrapped in the white bed sheets, I let myself fall into a deep sleep.

* * *

"Quack-quack! Quack-quack! Quack-quack! . . ."

The little duck woke me up. Now, how could one not open their eyes when hearing that ringtone? I had to set my alarm to duck mode in order to wake up as soft harp music or the likes would go unnoticed.

"Come on, get up," I said out loud.

With great difficulty, I pulled my heavy legs out of bed. I felt drugged on fatigue but I knew that a half-hour jog would sort me out and give me all the energy I needed to make the most of the evening. I quickly got dressed and started my Parisian routine.

I'll always remember in my interview with Americair when the interviewer asked me why I wanted to be a flight attendant. Among all the answers I provided, there was the fact that I didn't like routine. Surely, that made the job perfect for me.

Yet, every human, no matter how fickle, needs some sort of routine. Our body requires it after a while. As if to offer us comfort, some of life's components, as simple as breakfast for example, repeat themselves. In Rome, I have a routine, and in Vancouver too. Same for Paris. I appreciate it. I need it. And that is why, when possible, we keep the same crew hotels for a long time. That way, we can feel somewhat at home while away from home.

That day was no exception to the rule. Our hotel was located in one of the most beautiful neighborhoods of Paris, Saint-Germain-des-Prés, and I couldn't complain. So, I went for a run by the Seine. It only took a few minutes to feel revived. Becky didn't want to come along; she preferred yoga. When I got back, I jumped in the shower again, put some comfortable clothes on, went down to the lobby, and enjoyed a nice espresso. Then, I went for a walk around the neighboring streets to run some errands. I only had an hour to get everything done so I had to be efficient. I stopped at the bookstore Taschen on Rue de Buci. I love their books. Some list the greatest photographers' work on large prints, while others talk about quirky subjects such as big breasts. I had to allow for a quick stop.

Afterward, I made my way to some of my favorite stores just to see if they had gotten new arrivals in. I got lucky and found a nice pair of bohemian-style pants for a really good price. Walking by Boulevard Saint-Germain, I admired the church on my right-hand side, and in the many crossroads surrounding it I found time to wander a little before making it to the grocery store. I walked by the delicious macaroon store Ladurée, on Rue Bonaparte. Seeing the line, though, I didn't have a choice but to skip the stop, and continued straight on to Monoprix to get a salad for the return flight. I took the opportunity to also purchase some delicious yogurts and French cheese. While waiting at checkout, I looked at my watch. It was already five thirty p.m. I had to quickly get back to the hotel. I couldn't miss my "date."

* * *

After carefully putting my food in my room's mini-fridge, I put on my new baggy pants. They were made of a light, silky fabric and the tag was proudly marked MADE IN FRANCE. This was one of the reasons I chose it in the first place and it also made me look at once laid-back and very stylish, just the way I like it. I wore it with my everyday T-shirt and took a last look at myself in the mirror to make sure my walk hadn't messed up my hair. Everything was perfect and, most important, I felt like myself. I went down to the lobby.

When I arrived, Becky was already there, sitting on one of the sky-blue couches. She seemed enthralled by the words her handsome pilot Philip was saying to John. Shyly smiling, I got closer to them.

"Hi, guys! Did you sleep well?" I asked instinctively.

I wasn't expecting a very elaborate response from any of them as asking a flight attendant or a pilot how they slept was like asking the usual "How's it going?" to which no one really cares to hear the answer.

"Sure did, and you?" they all answered.

"I did too, thank you," I automatically replied. "By the way, my name is Scarlett," I added, looking at the first officer and the captain.

"Hi, Scarlett. I'm Philip."

I then turned toward John so that he could in turn introduce himself.

"I'm John. Nice to meet you, Scarlett," he said, with one the nicest smiles I had ever had the pleasure to witness.

"Where did you plan on going to eat?" I asked the first officer, way too shy still to ask the captain.

"We were thinking of going to a restaurant I know. It's very good and it has an outside patio."

"Yes, somewhere with a patio would be pretty *cool* on a day like today," I said, mentally smiling at the pun.

"All right, then, let's go!" said Philip.

We all followed him without adding a word, which made it a very satisfying agreement. In order to avoid conflict, a leader had to take charge. So many times, we would all agree to meet up for dinner but ended up splitting the crew in order to satisfy everyone. But when one of us stepped up as THE connoisseur of a restaurant, no one dared to doubt him or her for as long as they maintained their convictions. Like a herd of sheep, we would then follow to the suggested destination. However, if the connoisseur doubted his or her choice out of fear of not pleasing everyone, chaos would arise: "Is your restaurant still very far?"; "Well, I know a cheap spot."; "I really would have liked to have some paella."; "Honestly, I don't really feel like having tapas." Doubt would bring fear and panic, which, just like on a plane, were contagious.

Fortunately, that day, it wasn't the case. Everything was going for the best since our leader had faith in his own skills as a culinary guide. He had an exaggerated confidence, just like a pilot's. Ah! Well, look at that, he *was* a pilot, that's why!

As we were walking toward the restaurant, the group naturally split in two. The first half consisted of Becky and Philip, and the second of John and me. Walking on Boulevard Saint-Michel, I noticed that John opted for the side closest to the street. I didn't know if he had done it intentionally, but nevertheless I appreciated the gentlemanly act. Becky was in front with the first officer. We weren't far behind but I couldn't hear their conversation. John and I started talking about nothing in particular. The conversation was friendly.

Pulling out my favorite ice-breaker question, I asked, "Have you been with the company long?"

"Ten years already. Yourself?"

"Three years. But it also feels like it went by very quickly." I continued on with my second favorite question. "What were you doing before Americair?"

Everyone had a past and I was always intrigued by my colleagues'. Some had had children, a family, and then one day had realized they had always wanted to be a flight attendant, so had applied for the job. Others had been nurses. Tired of the health system, they had decided to make the most of life, all the while still taking care of others. Among my colleagues, there was also a stylist and an American athlete. Flight attendants come from all kinds of backgrounds. Many have degrees in law, management, or teaching, and evolve to working in aviation purely out of choice. If only passengers knew all of this, they might look at us differently.

As for pilots, prior to Americair some had flown rich men around to foreign countries on their private jets. Others were retired from the army but still wanted to keep in shape and thus had chosen to fly with us full-time. A few had even been flying above distant corners of America, where there is plenty of wildlife but not many people. I wondered about John's past.

"Well, I was up in Alaska," he said. "I was flying for a small charter company there. I was often with geologists who had to analyze the ground composition. By flying over the land they could, with the help of their weird machine, know if it contained gold or something. As far as I was concerned, though, I was flying, and that's all that mattered to me."

I had never heard of that technique. And although it was all very educational, I didn't really care to find out more about it. I wanted to know more about him instead, about his life.

"Interesting. How long would you be lost in the woods for? Surely time didn't fly up there?" I asked, to keep him talking.

"I would stay there for three months and then they would fly me home for two weeks so I could be among humankind. I can't deny the fact that after three months I needed to see people, women. But above all, I loved to fly the northern skies. It was flat calm. Peace and quiet. With only wolves howling. Can't put a price on that."

Listening to him, I let his words and thoughts sink in. As I was from Woodstock, Vermont, I also felt a strong love for nature. Actually, I wondered where he was from.

"What background is *Ross*?"

"It's from Ireland. My father is Irish and my mother American."

"Ah! That's where your subtle accent comes from?"

"Barely noticeable, right?" he said, in a very proud, nationalistic way.

"No, not at all! I hope I didn't offend you?" I said, worried it had come out as an insult.

"Just a little bit," he joked, flashing one of his charming smiles.

The more I listened to him, the more I was starting to understand my inexplicable attraction for him. I was really hoping nothing would go wrong until the end of the night as for once, I was interested in someone.

After only a few minutes, we arrived in front of a restaurant sign indicating Le Pré Verre. We made ourselves comfortable on the patio. Becky was sitting in front of me and Philip next to me, with John facing him, so diagonal to me. We started by ordering a bottle of the red wine the waiter had recommended. After a few sips, I finally became more at ease. I had no reason to be shy, especially since there had been zero intimacy. I couldn't tell if there was a slight chance he found me attractive. I could clearly see that Philip was attracted to Becky, but John hadn't given me any obvious sign, even though I could definitely feel some chemistry between us.

At dinner, we talked about, unsurprisingly, airplanes, passengers, and company gossip. John, on his end, kept mostly silent. He laughed with us but remained quiet, only speaking to add a few comments or a relevant statement here and there. At one point, out of the blue, or perhaps due to our alcohol consumption, the conversation strayed into a completely different direction: the mid-life crisis.

"Is it true that men start considering being unfaithful when they get close to their forties?" asked Becky, obviously trying to test the waters with Philip.

"Hum, maybe John could answer that," said Philip, avoiding the question.

We later learned that Philip was only thirty-four and single, so had no way to answer the question. But wait a minute! If Philip passed the question on to John, did that mean that John was in a relationship? I started freaking out internally. I could already sense disappointment growing. It was only a matter of seconds until I found out the truth.

"Ah the mid-life crisis! Well, I'm thirty-nine and strangely, the closer I get to forty, the more I feel like I just think differently."

I had just found out his age and according to me, he was too handsome to be single. But I had to make sure.

"Well, have you been with your girlfriend for a long time?" I asked, having forgotten to turn my filter on. I thought, *Surely, I'll know every detail of his life momentarily.*

"Eight years. But it's not really my wife, nor my kids, who are making me go through a mid-life crisis . . . but rather everything else that's going on in my life," he confided, quite naturally.

I was about to faint. A wife? But where was his ring? Maybe he wasn't wearing it out of fear of losing it? No matter the reason, I had to put an end to the interest I felt toward him. Not only had he been in a relationship for eight years, he had also mentioned having kids. Kids! Not kid, kidS! The "s" at the end of the word clearly indicated plural, therefore John must have had at least two kids. Possibly even more! Disaster! How could I have been so interested in a man I didn't know anything about and who was, above all, a pilot? Unfortunately, as attraction was often inexplicable, I couldn't hold it against myself. I'd be disappointed for a day or two and then would get over it. That's what I hoped, anyway.

I suddenly really wanted to go back to the hotel but Becky, after glancing at me with sadness in her eyes, tried to get some more information out of John, maybe some clues of infidelity to cheer me up. Knowing me, though, she should have realized that all my hopes were crushed and that even if he was open to frolicking, I would have never allowed myself to get involved. Nevertheless, she continued her search on the matter.

"According to what I've heard, the mid-life crisis has nothing to do with thinking differently. Men just want to get some with younger girls. They want to have an affair, it's that simple! Don't you?" said Becky, as eager and determined as Sherlock Holmes.

"Hm, mid-life crisis does imply exploring new territories, but not always. For me, it makes me question many aspects of my life. I feel like I haven't experienced enough in the past, so I want my future to be different. Let's just say that now, I want to put myself first," he explained genuinely.

I could appreciate his honesty. He didn't avoid the question, probably having realized that Becky and I would have only pressed on. Had he not said anything, we obviously would have searched deeper. We were, after all, flight attendants. Within crews, we tackle many very intimate subjects. We are, to some extent, a big family. The only thing is, our family can't keep a secret. And secrets get repeated as soon as we touch the ground. Either way, John had not shared very juicy life details so it was all going to stay here, around a pretty Parisian table. After all, he hadn't said anything explicit about being unfaithful, and I was satisfied. At least I had had a crush on a decent guy.

Philip took over the conversation, having suddenly decided to convince us of the many advantages of having an affair.

"Well, I believe that being unfaithful once in a while can actually save a lot of relationships," he declared, sticking out his chest. "I once cheated on my ex and when I admitted it to her, she understood the reasons why and saw the positive impact it had had on my mood. Once in a while, it can't hurt anyone."

I couldn't believe what I was hearing. There he was, the *Scumbag Pilot*, trying to convince us of the positive effects of cheating. If that was his opinion, he was not meant for Becky, as she still believed in fidelity. She looked at me, no longer interested in his remarks. I knew then that she had categorized him as a scumbag pilot, along with many of her nocturnal conquests. Perhaps one night with him was worth it. But no more than two.

I couldn't help but stir things up a little bit.

"By the way, you're no longer with her, you know! (Idiot.) So, I don't see how you can be so sure that cheating on someone you love once in a while can save the relationship. And did you ever think about *her* mood when she found out about your actions? Instead of being sensible and wondering what was wrong between the two of you, you decided to relegate the problem and blamed your testosterone. Like a coward."

Obviously, continuing the debate wasn't going to improve our evening. I looked at our waiter and asked for the bill. I wanted to get away as fast as I could. I allowed Scumbag Pilot to try and justify himself for a few minutes. Becky was no longer participating in the conversation. As for John, he listened to his first officer and laughed along at the libertine philosophy. I could see the way he looked at him. He didn't agree with his relationship ideals but as Philip expressed himself with so much confidence, he found it amusing. His first officer was acting like a bro detailing his sex life in the hockey locker room, hoping to impress his buddies. It was entertaining, but certainly very stupid, and my hotel room was waiting for me.

When the bill arrived, John, with Philip, took care of paying for the wine. That was much appreciated as even though pilots earn a lot more than flight attendants, they only rarely offer to get the wine. Tonight, being a pilot didn't mean being a cheapskate. We made our way to the hotel and despite everything, I still would have liked to extend my evening with John, even if no intimacy was in the cards. To my great despair, I was attracted to him; his energy hypnotized me.

Once in front of the hotel, Philip suggested we walk by the Seine. I thought to myself, *If John goes, I go*, but sadly, he declined the offer. He preferred going back to his room to rest before his flight the next day. As I no longer had any interest in going for a walk, I also declined the invitation and left Becky in the arms of Scumbag Pilot.

I entered the hotel lobby, making sure to walk a few steps in front of John, thus demonstrating my lack of interest in him. I went straight to the elevators, assuming he was following me. However, his room was in a completely different part of the hotel, so he wasn't following me at all. I heard his deep and captivating voice wishing me good night. I was unable to say anything, so I didn't. From the corner of my eye, I could see his silhouette standing still behind me, staring at my back, waiting for his *good night*. At that moment, knowing that I wouldn't get the chance to fly with him again the next day, I soaked up the memory of his shadow walking away, full of charm, as always. Only the future could tell if I'd be seeing him again soon. And despite my greatest efforts, I did hope it would be very soon.

Chapter 7

Boston (BOS) – Paris (CDG) – Philadelphia (PHL) – New York (JFK) – Barcelona (BCN)

I had been extremely busy flying all summer long, and so I had managed to bury deep the crush I had on my captain. It was far away from any of my conscious thoughts and I didn't expect it to come back to the surface any time soon. Within only a few months, I had traveled as far as Turkey and had visited some of the nicest cities Europe has to offer. Having a set schedule meant I could be gone for as long as a week at a time and thus never had any idea what day it was. I was now relying on the good old calendar days, actual dates, to plan my social life.

"Are you free next Saturday?" my friends would ask.

"Nah, if it's a Saturday I'm definitely working."

"All right, so are you free the following Thursday, then?"

"What date is that? The nineteenth? Yes, I think I'm free," I would answer, convinced that I was available. But then, looking at my daily planner, I'd realize I was coming back on the nineteenth at six p.m. Surely after my flight I would be pretty tired, and as there was always the possibility of encountering a delay, I would prefer to not plan anything in advance.

I hadn't seen my mommy-friends Paige and Rachel since our last catch-up in February. They had tried to organize a barbecue on a hot weekend in July but, once again, I had been flying and couldn't make it. To be honest, I was far from upset about it.

As for Becky, she had seen her pilot three more times, but had put a stop to it after hearing a colleague bragging about fooling around with a pilot whose name happened to be Philip Burns. She hadn't made a big deal out of it but she didn't wish to be number fifty on his long flight-attendant trophy list, so had cut all ties with Scumbag Pilot. I was pleased, of course.

Rupert-the-Jinx, on his end, made us laugh all summer long with his extraordinary stories. One day, a sick passenger on his way to the lavatories discharged his whole digested meal on Rupert's nice uniform. Another time, Rupert had to step in between two frustrated passengers who were ready to fight for the middle armrest; the ladies really didn't want to share. There was also an emergency situation where the indicator for the landing gear showed that it wasn't secured. The pilots had to navigate the aircraft as close to the control tower as possible in order for someone there to see if it was actually out. They landed on the lookout, not entirely convinced it was properly engaged.

I will never be able to scientifically explain how or why Rupert manages to jinx his aircrafts but, as far as I'm concerned, I'm convinced that's what he did on a particular day in August, as part of my crew. And above all, my charming pilot would also be there to witness our misfortunes.

* * *

If you ask me, a checked baggage equals constant frustration. After a flight, I'm too tired to allow myself the luxury of waiting around with my passengers for my big suitcase to appear on the belt. Obviously, depending on our destination, some ground agents make sure to remove our crew bags in priority and hand them over to us at the bottom of the stairs or in an area reserved for us. But, as I do not feel like worrying about losing my personal belongings (which does happen!), I prefer to only bring my carry-on and take it on board the aircraft with me. Therefore, I had agreed with Rupert that we would both proceed that way, allowing us to follow each other without having to wait around. He, obviously, had complained.

"Well then, I'm going to have to roll all my clothes tight and can only bring two pairs of jeans!" he moaned.

"Come on, Rupert, if I can compact all my clothes, I'm sure you can too. And you only need one pair of jeans anyway, not two!"

"Yeah but then I can't bring back any souvenirs!" he sighed.

"Just do whatever you want. You're the one who's going be stressed out if you lose your suitcase. We're not just going directly to Paris this week, you know. On the second part of the pairing we leave from Philadelphia, stop in New York, and then continue on to Barcelona. We're gonna have to wait for your big suitcase in JFK (New York) and then check it in at the counter again. And that's if it even makes it there!"

My mind was set. I would convince him to travel light, for his own good, my own good, and the good of our future crew, as it was a known fact: Rupert's suitcases get lost—all the time. He finally gave in after about half an hour.

We were leaving on a Wednesday evening and would get back to Boston the following Monday. This meant a six-day pairing worth many hours of flying, which would take us across the Atlantic Ocean a total of four times. I didn't know the flight details and relied on my colleagues to explain them to me. Neither Rupert nor I had printed our flight itinerary, so I didn't know then that my dear John Ross would eventually be added to the crew.

In reality, there were only four of us who would be together throughout the whole journey. For each flight, we would be joining different cabin crew members, which meant that over six days we would have to adjust to all sorts of personalities. At least I knew the other two colleagues coming with us very well, and I knew there would be no issue with them. There was Anna, a pretty, soft-spoken brunette with quite a delicate nature who got along with everyone. There was also Ishma, a cute Indian girl no taller than five feet three inches. She wore heels so high that a simple gust of wind could make her trip. She seemed gentle but was far from a pushover and would always ask me to close the overhead bins for her, claiming she was too short to do it herself. If I wasn't around, though, she would manage to close them by bouncing up and down in a very amusing way. The last member of our quartet was Rupert and, being a faithful servant to his passengers, there was no way he would be the cause of mayhem in our group.

During the first part of our pairing, we operated a flight to Paris. We spent twenty-four hours there and, the next day, crossed the ocean again to Philadelphia. So far so good. Rupert-the-Jinx had obediently stayed hidden away. Like a dream come true. But it wouldn't last long.

The very next day after arriving in Philly, we were flying off again. We were due to leave the hotel for the airport at three p.m. As planned, the hotel room phone rang at precisely two p.m. to wake me up. The voice recording announced:

"Hello, this is your wake-up call."

I immediately hung up. Per usual, I had tried to have a nap before my flight but as it was the middle of the day, I hadn't fallen asleep. Still, I had stayed under the warm covers, relaxing. After the automated call, I got up and jumped in the shower. That's when the misfortunes, or rather the disasters, started.

Ring, ring! Ring, ring! Ring, ring!

From the shower, I was able to pick up the receiver in the bathroom. As I had just gotten my wake-up call, I knew this time it wouldn't be a machine at the end of the line.

"Hello?" I answered.

"Good afternoon, Scarlett, it's crew sked. It's to let you know that there's a one-hour delay on your flight. The new departure time from the hotel is now four p.m.," announced one of the department's employees.

DISASTER No. 1! I wasn't surprised, nor disappointed, nor anything at all. Delays happen. I wished I had received that call before I got up or at least before my shower but oh well, I was simply going to relax and take my time getting ready in my room, until the new departure time. At four p.m., I made my way to the lobby to meet up with my three colleagues and we left for the airport.

What disgusted me the most had nothing to do with the delay itself, but rather that we had to start our workday on a dirty aircraft. DISASTER No. 2! The aircraft had arrived from Paris and was continuing on to New York. Some of the passengers were getting off in Philadelphia while others continued on to the Big Apple. Four of the cabin crew who had operated that inbound flight were being replaced by my quartet. Then we were to work the one-hour flight with the rest of the crew coming

71

from Paris, to finally join yet another crew in New York, to operate a flight to Barcelona. I was a bit lost, so I was better off just going with the flow.

Needless to say, it wasn't with great pleasure that we boarded the aircraft. First, the exhausted passengers didn't seem very welcoming, and I'm not even going to mention the musty smells floating around the cabin. As for the lavatories? How is a flight attendant supposed to be cheerful and joyful when they have to pick up little bits of paper soaked in pee before the flight has even started? Aviation always implies some level of adaptation, if not to say a *huge* amount of adaptation, so I did my job without a word. I had yet to perceive how long the upcoming day would be.

As no passenger was boarding for New York, we were waiting for the captain's okay to close the door. Suddenly, the chief purser got called into the cockpit. He came out somewhat frustrated.

"Hydraulic issue. Delay of at least an hour," he announced.

DISASTER No. 3! He then proceeded to make an announcement to the passengers to keep them informed. On our end, all we could do was wait patiently and hope the issue would get resolved quickly so that we wouldn't miss our flight to Barcelona. Meanwhile, Rupert came to the front of the aircraft to talk to me.

"I spoke to Ishma and Anna and they say we're gonna have to run in New York because if we don't take off within an hour, we might miss our flight to Barcelona."

Rupert was fidgeting, almost as if panicking. Regardless of the situation, that's the way it was. I tried to calm him down.

"The crew will just have to start boarding without us. No big deal. Anyway, crew sked knows we're stuck here, someone from the department will just have to call in some reserves if they don't want to delay the flight." I tried to put his mind at rest.

After almost an hour, things seemed to be progressing. A mechanic came in to talk to the captain and I heard an *okay*, meaning we would soon be able to leave. We closed the last door and took off. In-flight, we looked at our itinerary and realized that the aircraft taking us to Barcelona was the very same one we were on. Turns out, no one could leave without us.

Once landed in New York, all passengers disembarked in no time. It was now seven thirty p.m. We quickly said bye to the crew members leaving us. As this flight was, technically, coming from Paris, we also had to go through American customs. I was no longer worried about being late as the plane had to be cleaned, restocked, and refueled. In theory, we had plenty of time to go through customs and make our way back to the gate. But I did wonder which gate we had to go to.

To find out, I took a look at the board, aka FIDS (Flight Information Display System), in the waiting room where my future passengers were seated. Curiously, it indicated a time of eleven p.m., so I mentioned it to my colleagues.

"Um, guys! What's our flight number? Because it says departure at eleven p.m. on the board."

"Hold on. I'll check," Anna said softly.

She grabbed the unique copy of our itinerary and looked at the flight number.

"Six forty-two."

"Okay, it's the same number written on the board, except now it says eleven p.m. instead of eight p.m. What's the problem?"

Rupert, already worked up, was restless again and asked us to wait. He seemed to have the intention to solve the mystery as quickly as possible. He then stood in front of the gigantic window separating the departure area from the arrivals. He happened to be just behind the check-in counter. He violently knocked on the window located between him and the agent. The action made her jump and she quickly turned around, curious to see who was disturbing her. He brought his face close to the glass and yelled very loudly:

"Why is the flight to Barcelona now at eleven p.m.?"

She rolled her eyes with an obvious sigh and managed to tell us what we didn't want to hear.

"Delay! They planned a three-hour delay on that flight in order to fix a mechanical problem."

DISASTER No. 4! I couldn't believe it. Another delay! And there I was thinking that the hydraulic issue had been fixed in Philadelphia. We were already tired and hadn't even started our *real* flight. Rupert was beet-red. Anna was mute. Ishma's feet, with her heels, were already hurting. Our day, which in a way hadn't yet begun, looked like it was going to be long, *illegally* long. We started calculating while going through customs.

According to our union contract, if we went over a certain number of hours while on duty, we were no longer "legal" to operate a flight. We had to speak with crew sked immediately. Perhaps they had already replaced us and we would be spending the night in New York.

When are arrived in the crew room, our future colleagues were also there. They had just found out about the delay. I didn't know any of them and everyone was concerned with the wait so there wasn't much in the sense of introductions. Ishma, only slightly more experienced than us, contacted crew sked to clarify the situation. The conversation was heating up. When it came to the rules of our union contract, we were all inexperienced, so in some way, we blindly trusted the company. Ishma informed us that crew sked hadn't called in other flight attendants to replace us even though it was obvious that the new delay would make us go over our legal duty time. They were asking us to still operate the flight. In order to make an informed decision, Ishma requested they send us a new flight itinerary. In the meantime, I walked toward the restrooms, passing by the room reserved for pilots. As I walked by, I froze. Someone who looked quite familiar was seated there. Without thinking, I entered.

"Hi, John!" I said, shyly, as usual.

He looked up. His gaze penetrated mine. He smiled brightly at me, as if my surprise visit truly pleased him. I got weak in the knees.

"Hey, you! How are you?"

"Hm, so-so. Our flight's been delayed by three hours. We're gonna go over our duty time and crew sked hasn't replaced us," I confided.

"How come? Are you by any chance coming with me to Barcelona?" he asked, looking happy.

"Eh, looks like it. But I have no idea how this whole story is going to end."

Suddenly, I felt a little bit more motivated to operate the flight, even though we weren't legally supposed to do so.

"I don't understand why they didn't replace you . . . they called in a third pilot for us to be legal to leave."

I simply couldn't understand either. I knew that a pilot needed all of his concentration to fly, but that was no excuse to ignore flight attendants, who were also going to be drained within eight hours, right during our decent into Barcelona. If the union had determined a specific maximum number of duty hours, it was certainly for a reason. Regardless of my handsome captain's presence, I was eager to clarify the matter. If I couldn't go, I wouldn't go, even if John was going. I returned to my group, where Ishma, Anna, and Rupert had just received the anticipated itinerary.

"Crew sked just sent us a flight itinerary indicating an eight p.m. departure time. It is not the real departure time. We have to find out when we'll be landing in Barcelona in order to know if we must refuse to operate the flight!" explained Ishma.

"I'm gonna go see the captain!" I said, pretending to be just as infuriated as them and making my way back toward John.

I was glad to be able to talk to him twice within such a short period of time. I asked him the expected flight time to Barcelona and came back to the group with the information.

"The captain told me we're due to land there at twelve fifty," I said, not really knowing what to think of this new piece of information.

Rupert lifted his hands up to his temples and looked down. He was calculating. Anna was watching the group with an empty gaze. So was I. Until now, I had never had to understand the union rules. I knew a couple of them, of course, but I had no idea how to handle such a situation. Therefore, I preferred to let the more experienced ones do the complex math. During this short moment of silence, I attempted to fully understand the situation myself. *At two p.m., I showered as planned. At three p.m., I was supposed to leave for the airport but left at four p.m. instead. At five p.m., we got another delay. And then, another one. It is now nine p.m. I have already been "working" for seven hours, although I haven't started my real eight-hour long-haul. Whoa! So, I'll be working a 1sixteen-hour day? I'm lost!* I thought, feeling overwhelmed. Then Rupert interrupted:

"We're not legal!" he finally declared.

We had to call crew sked again. Besides, they still had time to get ahold of other flight attendants and replace us. Why hadn't they done so already? Ishma grabbed the phone and pressed nine to be directed to the crew scheduling department. Vanessa answered again.

"Vanessa at crew scheduling?"

"Yes, hi, it's Ishma in New York. We're scheduled for the eleven p.m. flight to Barcelona. We calculated our duty time and aren't legal, therefore we refuse to operate the flight," she said very professionally.

The woman at the end of the line seemed to be going mad.

"You said earlier you would do it. It's too late now to call reserves. You'll get your bonus, but you must do it," Vanessa replied with much authority.

"We are going over our duty time. We're tired. We have the right to refuse and are exercising our right," Ishma pressed on.

"Okay. I'll replace you," she finally replied angrily. "Stay in the crew room. I'll call back to tell you where you'll be sleeping."

Ishma hung up and gave us a summary of her conversation. In a way, I was relieved this would be over as we were already worn out. I couldn't imagine serving loud Spanish passengers and picking up dirty trays all night long. While waiting to find out which hotel we'd be sleeping in, I went to the couch to try to relax. That's when I saw John's silhouette in the next room. I suddenly felt disappointed. I thought it was better this way, though. I was better off not flying with him as I didn't want to be tormented again. From the simple look he gave me, my knees had gone weak. I didn't dare imagine what else could happen.

Next to me on the couch, there were a couple of other crew members. One of them introduced himself as Roberto, today's chief purser. At last, he found out more about the situation and seemed to agree with our decision. We were going to exceed our duty time and knowing this, we were allowed to refuse to operate the flight. He kindly assured us we shouldn't feel bad. Suddenly, the phone rang again. Ishma answered.

"Hello, Ishma speaking."

"Yes, it's Vanessa at crew sked. I'd like to speak with Roberto, your chief purser."

Roberto took over the call. I was observing him, intrigued by the conversation. After a few seconds, his whole body language completely changed. A few minutes earlier, Roberto had seemed very friendly, understanding, and pleasant to work with. He had just told me we were perfectly allowed to respect our union contract. I had appreciated his solidarity but somehow, now I didn't feel as much empathy from him. The kind and respectful look he had had toward our group had suddenly transformed into a terrifying one. I found myself feeling scared of what he was about to tell us and doubted his opinion had remained the same about our decision. After a couple of *okays*, he hung up. His mind was set. He pointed at us angrily, almost like a maniac.

"The four of you are coming with me! You're operating the flight. End of story. GOT IT?"

Roberto was clearly not asking us a question. There was no room for discussion and I got the message. In other words, he meant SHUT UP and TO HELL WITH YOUR FATIGUE TONIGHT! We were baffled. It had already been at least an hour since we had refused to operate the flight and he had even confirmed it was our right to do so. Now he was ordering us to get on the plane with him. It was beyond my understanding. Looks like no one had cared to listen to us. DISASTER No. 5! 6! 7! 8!

After having ordered us to follow him, Roberto grabbed his carry-on and all his paperwork, then yelled like a mad dog:

"Let's go! Everybody on the plane! NOW!"

The rest of the crew followed him. We were still in shock. As I didn't want to lose my job, I followed him as well. Perhaps Vanessa had threatened Roberto? I had no clue what her argument had been but it had obviously worked. My feet were moving forward out of fear. Fear of authority. I didn't know my rights. Rupert either. Anna was following behind and Ishma was struggling to walk with her high heels. Legally, we could leave, and at the same time, we very well knew that refusing to operate the flight would possibly result in additional delays. We pressed on, listening to other crew members express their opinion on the matter.

"If you step foot on that plane, you won't be able to get off and you'll have to operate the flight," one of them was saying.

"You have the right to leave. You're at an American base. We have to follow our union contract!" said a pro-unioner.

Neither I nor the others wanted to make the situation worse. Our intention had never been to insult anyone. We had done things the right way and had notified them of our refusal within reasonable delay, but to no avail. No we were being pulled toward the damn aircraft against our will, as if attached to an invisible string. All the love I felt for my job had suddenly vanished. I hated Roberto for acting that way. I despised him. I loathed him. I hated Americair, the airport, airplanes, everything!

Nevertheless, we made it on board. I was so angry I had tears in my eyes, knowing that I wouldn't get any sleep but would be flying to Barcelona instead. My tears represented my helplessness facing the Final Judgment. I stored my suitcase in an overhead bin and started my pre-flight checks. I was barely checking under the seats. I forgot to check my first-aid kit. I wasn't really looking for any firearms in the seat pockets. I no longer cared. I actually couldn't care less!

Per usual, I went to the front to sign my name on the emergency sheet, certifying that I had done my pre-flight checks according to regulations. When I got to the front, Roberto was holding the sheet and handed it over to me. Before signing it, I looked at him and decided to face him.

"You know, if I wanted, I could not sign this sheet," I said, hoping to have him understand that him yelling orders hadn't played any role in my decision to board the plane.

Roberto looked at me, skeptical. I noticed his left eyebrow arch up before he opened his mouth to reply.

"Sorry, I don't understand your moaning," he said in a very condescending way.

I wasn't sure I heard him correctly so wanted to make sure.

"What do you mean, moaning?"

I couldn't believe it! He was treating me like a child! I could feel the tension increase between us. I thought maybe I shouldn't have said anything. But I didn't feel like it. I was going to stand up for myself, or at least try to. Hearing my question loaded with attitude, he moved in closer and rested his hands on the back of a seat. He frowned and declared:

"No, I don't have to deal with your moaning. I have a real job to do and it doesn't include babysitting children like yourself. You have a problem with that?"

I was dying to start a conversation about that because yes, yes I had a problem with that. He was our chief purser. His job included having to look after us, after every single one of us. He was supposed to be there to support and help us in situations like these. Not wanting to get into a really bad argument, I answered that I didn't have a problem with that. However, wanting to push it just a little more, I decided to repeat my statement.

"Well, I just want to make sure you understand that I could refuse to sign this sheet if I wanted to!"

My comment had the effect of a nuclear bomb. I should have seen it coming. His eyes became big and round, like golf balls, and I could see red veins popping out of them. Roberto was transforming into an in-flight monster. Suddenly, he looked down at his victim, which happened to be me, and roared with all his power, extending his claws:

"Sign this fucking sheet! NOW!"

I remained calm and stood up straight but internally, I was terrified by the man. DISASTER! DISASTER! DISASTER! I replied one more time but this time, to myself, just to make myself feel stronger. And maybe to continue my "moaning."

"I'm gonna sign the sheet, but you have no right to talk to me this way!"

I finally signed the document and quickly left into hiding. I had no desire to see his arrogance bite me again. Maybe he could even spit fire, who knows? I was scared of this Roberto IN-FLIGHT MONSTER so I hurriedly found Rupert to tell him all about the situation.

When I found him, he seemed to have gathered his strength. He was already working away, counting the trays in the central galley located between the second set of doors of the aircraft. I explained my recent trauma. He rubbed my back, telling me everything would be okay. I wasn't so sure but looked down in agreement. Again, my eyes filled with tears. I rested my elbows on the counter, trying to get my wits back. I concentrated and visualized the busy gardens of Barcelona. I pictured myself holding a glass of delicious *rioja*. How comforting! As I was getting carried away by my thoughts, I felt a hand on my shoulder. I was convinced it belonged to Rupert and held it tight. Then I heard a comforting voice that sounded nothing like my roommate's.

"Everything will be fine, Scarlett . . . "

I recognized the kind and reassuring voice right away. A manly and hoarse voice. My knees went weak again. It looked like Captain Ross had sensed my breakdown. The shivers I got from Roberto-the-In-Flight-Monster were nothing compared to the ones I got from my captain.

"I know it's not easy right now and you're not legal for takeoff. However, I want to thank you for coming with us. In return, I'd like to take you guys out to dinner when we get to Barcelona. What do you think?"

The invitation was more than tempting, it was irresistible. I was delighted but made sure not to reveal it. I dried my tears. I was stuck on this aircraft so might as well be a prisoner along with the endearing John Ross. I smiled and gathered all the energy I had left, which I needed to go through the next seven hours and forty minutes.

Chapter 8

2,000 feet above Barcelona (BCN)

W hen on a plane, some individuals seem to make it their own personal mission to annoy the cabin crew. I'm referring to the "friendly" passengers who never go unnoticed and always find a way to be distracting on board. It's inevitable; even when they're sleeping, eyes closed and tucked in their blankets, one of them will manage to be annoying. He'll either have both his feet in the aisle, meaning we have to wake him up every time we have to get through with our cart, or he'll come to the back of the aircraft, hours after the meal service, to advise us we forgot his dinner. Of course, it'll be *our* fault, not his.

In fact, many passengers have the bad habit of putting the blame on the flight attendant. It must be nice to live life without any self-criticism, right? They're quick to point their finger at us: "You forgot me!" or "You didn't come down the aisle with the duty-free!" Why are they so adamant about immediately attacking us? They would simply need to ask and I'd be right back with perfume for them to buy. No need to attack me. I've got proof of my innocence anyway. It was actually me who, earlier, walked down the aisle with my cart and witnessed the same accusatory lady with her eyes wide open, chatting away with her neighbor. I saw her peek at my Chanel and Givenchy perfume bottles. But oh well, memory has a way of fading, so I won't mention it.

Me, Myself, and I passengers, as I like to call them, usually manifest themselves early on in a flight. I would even say they show themselves right from the beginning, during boarding. Strangely though, flight 642 from New York to Barcelona didn't appear to carry any of them. It was much better that way as I didn't feel like handling their tantrums. The various disasters we had just been through were enough and I truly believed, or at least hoped, that I had had my share of *Ruperian* adventures.

Even after our three-hour delay, passengers had obediently taken their seats. None had seemed to be bringing every single thing they owned on board and the overhead bins had seemed almost empty when we went about closing them. I hadn't had to play my usual role of the Weightlifter Flight Attendant for my high-maintenance passengers; they lifted their bags themselves. I hadn't received an excessive amount of requests from them either. When I made it to my jump seat for landing, I almost, *almost*, had a smile on my face.

Once seated with my seatbelt fastened, ready for our arrival into Barcelona, I started thinking about my upcoming evening with John. I was still hoping to find out more about him. *There's no harm in being friends*, I thought, lying to myself. At least thinking about him was helping me stay awake. As I was seated in front of passengers, it was very important to look awake. I definitely couldn't fall asleep, even a little, as my main task was to remain alert and ready in case of an emergency. The descent went smoothly, and looking out the window, I could see the

Mediterranean stretch out along the coast. Then, I heard the landing gear engage. The wheels were well in place for landing.

Suddenly, three rows down, a woman jumped from her seat and started walking toward me. Dressed like Coco Chanel, she didn't seem ill or anything. Her complexion looked quite fresh and pink. Actually, she appeared to be a Me, Myself, and I passenger. I should have known better. A flight without any creature like herself was simply impossible. There would always be one appearing before the end, but thirty seconds prior to landing was definitely not a good time.

I remained in my jump seat as there was no way I was going to hurt myself for this Lady Coco. She was moving toward me, so I decided to stop her as she passed by. She was barely looking at me, staring at the lavatories my jump seat was attached to instead. I called out to her.

"Ma'am, we'll be landing in a second, please go back to your seat."

Lady Coco looked down at me, determined to not go back to her seat and continue on with her game plan. She lifted her hand up to her mouth and announced:

"I'm gonna puke!"

Really? I didn't believe her. It was obvious she wasn't sick. She just wanted to use the lavatories here and now, at 2,000 feet above ground, going at a speed of 180 miles an hour. I couldn't let her go past, as my duty was to look after everyone's safety. I had to make sure she didn't hurt her pretty little self. I reinstated my request more firmly.

"Ma'am, you need to be seated for landing."

Lady Coco then looked at me in a sneaky way, put on a pitiful, ill face, and repeated she was about to vomit. At that moment, I became utterly uninterested in her safety. I had informed her of the procedures but she had refused to respect them. *She might as well hit her head on the toilet seat!* I thought, rolling my eyes at her. I lifted my hand toward her to show her through.

"Just go!" I declared, not bothered anymore.

I no longer felt like myself. I wasn't worried about the woman's safety. I was almost hoping she would hurt herself. I really needed to get some rest! I glanced out the window to see how close we were to the landing strip. We were already on it. We landed ever so gently, without any bump. I was disappointed. I would have appreciated a nice gust of wind. We were quickly driving down the runway when I heard the toilet flush. Barely a minute after she went in, Lady Coco came right out. She walked by and as if landing in the lavatories wasn't out of the ordinary enough for her, she turned around and faced me. As I was still on my jump seat, the height difference gave her a feeling of superiority. She pointed a finger at me, as if telling off a child.

"Don't you dare ever speak to me like that again!"

I couldn't believe what I was hearing. I was the flight attendant, the one with authority on this aircraft. But Mrs. Me, Myself, and I was commanding me to not speak to her like that! Was she now trying to teach me a lesson? I wasn't ready to lash out at her so with a calm, yet authoritarian tone, I justified myself.

"I did that for your own safety, ma'am.'

That woman must have had a problem with authority and surely must have behaved like a queen her whole life as she pressed on:

"I refuse to be spoken to this way!"

And she was insisting too! Now, that was enough! She had dared to get up in the middle of our descent just to use the lavatories. She had even landed while still inside them. I knew she hadn't vomited as my head was right next to the wall and

I could hear every little sound coming through it. Lady Coco had come out after a millisecond and instead of returning to her seat without a word, she had positioned herself right in the emergency exit, in front of the passengers seated across from me. Now she was lecturing me in front of everyone as if I was just a little girl, and above all while we were still moving fast on the ground. I exploded!

On the spur of the moment, I turned into an animal. A dragon was born in the sky. My nostrils flared and smoke was coming out of them. I could spit fire. I unfastened my seatbelt and literally leaped in front of her. I was now about three heads taller than Lady Coco. She was just a little bug, a small grape I could easily crush. I stood straight, shoulders back. My eyes turned red and my eyesight sharpened. I could see everything, every little piece of dust floating about the cabin. The former pretty air stewardess was nowhere to be seen. I was now the devil himself. I was no longer whispering, but shouting instead.

"ENOUGH! Go back to your seat NOW!"

My voice traveled through the whole plane. Rupert, who was seated at the door across from me, looked at me, astonished and amazed. I had yelled so loud at her to go back to her seat that my throat was hurting. I had actually spat fire. Tiny Lady Coco looked up at me. She looked like a poor stray dog. The dark rings around her eyes seemed even darker. She hesitated, her paws trembling, the hair standing on her back. She searched for a comeback, but none came to her. Then, silence. Without a word, at least for the moment, she turned around and went back to her seat. I had won. The aircraft was still moving, so I returned to my jump seat. I was hoping this would be the end of the story. I was exhausted. I had gone through enough for the day. However, I knew very well the Lady Cocos of this world and I knew that this one wouldn't call it quits so easily. This was only the beginning.

* * *

"Ladies and gentlemen, Americair would like to welcome you to Barcelona, where the local time is one p.m. and the outside temperature is eighty-two degrees Fahrenheit. We ask you to please remain seated with your seatbelt fastened until the captain turns off the seatbelt sign."

The aircraft finally came to a stop. I immediately unfastened by seatbelt, eager to stand up. I was about to faint out of fatigue. With itchy eyes, I disarmed my door and ensured that Rupert, my counterpart, had disarmed his as well. Soon, I'd be able to lie down in a comfy bed and snore away the exhaustion. Although, I suspected I'd first have to neutralize my opponent.

Our passengers were about to get off. Rupert opened his door. An announcement was made.

"Ladies and gentlemen, you may now disembark through the second door on the left. Thank you!"

I started sending off my passengers with a great smile and relaxed *thank-yous* and *goodbyes.* I was trying to look Zen, hoping that Lady Coco would come to her senses. I didn't want our showdown to go any further. She had gotten on my nerves and I had cracked. I was ready to overlook her behavior and was hoping she'd do the same and would keep walking by, silently, until she was out of my sight. I tried my best not to look in her direction, but her seat was only three rows away. It was difficult not to notice her stately demeanor slowly approaching.

Lady Coco had thrown her shoulders back, lifted her chin, and buttoned up her jacket. I could feel her eagerness to get past the other passengers and reach me, her prey. She hadn't laid down her arms like I had hoped. Instead, she was fully charged and ready to pounce. She slowly made her way to where I was standing.

Passengers were trickling off the aircraft, giving me time to observe Lady Coco approaching. I had no idea what was to come but I was dreading it. It was down to just one passenger between me and her. He thanked me and turned to his left, toward the exit, thus unveiling my dear enemy. Lady Coco, as planned, moved forward, but before turning toward the exit, she stopped. She was now blocking the other passengers' way. She waited a moment, then exploded.

"I want to see the captain! I want to make a complaint! What is your name?" she barked at me.

I wasn't going to give her my name just to have her falsify the facts in her favor. I had run out of empathy a long time ago, so I put on a more arrogant attitude and told her:

"Sorry, but I won't give you my name."

My refusal to provide my name made her go even wilder. Still blocking the exit for the other passengers, she insisted.

"I want to see the captain now! I want to make a complaint!"

Aw! She wanted to complain to the captain! She obviously knew nothing about aviation rules as a pilot is here not to hear out the passengers' complaints but to take them to their destination. The purpose of having flight attendants on board is to manage human crisis, but since she wanted to see a captain, I thought I'd introduce her to one right away. I responded to her request.

"All right, you may see the captain. However, you'll have to wait for all other passengers to deplane. Have a seat," I firmly ordered her.

She took a seat, livid with anger at me for making her wait to see the "captain". Meanwhile, I put on my loveliest smile and continued wishing the best to my passengers.

"Thank you! See you soon! *Gracias!* Enjoy! *Hasta luego!*"

The aircraft was finally empty. I gestured to Lady Coco to follow me and walked to the front of the plane. I commanded her to sit at row four, just before the first-class section. She complied. I made my way to Roberto-the-In-Flight-Monster and quickly explained the situation. As I had hoped, he listened. I knew I wasn't to blame for anything as I had simply done what I had been hired to do: ensure everyone's safety. Regardless of our pre-flight disagreements, flight attendants would always obey the unwritten rule of solidarity. Roberto, although he had been a horrible creature to rub shoulders with, would certainly ignore our small dispute and join forces with me in front of the passenger. Victory was within my reach.

He moved toward Lady Coco, who was still waiting on her seat. I followed.

"What is going on, ma'am?" he asked, to find out her version of the story.

"I went to the restroom and that girl was impolite with me!" she announced, stuttering with emotions.

"Ma'am, was the seatbelt sign on?" he asked innocently, knowing that if it was on, Lady Coco would be in the wrong.

"Hm, hm, it's that nobody has ever spoken to me like that before! I want to make a complaint and—"

Roberto cut her off.

"Was the seatbelt sign on when you got up to use the restroom?" he asked again.

Lady Coco was stammering. She was refusing to answer the

question but at last had no choice but to do so, as Roberto, now called Roberto-the-Loyal-Accomplice, was insistent.

"Was the seatbelt sign on, ma'am?"

She finally yielded.

"Yes, it was on but . . . "

Still, she refused to understand. The situation had become quite ridiculous and it was about time it ended. Roberto finished her up.

"My colleague was just doing her job. Now, I will ask you to leave the aircraft. Have a nice day!"

Lady Coco was in a fury. Roberto had just interrupted her and had declared that I had been right to use a little authority toward her. He escorted her to the exit. Angry, she managed to set foot on the bridge. From inside the aircraft, I could hear her shouting and kicking up a fuss. Then, the yelling stopped. The threat had cleared. I happily picked up my suitcase, ready to leave the last fifteen hours of disaster behind. I opened the door on the bridge, the one leading down to the tarmac. The sun blinded me and I could barely see the steps taking me to the bottom. I came to a halt to allow my eyes to adjust to daylight. And then, I saw him. Down by the aircraft, John was putting his bags in the back of our private transportation. He turned around and saw me. He flashed a wonderful smile and gestured for me to come join him. I was the last one to arrive. Close to him, the previous nightmarish hours were now forgotten. I had never been so hungry for tapas.

Chapter 9

Boston (BOS) – Returning from Barcelona (BCN)

H e grabbed the back of my neck and slid his hand through my long hair. He strongly pulled me toward him. His piercing gaze was tearing me apart. His dark eyes reached deep into my soul. I could feel my body weaken. He owned me. I was pulled toward him like a magnet. My mouth opened softly, naturally. I was ready and he could feel it. He wanted me just as much. He opened his mouth too. Our tongues, impatient; our bodies, finally coming together. We became one. And then, abruptly, someone opened the door to my apartment and I woke up.

Becky entered, fresh from her yoga class. And I, having just gotten back from Barcelona, had fallen asleep on the couch, absolutely drained. Rupert was sleeping across the room. The last twenty-four hours had gone so fast. In my dreams, I had tried to remember the recent events, tweaking just a couple details. Ten more minutes of sleeping and I would have been in heaven. Unfortunately, Becky had made me wake up to reality. John wasn't here. He wasn't holding me in his arms, he was holding another woman instead. His wife. Regardless of the nice evening we had spent together, the situation remained the same. I could never be with him. I had to move on and forget him.

I rubbed my eyes and sat up on my comfy cushion. Rupert was yawning, still half asleep. Becky, after apologizing for waking us up, went to the kitchen for a drink of water. I couldn't wait any longer; I had to pique her interest.

"Guess who I spent the evening with yesterday, in Barcelona?" She drank her water and glanced at me, clearly intrigued.

"I don't know, who?" she asked, with an overly interested tone.

"I was so happy he was there!" I added, intentionally omitting the mysterious person's name.

"Do you mean to say that you spent the evening with Mr. Inaccessible?" she asked, not wanting to mention John's name in front of Rupert, who was listening in.

From the kitchen, I could see Becky's beautiful dark eyes grow big. She subtly pointed toward Rupert to find out if he was already in the loop. I confirmed that he was indeed, and proceeded to provide more details.

"He knows the full story. He was with us last night so it was hard to pretend. He promised not to say anything, though. The crush I have on John must remain a secret, right, Rupert?"

I knew that Rupert was the biggest gossiper of all flight attendants but he needed to understand that stories about Becky and me were completely confidential and should not go around the airline. He agreed, somewhat insulted.

"Come on, Scarlett! You can trust me! I won't tell anyone that you're fantasizing about the guy," he replied. And then, to annoy me he added, "What would people think if they knew that the *idealistic* Scarlett had fallen for a married pilot who has kids?"

I simply laughed at his comment. Internally, I knew very well he was right. I truly had fallen for a man who was the complete opposite to my ideal. It didn't make sense and I couldn't get my head around it. At least Rupert had grabbed Becky's attention.

"Does that mean, Scarlett, that you set aside your principles to have fun, just for one night, with someone you like?" she asked, happy to finally imagine me putting myself first.

Becky was picturing the same adultery scenario most people would. But that's not exactly what had happened. I had to explain the evening's events. I suggested she come sit between Rupert and me so that I could unravel the mystery.

Just as I was about to start telling my story, my phone rang. It was my mom calling. I didn't answer as I knew she would earnestly question me about my last trip and I would have to interrupt her in order to continue my conversation with Becky and Rupert. I thought I was better off calling her back once I was well rested. I put my phone down and noticed four missed calls in the last hour. My phone had been on silent and I had not heard it while asleep. All four were from my parents. What a surprise! When mom wanted something, she persisted. In a way, I felt like part of me was just like her. When I set a goal for myself, I fight to the end. Internally, I was hoping John wasn't one of my ambitions, though. What would the consequences be? I knew I shouldn't look for the answer to that question. Becky was getting impatient so I hastened to tell her about my night.

"First, we went to the old part of Barcelona for an aperitif. The evening was promising since the whole group was getting along very well. There was Anna, Ishma, Rupert, and three pilots, including John of course."

"Which pilots were they?" asked Becky, to further understand the group dynamic.

"Uh! I can't really remember but I think there was an Anthony and a Charles."

"Hm, don't know them . . . Sorry for interrupting. I'm listening now!"

"Honestly, Becky, I was so happy that John was with us, I wasn't concerned with the other group members. He's the only one I wanted to speak with," I admitted before Rupert jumped in.

"I'm telling you, Becky, I had never seen Scarlett like that. I tried to talk to her twice while she was talking with that John guy and she completely ignored me. I could have screamed in her ears and she wouldn't have noticed!"

"Okay, now you're exaggerating! I was, I'll admit, a bit too interested in what he was saying, but I still managed to look independent," I said, mostly trying to convince myself that I had been able to hide my true feelings.

"Maybe at first, for the pre-drinks, but afterward? And at dinner? And in the elevator?" Rupert jumped in again, refreshing my memory.

"Whoa! Okay, now you're stealing my thunder! Let me tell my story."

Once lectured, Rupert laid back down on the couch and folded his arms behind his head, indicating he would no longer participate. He looked really bored. *He can just leave if he's so uninterested!* I thought to myself. Still, he didn't move an inch. So, I continued on with more details.

"We shared a pitcher of sangria on a nice patio. After the very first glass, Rupert was already tipsy and I was almost the same. It made sense, after the night we had gone through," I said, giving a knowing tap on Rupert's shoulder.

"What happened?" asked Becky.

"Ah! A delay, but we'll tell you about it later. Let's not put a halt on Scarlett's precious little story," added Rupert, to push my buttons.

I ignored his comment and continued my story.

"I was already tired so quickly felt the effect of alcohol in my blood. Actually, we were all pretty much on the same page so you can imagine our conversations!" I exclaimed, remembering the scene.

"I hope you weren't talking about sex?" Becky asked quickly.

"Ha! Ha! Nope! Not this time. Just mammary implants!"

"Okay . . . the boys wanted to know if you'd had a boob job?"

"That conversation was so ridiculous, I couldn't even get involved!" mentioned Rupert, as if it had really bothered him.

"Aw, come on! You thought it was funny. And we didn't talk about it for long."

"Actually, I don't even know how we got talking about implants."

"What was being said about them?" asked Becky, interested.

"I think Ishma brought it up when she mentioned that her boyfriend loved her new boobs. And then, one of the pilots added that he liked implants too, and so on."

"What! Nonsense!" exclaimed Becky. "And what about John? What was his preference?"

"Oh, John!" I answered, still under his spell. "He was mute for most of the conversation. I was the one who had to pry."

"That's good! A reserved pilot. I like it. So, what did he answer?"

"He said he liked natural women."

"That's it?"

"Yep, nothing else."

"Awesome!"

"Why?" I asked, skeptical.

"Well, there's none more natural than you, Scarlett! You're a *what you see is what you get* kind of girl."

"So, you think he could possibly like me?" I asked, full of insecurities.

"Yeah, but keep going with your story and then we'll see."

I obliged.

"After the weird conversation, we turned it around and started asking basic questions such as *tea or coffee?* or *white or red wine?* Silly questions to keep the conversation going."

"Not at all!" Rupert cut in. "At least I could join!"

"Yeah, true," I admitted. "And it's a good thing we started talking about that because that's when I had a strange feeling."

"What?" asked Becky.

"Well, it's as if I could predict all of John's answers. I felt like I was inside his head. I can't really explain it, Becky, but that had never happened to me before."

"Hm, I read somewhere that soulmates are so connected through their spirits that sometimes they don't even need to speak to communicate. They understand each other through their thoughts."

Now that was a very irrational thought, but I did like to think that John and I were meant for each other. Rupert, on the other hand, was quick to burst my bubble.

"Oh dear! Girls, you've lost it! Soulmates? We're connected through our spirits? Blah! Blah! Blah! That's bullshit!" he declared, somehow offended by the analysis.

I didn't agree with him but I had no energy to get into an argument. I also knew why he had reacted that way so I didn't want to add anything. Rupert had never gotten over his first love and, not wanting to admit it, had skipped from lover to lover for the last few years. It was best not to dig up old memories. I simply rolled my eyes to indicate the irrelevance of his intervention and went on.

"After the pre-drinks, we found a small restaurant close to where we were. Nothing too complicated. At the back, there was one table left. We all sat down without putting too much thought into who sat where. Or so I think . . . "

I paused. I wondered if what was to come had only happened out of luck.

"Regardless, guess who sat in front of me?" I asked Becky, keeping her guessing.

"Well, John!" she squealed.

"Exactly!" I said, smiling.

"He chose to sit in front of you or it just happened?" she inquired, as if the answer could change the outcome.

"A coincidence, I think. There was only one seat left and it was in front of me."

"Oh, I wouldn't be so sure!" added Becky. "I saw the way he looked at you in Paris. He was far from indifferent. Obviously, *you* can't see it. Rupert, what do you think?"

"Ah! Now you girls care about my opinion, huh?" he said, again a bit insulted to have been excluded.

Rupert seemed overly sensitive. It must have been the after-flight frustration. I totally understood. I also had to be handled with care after a flight. Knowing this, I tried to reassure him.

"Of course I want your opinion! You know that! You were there with me; surely you noticed something. Right?"

"Well, if you really want my opinion, I think you're crazy about him!" he said, bursting into laughter.

"Eh, yes! That, I already know, Rupert. That's all you've noticed?"

"Truthfully, Scarlett, seeing how he was looking at you, I think he likes you. But he remained so conventional, it's hard to tell."

"So, he was sitting in front of me purely out of chance?" I asked, disappointed.

"I'm not so sure! Really!" insisted Becky.

"Yeah, you're probably right. Problem is, in Barcelona, just like in Paris, John and I only talked as colleagues, so I don't have proof of anything."

I could definitely feel a mutual attraction but I couldn't be entirely certain, even after our two surprise encounters. Anyway, even if he was interested, he wasn't the kind of guy to bend the rules. He must have sat in front of me simply because it would make the evening more pleasant.

"I know that John doesn't look like a scumbag pilot, but still, I wouldn't say he talked to you as just a colleague," Becky declared before listening to the rest of my story.

She might have been right but, then again, John had given me no clue indicating that I should think otherwise. I was probably the only one seeing a strong electric current traveling within our non-existent couple. Most likely a one-way connection going nowhere. The thought of not finding a way to be with him saddened me but, at the same time, I was glad he hadn't shown me any clear sign of interest. I wouldn't have wanted a cheater, an unfaithful man. So, either way, I was doomed.

"The meal was delicious. We even shared an appetizer. And that's when Rupert started glancing at me suspiciously, which made me blush."

"Ha! Ha! Ha!" Rupert laughed again, looking at Becky. "It was way too obvious for me not to notice. Even after three years of living together, Scarlett won't drink out of the same water bottle as me, yet there she was laughing away, picking at the food on the captain's plate. The world upside down!"

Becky started laughing as well.

"You're exposed, Scarlett! Did the other flight attendants notice anything?"

"No, I don't think so. But anyway, what difference does it make if they noticed our complicity or not? We weren't making out or anything!"

"No, that's right, it's none of their business. Plus, he's so good-looking they would have just been jealous anyway," said Becky, still laughing.

"Ha! Ha! Ha! Maybe Rupert would have been!" I joined in.

"Nah, he's not my type. I must admit that he's very charismatic but I prefer the big and strong. The tough guys."

"He's mine anyways," I replied unconsciously.

Oops! Had I really said that? He's mine? Hm! If John was mine, I was sharing him with another woman. I couldn't believe that I was imagining myself owning him. We hadn't even touched lips. But that's exactly what I wanted, to own him. I wanted him to be mine, mine only, and I had to face the facts: It was impossible. The conversation had strayed a little so I brought it back to the main topic.

"After dinner, we all walked to the hotel. Of course, I was next to John. We were chatting away. He was so easy to talk to. He didn't mention his wife, nor his kids, so I didn't want to mention them either. I'm sure that had he not been interested, he probably would have referred to them at some point. I don't know and don't want to know about them. We stopped to get some ice cream. He paid for my cone but not for the others."

I paused to take a breath. Becky took advantage of this to recap.

"So, he paid for your ice cream but not for Rupert's, nor for anyone else's? He wanted to be nice to you, it's obvious. I knew he liked you!" she concluded.

"You're jumping to conclusions pretty quick, don't you think?" I asked.

"No, not at all! Why wasn't it one of the other pilots you were with who paid for your ice cream? Or why didn't John pay for Rupert's, Anna's or Ishma's?"

"To demonstrate some interest?" I, in turn, concluded.

"There you go! It's a tiny detail, but you're the one who keeps complaining about men not paying and he proved you wrong," said Becky, happy to see that my captain had looked after me and my ice cream consumption.

"Anyway, it was greatly appreciated and I thanked him. He seemed quite happy to spend three euros to treat me," I added jokingly.

Rupert, still under the influence of the after-flight frustration, started judging our feminine reasoning.

"Bah! You girls are unbelievable! Hilarious! All a guy needs to do to impress you is to pay for ice cream!" he said, making fun of us.

I refrained from justifying myself as I knew very well he also appreciated this sort of attention when he was in a relationship. I motioned for him to be quiet and he sprawled further out onto the couch, fully relaxed. Becky urged me to continue my story. The end was near.

"Well, it's on the way back to the hotel that I started to weaken. I didn't have any proof, of course, but I was under the impression that there was a clear complicity between John and me . . . "

"If I can be of any help," interrupted Rupert, "I don't think you were dreaming."

"Yeah, I think the same," confirmed Becky.

"Well, even so, there's nothing I could do! My hands were tied. I wasn't gonna be like, *Hey, hot stuff, wanna come up to my room?*"

"Why not?" exclaimed Rupert.

"Come on! That doesn't make any sense. I know I'm quite picky and don't normally like anyone but that's no excuse to jump on the first man I like, especially when the lucky one is a married forty-year-old pilot who has kids!"

"Yeah..." sighed the pair.

"And, apart from the ice cream move, John didn't give me any sign. Imaginary electric connections aren't enough to act on!" I added, disheartened.

My two friends were stroking my back out of compassion. Had I been able to travel back in time, I would have never wanted to meet John in the first place. *It would have saved me the heartache,* I thought, before continuing.

"Once at the hotel, we all got on the elevator. I was still pondering the strange chemistry I had felt between John and me. I was wondering if I had dreamed it all up. The elevator stopped on the first level and Rupert and Ishma got off. Then, the two first officers got off on level two. It was just Anna, John, and me when the door opened again, on level three."

"I hope Anna got out of there as fast as she could," let out Becky, looking at me impatiently.

"Well, I thought John would get off. I was mentally prepared to say, *Bye, see you tomorrow,* but no! It's Anna who got off and then the door closed behind her. At that point, it was only John and me inside the elevator. I was so surprised, I was speechless and completely uncomfortable."

"You mean you were shy," clarified Rupert, based on the version I had given him on the plane.

"Yes! Shy! Completely intimidated. And so was he, because he wasn't saying a word. I quickly understood that we were the only ones sleeping on level four. Just me and him. No one else."

Suddenly, it all dawned on Becky.

"You mean to say, you could have slept in his room and no one would have known? Please tell me that's what you did!" she pleaded.

I smiled.

"Actually, it had become so silent in there I started to have doubts. Normally, whether we were with Ishma, or Anna, or even the other pilots, someone would say something, anything, to break the silence. But at that moment, nothing! I was no longer breathing, and John neither. I'm telling you, there was an indescribable tension in the air. A direct result of attraction? I can't say, but it was as if the seconds had stopped and the damn door would never open. If I didn't get out of there quickly, I was going to be pulled toward him like a magnet."

Rupert interrupted and I grabbed the opportunity to catch my breath.

"You mean, if you stayed any longer in the elevator, you were going to betray your mighty principles."

"He isn't wrong . . . I like taking risks but I wasn't ready to betray what I believe in: fidelity. However, feelings were jostling inside me and I felt an inexplicable desire to express the attraction I had for him. My spontaneity was about to take over."

I took a few seconds to catch my breath again and continued on.

"The door hadn't opened on level four yet so I decided to observe his body language. He was standing straight, confident, gently smiling. He looked so handsome, so manly. I could sense the man in him but still, he wasn't doing anything to indicate that he was attracted to me."

"Yeah, sure, but, Scarlett, those things can usually be felt," said Becky. "Didn't you notice anything?"

"Yes and no! I definitely noticed that we were both uncomfortable but he stayed quiet. Not a word! I was dying inside and finally decided to do the same as him and not say anything."

"I get it," said Becky encouragingly.

"An eternity later, the door opened. I was so eager to get out that I quickly slid through the small gap to make it to my room. He did the same and headed to my right, three doors down from me. We were both nervously looking for our keys and I could still feel the intimidating chemistry between us. And then, don't ask me why, but I lost it."

I paused to collect my thoughts. I was so ashamed of what I was about to say. I really could have done better. I refused to completely expose my disgrace to my friends but Becky forced me to.

"So, Scarlett, what did you say? It can't be that bad, come on! Admitting our weakness for the opposite sex has never been shameful. Go on!"

"All right, all right! Well, I had just found my key in my bag and saw from the corner of my eye that John had opened his door. As he was entering his room, he turned his head toward me. I looked at him and heard him say, *Good night! See you tomorrow!* I wanted to answer but instead of wishing him sweet dreams I said something else. Dammit!"

"And?" asked Becky, hanging on my every word.

"Well, I said: *You get on my nerves!* and I entered my room quickly, like a coward."

"Wow! You didn't sugarcoat it!"

"Spontaneous, per usual. No idea how I came up with that!"

As a matter of fact, I have the tendency to act on the spur of the moment, without thinking. Once I had made the mistake, I had to rectify the situation, which was quite embarrassing. The *you get on my nerves* shouldn't be taken literally but it was already too late to explain myself. Anyway, seeing the smile on John's face when he heard me, I assume he knew exactly what I meant. I was sure he now knew I had a soft spot for him. And then, not wanting to elaborate my statement, I had escaped to my room.

Once inside, a mix of ridicule and relief had come over me. I had automatically banged my head on the wall. The *bang* had resonated throughout the room. I could only imagine the aftershock that made it to the neighboring walls. *As long as it didn't go as far as the third room down the hall*, I thought.

I had to get a grip. I wanted the man. Not in two days, nor two weeks, but right at that moment! The impossible separating us no longer mattered. Thoughts were rushing through my mind. I started breathing deeply, pacing around the room. My feet, rubbing against the carpet, were literally raising dust as I walked. I analyzed my options:

1. Run to his room and seduce him;
2. Call his room and evaluate my chances or;
3. Stay put and do nothing.

I had chosen the third option. Becky was offended.

"Scarlett! He wouldn't have said no, he's a man! It may be months until you see him again, you know that. Still, you preferred to not do anything?" she scolded.

"Yes! Exactly! That's what I chose to do! Nothing. I wouldn't have felt good about myself. He's married, Becky! I would have slept with him, then what? Nothing! I would have been the one with a broken heart. And, had he wanted something to happen, he would have taken the opportunity to make a move since I had just revealed my feelings for him," I explained, convinced I had made the right decision.

"You're right. I've had dozens of married men make a move

without me trying. When that's what they want, they go for it."

Becky was proud of me while still being disappointed that nothing had happened. I was saddened but also relieved to have stuck to my convictions. I didn't know when I'd see him again but it was better not be too soon. It was about time I met other people and fell for another man. At that moment, I vowed to accept all invitations coming my way. Surely, it was only a matter of time before another man would steal my heart. It was worth the time and effort, so I had to give it a try.

Chapter 10

Nice (NCE) – Boston (BOS)

I called it the *Extreme Flirt Game* and swore to accept every invitation I received. It was an improvised detox with one aim: forgetting about the handsome John Ross. My mind was set on going all the way with this and I stubbornly wanted to have fun with men, putting aside my restricting principles. Therefore, my choice of eligible candidates, although subject to a short list of criteria, would be almost unlimited.

The candidates had to be, first and foremost, single. All who were in the process of getting a divorce, on a *break*, or separated were not eligible for my flirt sessions. And lastly, they had to be between the ages of twenty-five and forty-five years old. In short: I was ready to meet just about anyone.

Seeing the large number of candidates, the upcoming months promised to be quite entertaining. I was ready, no matter the cost, to gamble. Who knows, maybe my tender feelings for the Inaccessible Pilot would be banished once and for all? That's what I was hoping anyway.

Becky had introduced me to a couple of eligible men through-out the month of September but none had me really interested.

Like a big girl, I had accepted some of their invitations. Our dates hadn't led anywhere but at least it had helped lighten my mood. I was acquiring a taste for the game and actually wanted to continue playing.

Then, one day, I ended up receiving an email from a senior colleague named Ben. It read: *Hi, Scarlett, we do not know each other but I have a flight to switch. If you're interested, it's a seventy-two-hour layover in Nice.* Wow! Of course, I was interested! Seventy-two hours in Nice! I read the email again and suddenly panicked. Surely I wasn't the only one Ben thought of. He must have sent a message to other flight attendants as well in order to make the switch as quickly as possible. Therefore, I hurriedly replied to him. Such an offer could disappear in the blink of an eye and I didn't want anyone to beat me to it.

The flight exchange had great timing. Now that I had adopted my new Extreme Flirt philosophy, little *getaways* abroad could be perfect opportunities to meet some candidates from across the Atlantic Ocean. Who knows? I waited impatiently for Ben's confirmation and after a whole day, found out that the switch had been approved. I felt as if I had won the jackpot! Even after just over three years of flying, I had never seen such a pairing on my own schedule. Ben, for some reason, was taking my Paris-no sleep-deadhead-Istanbul with nineteen hours rest, from Friday to Sunday (ew!) and I was to take his seventy-two hours in Nice with direct flights, from Monday to Friday (yeah!).

That night, I got ready for work thinking about Nice and its pebble beach. Although it was October, I was hoping it would be warm enough to enjoy the Mediterranean Sea. I hadn't even left yet and was looking forward to being there.

I looked at my watch and realized I still had half an hour before I had to leave for the airport. I settled in on the couch with my laptop and had a look at my crew. Hypocritically, I was hoping to see John's name on the list. I was disappointed with myself but fortunately did not see any familiar names. I was curious to find out who Samantha and Cecilia were, though. Their names rang a bell. Only one person could help in this situation and luckily, he could be found in the next room.

"Rupert, can you come here a minute, please?" I yelled with urgency.

I looked at my screen again and stared at the seniority numbers next to each of the names: 2, 20, 25, 45, 68, 70, and then mine, 1014! I was definitely dealing with a crew of old bags. I got scared.

Ever since I started working in aviation, urban legends were going around the airline. Many of them were about flight attendants with a lot, a lot of seniority. We called them *old bags* and I heard that some were nice and sturdy, while others were just shabby old bags.

I also knew that some of these cabin crew's reputations were true as I had often flown with a couple of them. Luckily, I had stumbled on a good bunch: men and women who had been flying for twenty years or so and who were still passionate about their jobs. Out of love for their work, they had served an inconceivable number of passengers and had put up with cigarette smoke, back when it was still allowed to smoke on board. Even after thousands of hours of flying, they were still smiling and dedicated. They were Top Quality Bags.

Unfortunately, the opposite was also true. Like night and day. Birth and death. Cold and heat. *Sturdy* and *Shabby* bags.

On the flip side, shabby bags are self-centered and act as such from takeoff to landing. They are, just like the vigorous kind, men and women who have been flying for a number of years and have helped thousands of passengers. However, these flight attendants no longer love their work. They keep their jobs out of need. They don't appreciate the passengers' needs and a single request from them can send them over the edge. They do not smile and as soon as their side of the aircraft has been served, they prefer to sit on the crew seats instead of helping their colleagues. Like useless old bags! I was really hoping none of them were on my flight itinerary. Again, I got worried.

"Rupert! What are you doing? Come here, quick!" I panicked again.

Still half naked, he came out of his room.

"What's wrong with you? Where's the fire?"

"No fire, but almost. I'm leaving tonight for Nice and just had a look at the crew list. The flight attendants flying with me are way too senior! I need to know what you know about them. I'm worried they're all old bags who aren't gonna do anything," I explained.

"Ah! I see. Let me have a look at the names."

Rupert was behind me. He bent down and rested his head on my shoulder to look at my screen.

"The chief purser is Nate Martin. He's number two in the company. He's awesome. He's gonna like you. He's a bit serious but works hard and commands respect."

What a relief! A purser should always lead by example and create a good workspace. If, inadvertently, a rotten old bag was among us, she wouldn't dare lag behind with a purser who commands respect. *Although, urban legends exist for a reason*, I thought. Rupert then continued.

"George is also very nice. He might spend most of the flight talking to you about the flowers he cultivates in his sunroom but it could be worse. As for Michelle, she's as gentle as a lamb, so you've got nothing to fear. She always brings her lunch on board and it always looks delicious."

Until then, it looked as if I had come across a crew of nice old hags. I was almost looking forward to meeting them. It was soon time for me to leave, so I urged Rupert to finish his analysis.

"Lucky! You're flying with Mary Andrews. An angel! Always ready to help. You're gonna like her."

"All right. Looks like everyone's nice. Great! Do you know Cecilia and Samantha?" I asked, as my last question.

"Cecilia Dawson? And Samantha Brown?" he quickly clarified.

The look in his eyes completely changed. He seemed surprised to hear me pronounce their names. I looked at the crew list again and read the last two names again.

"Yes, exactly. Dawson and Brown," I confirmed.

"Oh my God! Oh my God! Oh my God!" he let out sharply.

Surprised by his reaction, I closed my laptop and looked up to try and understand what he meant.

"Scarlett, those two women . . . they're . . . they're . . . Ah! I don't know how to explain . . . "

I didn't know where he was going with this. He seemed surprised, yet embarrassed to hear their names. I needed more details.

"Rupert, what happened with Cecilia and Samantha? Did you sleep with them or what?" I exclaimed.

"Come on, Scarlett! Me, sleep with women?"

"What did they do to you, then?"

"Well, it's actually what *we* did . . . "

"Fine! What did you all do, then?" I quickly asked.

"Bad, bad things!" he said, embarrassed but also smiling.

"Such as?"

"I was young, drunk, and stupid that night!" he justified,

without offering any more details.

"Rupert, we were all very naïve when we started with Americair. I'll understand. Go on, tell me what happened."

"Hm, I don't know if I should tell you," he teased, suddenly amused by my curiosity.

His little secrets were starting to seriously get on my nerves. Why wouldn't he tell me what he had done? I had been his roommate for three years! It was irritating!

"Rupert! Just tell me! The suspense is annoying. I'm your friend. It can't be that bad. If you don't tell me, I'll ask them. I'm flying with them tonight, you know," I said, trying to manipulate him into revealing his secret.

"Don't you dare ask them anything. And don't even mention we're friends. If I tell you the story, you can never ever mention it on board," he warned.

"Why? They hate you?"

"No! But what happened that night created a huge commotion. Since then, they allowed rumors to go around, but I've never said anything. I decided to hide the truth. Nobody should ever find out.

"Rupert-the-Gossiper keeping a secret! What's so precious about it?" I asked.

"It's because it implies a pilot and the whole thing turned sour for him."

"Ooh! Interesting! Who's the pilot?"

"Remember, a few years back, the handsome pilot who quit out of the blue, after having worked a mere three months at Americair?"

"The one who had decided not to operate a flight back from Paris, without any explanation?" I asked, increasingly more interested.

112

"Yes, him."

"Weren't you there actually?"

"Well, that's exactly why I know the reason he left," he admitted, still without providing more details.

"So, tell me! Quick, Rupert, please! I have to leave in fifteen minutes. I swear I won't tell anyone. Not even Becky," I pleaded, tired of waiting.

"You can tell Becky, but not another soul!"

"I swear on my mother's grave!"

I sat back down on the couch and Rupert quickly stepped out to put on a sweater. He came right back and sat next to me in the living room. His story seemed really weird and I was hoping he'd quickly reveal the details so that I could be on my way.

"All right, let me remind you that when I first started in aviation, I screwed up, I did stupid things. You kissed pilots who had girlfriends and I did things too, okay?"

"Yes, Rupert, I won't judge you. I promise!" I assured him.

"The story takes place in Paris, a few months after my very first flight. There was a captain, a first officer, Cecilia, Samantha, and me."

"What do those two women look like, so that I can have a clear picture?"

"Fifties, platinum blond, too much makeup. They were probably pretty when they were young but now they just look like they've partied too much."

"I see. And who was the other pilot?"

"Ah! Well that I won't say!" he quickly stated.

"What! So, what's the secret you're sharing, then?"

"No, I'm not telling you his name. It doesn't change anything to the story anyway."

I pouted childishly and let him continue.

"The later it got, the more alcohol there was. Once we were all nicely drunk, the topic of sex joined in."

"What a surprise!"

"Yep, always a popular topic. We could have just talked about it but Cecilia and Samantha had a better idea."

Rupert paused voluntarily. I couldn't wait to find out more.

"Come on! What did they suggest?" I questioned him again.

"They proposed a blowjob contest," he finally exclaimed, giving me a shove.

"You're kidding me! What a couple of perverts!"

"Yes, I agree!"

I was shocked yet impatient to know how the story went. I could never have participated in such a tournament to prove how I handle a stick. Although, I might have liked to be a fly on the wall. Rupert had to get on with his story. If there was the slightest traffic on the road I'd be late.

"The captain was married, so when he heard the proposition, he decided to leave."

"Very responsible of him. Surely, he missed out. Cecilia and Samantha must have been disappointed it was just you and the first officer?"

"I don't think they cared. Since the handsome pilot was new in the company, they had wanted him all to themselves. They could finally have fun with him."

"And what about you? You didn't fall under the two ladies' charm, I hope?" I asked, baffled.

"Of course not! I also thought about leaving but the first officer was quite attractive so I offered to be the referee and viciously observe the competition."

"Oh, you must have gotten quite the show!" I exclaimed.

"Sure did!" confirmed Rupert, with a shy smile, and then

continued.

"Cecilia pulled an eye mask out of her purse, as if she had planned it all along. She blind-folded the pilot. He was ready to start and had already pulled his pants down. In the red corner, we had Cecilia Dawson and in the blue, Samantha Brown."

"Oh! Stop it! Stop it! Such a demeaning story. I can't believe they'd do that to impress a guy," I declared, outraged.

"You want me to stop? The best part has yet to come, Scarlett," said Rupert, luring me in further.

"No, no! Go on! I definitely wanna know who won!"

"Samantha went in first. She kneeled down and did exactly what had to be done. The pilot was going nuts. She kept going until I announced Cecilia's turn. It was her turn to give everything her mouth had. The first officer got his money's worth. He was in heaven. I finally declared the end of the match. The result appeared to be a tight one."

"Who won?"

"The pilot couldn't make up his mind, so he asked for overtime."

"Ah! Bastard!" I exclaimed, offended.

"You mean, clever?"

"Yeah, cunning as a fox," I admitted.

I really had to go. I started getting dressed as Rupert continued detailing how the competition went down.

"So, Samantha went at it again. She was loving it and was taking great delight in the game. Her throat was taking it all in, very deeply. Eventually, her time ran out. One last chance was given to her opponent. It was all or nothing!" said Rupert, really into it.

"And what about the pilot? Surely, he wouldn't last much longer," I added from the doorway.

"Ah! He was in ecstasy. Samantha had given it her best.

But it's when her opponent started the second round that he found real pleasure. There was no more competition. Real professionalism. The first officer didn't last long. He exploded within two seconds!" declared Rupert, red-faced.

"Oh, why are you even blushing? So, Cecilia was declared the queen of blowjobs?"

Halfway through my sentence Rupert burst out laughing. He was doubled up with laughter. I didn't understand why he was laughing so hard but I really had to go. I couldn't wait any longer. I opened the front door to show my imminent departure. *Who cares who won the stupid competition anyway, those two women are equally queens of blowjobs!* I thought.

Seeing that I was leaving without waiting for the official winner, Rupert breathed deeply and tried to get serious again. After a deep inhale, he could finally speak again. He flashed an embarrassed smile, winked knowingly at me, and finally concluded.

"What if it was actually a king of blowjobs who had won the tournament?"

Chapter 11

Boarding – Flight to Nice (NCE)

W hen I got to the aircraft, the pilots had not arrived yet. Only two male flight attendants were already there. I assumed they were Nate and George. I introduced myself and they did the same. Just like Rupert had mentioned, they both looked very friendly. Nate was tall and skinny, and wore a beard. As for George, he looked a little bit older: smooth gray hair, somewhat effeminate mannerism. He was already talking about his flowers when I introduced myself.

I didn't speak with them any longer, preferring to sit at row three to wait for the usual briefing to start. I waited for the rest of the crew to arrive and was ridiculously eager to see what Cecilia and Samantha looked like.

Seated on my passenger seat, I remembered Rupert's last words: *What if it was actually a king of blowjobs who had won the tournament?* So, it turns out the rumor about blowjob contests with pilots was true. I couldn't believe that Rupert had played a role in it all. It's no surprise the first officer had quit his job right there. How embarrassing for him! In order to congratulate the talented winner, he must have lifted the eye mask as soon as he had relieved himself, but immediately realized that Rupert had failed as a referee. What a shock it must have been! And with the two queens laughing . . . At least the other pilot had been reasonable and had left before the competition even started. *My John would also have left*, I thought, absolutely convinced.

As I was pondering the whole story, my other colleagues arrived. They were laughing heartily. I quickly eyed them up. Two pretty ladies with soft traits and nicely styled hair sat in the row in front of me. They were talking about their kids, so I assumed they were Mary and Michelle. As for Cecilia and Samantha, I was convinced they were the ones who had just taken their seats in the front row. Their hair was in fact an immaculate platinum blond and their skin had clearly been exposed to too many UV rays, tainting the little class they had left. Their caked-up faces didn't lie; they had had many life experiences. One of which was quite fascinating too! *If only they knew what I know*, I thought.

The chief purser started his briefing. As the captain had personally provided him with the flight details, he could get started immediately.

"Good evening, everybody! I see that everyone knows each other so let's skip the introductions."

No! That's not true! I don't know anyone, and no one knows me, I thought. Perhaps they had ignored me because I was seated at the back of the third row? Still, I had made sure to introduce myself to the purser when I arrived. I had to say something now to avoid making a bad impression and dealing with the consequences. As I was about to speak up, one of the blondes interrupted Nate and pointed her red-polished finger at me.

"Sorry, Nate, but I don't know *her*," she said, with a despising tone.

I felt as if I was intruding her personal aircraft and as if my young and clear skin maliciously bothered her. All eyes were suddenly on me, as if seeing me for the first time. Nate rectified.

"Ah yes! Sorry! I had forgotten about the newbie."

Hm, excuse me? Newbie? Sure, I hadn't been in aviation for twenty years yet but still, I had started over three years ago. Now was not the time to get offended, though. I put on the friendliest of smiles and spoke with confidence.

"Hi, I'm Scarlett!"

I looked at the two women in front of me so that they could introduce themselves as well. Then I looked at the purser and repeated his name to indicate I remembered it. I did the same for George and finished my round with the two platinum blondes. I wondered which one was Samantha and which one was Cecilia. I suspected that the accusing index finger belonged to Samantha.

The first blonde looked me straight in the eye and with a great smile, introduced herself.

"I'm Cecilia. Nice to meet you, Scarlett," she said.

I then looked at the second blonde, waiting for her to confirm my intuition.

"Hi, Scarlett. I'm Samantha," she said, uninterested.

I knew it! I didn't ask for more. Everyone now knew my name and I knew theirs. We could continue, which is what Nate did at once.

"Now that we all know each other, I'll hurry up so we can get the boarding underway within the next fifteen minutes. Let's start with positions."

What a surprise! It was common procedure. Before having even heard the flight details, each flight attendant had to choose their position on the aircraft, according to their seniority. The most senior crew member would choose first, and so on. As I was the most junior crew member, I would get the last choice, but that didn't mean I wouldn't get a position I liked.

George was first. Then Michelle and Mary. Cecilia was more senior than her *best friend* and chose to work at the back, with Mary. There was only Samantha left before me. She had to decide between the two remaining positions.

One position implied having to work in the main cabin, but sit in the middle of the aircraft, in front of passengers. The other meant sitting at the very back, away from passengers and being able to chat with colleagues while preparing the meal and drinks carts. Seeing her perfect manicure, I suspected Samantha wouldn't risk working in the back galley and lifting heavy containers. She would likely have a fit if she broke a nail. So, as I suspected, she chose the position where she'd have to sit in front of the passengers, leaving me in charge of the back galley. The chief purser then continued his speech.

"Tonight, we will be operating flight 234 for Nice, with an estimated flight time of seven hours and fifty-five minutes . . . "

"Arrrggg!" complained Samantha.

Her reaction didn't come as a surprise. She looked like the type of flight attendant who belonged to the second group of old bags. Shabby bags who rarely went the extra mile. I must admit that eight hours did seem unusually long for a flight to Nice. Seven and a half hours would have been more reasonable and I could understand her disappointment. To me, thirty extra minutes meant that I'd have to fight longer to stay awake. But I doubted that Samantha was whining for the same reason. To her, the same additional thirty minutes simply meant that she'd have to work for longer. I could feel her sorrow. Nate ignored her reaction and went on.

"The flight is full. Three wheelchairs and two infants," he

added.

"Arrrggg!" she let out again.

The Crew Queen had complained again. Certainly, now, she had too many passengers to serve. She probably would have preferred an empty aircraft so she could sleep the whole flight. But without any passengers, would she still have a job? Surely, she hadn't thought about that little detail. She asked for some clarification.

"Ah, really! Do we at least have our crew seats?"

"Yes, Samantha. Don't worry. You'll get your seats at the back so you can have a rest on your breaks," confirmed Nate.

She finally calmed down and let our purser finish his long briefing. Strangely, I hadn't heard Cecilia complain the way her platinum twin had. Perhaps I had jumped to conclusions about her. Cecilia possibly swayed between the two groups. Sometimes sturdy, sometimes shabby. I would soon find out. As for Samantha, there was no doubt she belonged with the useless bunch.

* * *

The meal service was completed in no time. The carts were already filled with used, dirty trays. I was dripping with sweat, having been opening all the ovens to take out the hot passenger dishes. I hadn't had one minute to spare. I couldn't remember ever having been so busy before. Had the flight attendants really put the meals on the tray tables? Or had they thrown them at the passengers' faces to get the job done quicker? I was baffled. Cecilia arrived at the back, ready to eat her dinner. I investigated the matter.

"I couldn't stop for a minute during the meal service. Is it just me or did everyone get served unbelievably fast?" I asked, as if I had just witnessed an extraordinary feat.

"Yeah, the faster they're served, the faster we pick up, the faster we can sleep," she explained, as if it was very obvious.

"Ah! I see . . . "

So, it wasn't just an impression. I had given everything I had into my work just so that the rest of the crew could go to sleep sooner! I buried my frustration and pulled out the crew meal cart so that my dear offspring could finally eat.

I had barely opened the compartment when Samantha threw herself onto it. She started taking out a tray, then another, and proceeded to making up her own personal selection. I could see that the chickpea salad didn't appeal to her since she replaced it with the green leaves. She needed a vinaigrette for her new salad but the Italian one already on her tray didn't seem to please her. So she grabbed the sundried tomato dressing from another tray. However, she seemed to like the dessert. It's as if I was observing a wolf devouring a deer. Her cute little cubs were patiently waiting in the background for their share of the feast.

The she-wolf finally sat down to eat. I would have liked her to make herself comfortable on one of the crew seats, away from me, but she decided to sit on a jump seat at the back instead. Between each bite, I could see her scrutinizing me, sneering. I didn't make a big deal out of it and continued cleaning the wet counter. Suddenly, she resolved to talking to me.

"Scarlett, right?"

"Yes, that's right."

"Have you been with the company long?" she asked.

"Just over three years."

"Do you have a boyfriend?"

"Nope, no one in my life."

Her questioning didn't surprise me. I even liked it. Clearly, Samantha wanted to have a chat. By asking this key question, the conversation could open up on different topics: where had I met my man; who was he; what did he do; what were our life plans. Unfortunately for her, though, she'd have to ask me another question as I didn't have anything to say on the subject.

"Ah really! A pretty girl like you! Single! How come?" she asked, as if I held a logical explanation.

"Hm, apparently I'm too picky" I admitted self-consciously.

"No way! How old are you? Twenty-six?"

"No, twenty-nine!" I said, relieved to look younger.

"Ah! My love, if I was your age, I'd get a taste of just any man and wouldn't bother finding a husband."

"Yeah but soon I'll be thirty!"

"Come on, darling! Thirty is the new twenty! Have some fun before it's too late," she advised.

Have some fun? Sure! But a taste? Whoa! *Definitely not the way she did!* I thought. Samantha wasn't wrong, though. I should have fun. And that's exactly what I attempted to do with my Extreme Flirt Game. I just hadn't met anyone who turned me on enough to take it any further. *Apart from John,* I secretly thought. But I wasn't allowed to think such things. Strangely, in the end, I kind of liked Samantha. A woman who literally had a taste for men, sure, but also a woman who knew how to have fun!

* * *

The flight went well and my crew worked very hard, apart from the two shabby old bags who had fallen asleep for almost two hours on the crew seats, keeping the others from having a rest. Regardless of Samantha's selfish behavior throughout the flight, I still appreciated our conversation.

Anyway, the bad habits she had acquired over the years were certainly not about to change. And I had no desire to rise up against them.

I had spent some of the flight in the back galley, chatting away with Mary and Michelle. They had congratulated me for my Zen attitude toward my single life and had predicted that this attitude would inevitably put men in my path without me having to lift a finger. I was thrilled. What if they were right?

Chapter 12

Nice, France (NCE)

"Ladies and gentlemen, welcome to Nice, where the local time is seven thirty a.m. and the outside temperature is sixty degrees Fahrenheit. We ask you to please remain seated, with your seatbelt fastened . . . "

Sixty degrees! A bit cold for the beach. Although, it was still early and I was there for three full days. Surely, the day would warm up. *The perfect temperature to go explore,* I thought, picking up my carry-on.

Passengers had now disembarked and I quickly made my way to the exit. I was looking forward to being seated on the crew bus. My eyes were itchy and I suspected they were also bloodshot. *And this is precisely why we call night flights red-eyes!* I thought, stepping out of the plane.

I was the first one outside. I started to wonder how Samantha had not been out before me. She seemed to be the type who would run out before the passengers just to make sure she'd be on the bus before everyone else. Nevertheless, I walked straight out, rolling my little black suitcase behind me.

When I arrived at French customs, I noticed that the passengers were standing in my way. I went around them and walked all the way to the last customs agent, waiting for him to look at me. He immediately saw me and gestured for me to pass between his cubicle and his colleague's so that I could get to the other side of security. I lifted my Aircrew Identification Card up so he could see it but he simply lowered his chin to show his approval. He barely even had a look. *How pleasant is it to be landing in France!* I thought.

I was used to traveling light and therefore didn't have to wait for a suitcase at the luggage conveyor belt. I quickly spotted the exit sign and made my way toward it. I would soon arrive in front of two gigantic silver doors, which would automatically open as I approached them. They were made of shiny thick matter, keeping me from seeing through them and reflecting an image of myself instead.

The closer I got to the silver doors, the clearer the reflection facing me became. I could see in it my proud figure; from the curve of my hips to my shoulder span. My hair appeared to still be smooth and intact; its glow shimmering in the mirror. My red lips brought color to my face. Behind me, not a soul. Of all the passengers and crew members, I was the first one using these doors.

I approached the dazzling mirrors. One more step and they would let me through. They finally opened and I reached the arrivals area. All of a sudden, I felt as if I was a movie star arriving in Nice for the Cannes Film Festival. Paparazzi were waiting. Flowers were presented. Autograph requests were called out. All the people standing there were waiting for me! All I needed was a pair of sunglasses resting on the tip of my nose and I'd start waving at my fans.

Sadly, I was dreaming. No one was waiting for me. I was

obviously hallucinating. Despite my disappointing anonymity, my fake admirers let me through, drawing a path for me to walk through. I split through the crowd with a superior air, taking in the sights. Then, abruptly, my gaze was caught by the sole piece of red clothing worn amidst the group of people.

I automatically lifted my eyes up to get a look at the person wearing the red sweater. It was a man. A Greek god. His long brown hair fell on his broad shoulders. He looked like a deliciously splendid hippie. He was observing me closely. I was staring back. He looked familiar. But how could I possibly know him? I was in Nice! On the other side of the Atlantic Ocean!

He was still staring and the closer I got to him, the more familiar he seemed. I was by his side when I finally remembered.

"Hm, Arnaud? Hi!" I said, a bit shocked.

"Scarlett? Is that you? Hi!" he responded, equally surprised.

I was frozen in place. The hottest guy I had hung out with in my first year of college was standing in front of me. He was French and had come to the States on a school exchange. Back then, I had never wanted to have any sort of adventure with him as I knew he was a true Casanova, always showing off a new conquest. Being the reserved Scarlett I was then, I had declined his many attempts to seduce me during his time in the US. Eventually, he had gone back to live in France. I had never regretted not being one of the hundred ladies he had shared his bed with. However, now that I was committed to my Extreme Flirt, I suddenly felt ready to jump in. Hopefully, I was no longer hallucinating.

"You live in Nice?" I quickly inquired.

"Actually, I live in Monaco. What about you, what are you doing here?"

What kind of question is that? I thought. *I'm working, of course!* As if the color of my uniform and the scarf around my neck were my daily go-to outfit. Still, I made an effort to kindly reply and investigate his situation further.

"Well, I'm working . . . I'm a flight attendant, Arnaud," I specified, in case he hadn't noticed.

"Wow! You work on a plane?" he asked, to verify the meaning of *flight attendant.*

"Exactly, you got it, Arnaud" I replied, annoyed with having to state the obvious. "And you? Are you here to pick up someone?"

Obviously, the person he was waiting for had flown with me on my aircraft. Who was it? An old flame? A friend? His girlfriend? That last option would see me disappointed. I couldn't wait to hear his answer.

"A client," he said, running his hand through his hair.

I was relieved. The coast was clear. And seeing the way he looked at me, I knew he had the same sort of idea in mind I did.

Then I saw the rest of my crew come through the silver doors. Samantha was leading the pack and Cecilia was close behind. She walked by and noticed me talking with Arnaud. She didn't stop but she still glanced at us, smiled knowingly, and subtly winked. I got her message.

"Arnaud, I have to go. My crew is here" I said, hoping to speed up the conversation. I didn't need to say more, which was a relief.

"Are you in Nice long?" he quickly asked.

"Three nights."

"Well, we'd be crazy not to see each other again! Look, here's my number, call me later. I'll come meet you tonight, wherever you are, okay?"

"Great! See you tonight!" I said, leaving to go meet my crew on the bus.

* * *

As soon as I sat on the bus, eight pairs of eyes, including the pilots', turned toward me. I shrugged and didn't say anything. I, myself, was astonished at life's coincidences. Had I been asked to imagine who I would be running into today, Arnaud would have been the last person I would have thought of. Silence reigned over the bus, but not for long.

"Well, well, well, looks like our little newbie has contacts all over the world," teased Samantha.

"Eh, well! I truly don't know what to say. I met the guy ten years ago. I really had no idea I'd bump into him just like that, first thing in the morning, after landing in Nice," I explained, as if justifying my role of the victim in life's random acts.

"You're seeing him tonight, I hope?"

The tone Samantha had used suggested that if I wasn't the one making the most of Arnaud tonight, she would be. The look on her face made me smile but I didn't respond.

"Anyway, Scarlett, you can't say that your aura didn't hand him to you on a silver platter!" added Mary, referring to our earlier conversation with Michelle.

"Whoa, girls! Calm down! I'll call him after my nap and then we'll see if he comes over to see me. He's an old college friend, so we just have some catching up to do," I declared, only half believing my own words.

"Oh! Give me a break!" Cecilia jumped in. "He's handsome as hell. Surely you won't just be chatting!"

"Hm, we'll see. He's the biggest womanizer I've ever known," I added, still unsure of what to think of the upcoming evening.

"Scarlett, a womanizer, that's perfect! You couldn't have hoped for better! We already know how your night's going to end. Have fun for me, kiddo!" exclaimed Samantha.

Now the whole crew knew who I'd possibly be spending the night with. Awkward! They were all laughing along, picturing me in bed with Arnaud-the-Greek-God. They were even cheering me on!

"Come on, Scarlett! Come on!" they all yelled, clapping their hands.

"Come on, Scarlett! Come on!" they cried, even louder.

Clearly, I had inadvertently generated a strong team spirit in the company, for which I should get a prize! Listening to their cries, I couldn't help but laugh as well.

"All right, all right! Chill out! I'll try my best not to disappoint you," I announced, amused by the outcome.

"Good girl!" said Samantha before shutting her eyes.

I put my headphones on, turned on my iPod, and closed my eyes as well.

* * *

Ring! Ring! Ring!
  "*Bonjour?*"
  "Arnaud?"
  "*Oui.*"
  "Hi, it's Scarlett!"
  "Ah! Scarlett! Hi . . . "
  "Is this a good time?"
  "Actually, I'm just with a client at the moment. Can you call

back in about an hour?"

"Hm . . . Yes, no problem. Talk to you then."

Was it just me or had he cut the conversation short? *When you're ready, YOU call me back!* I grumbled, after having hung up. His tone had been really dry. Nothing like what I had expected. He hadn't even said *bye* before ending the call. I hated when a guy acted that way, especially when he had been the one suggesting I call him to set a time to meet up. Not wanting to jump to conclusions, I decided I would still call him back later and went for a run along the Promenade des Anglais.

When I got back to my room, I jumped in the shower, then tried calling a second time. Just before dialing his number, I promised myself that if Arnaud didn't pick up, it would be end of story. After all, I didn't intend on forcing things . . . but I still hoped he would answer.

Ring! Ring! Ring! The ringtone started.

Ring! Ring! Ring! It resounded.

Ring! Ring! Ring! Still no answer.

I hung up. ARRRG! I was absolutely furious! He had been the one offering to come and see me and now he was acting all independent. The last thing I wanted was to chase after him but still, I was in Nice and had met him out of nowhere. What did I have to lose? My dignity? Not even! I ignored the promise I had made to myself two seconds earlier and dialed his number for the third time.

Ring! Ring! Ring!

Really, I look like a stalker! I thought.

Ring! Ring! Ring!

This is getting embarrassing! Continuing my attempt.

Ring! Ring! Ring! He finally answered.

"*Bonjour?*"

131

"Hi, Arnaud. It's Scarlett!"

"Hi, Scarlett!" he answered, sounding more outgoing.

Now that was a bit reassuring. Turns out, I may have freaked out for no reason.

"Are you able to talk now?" I asked, a bit sarcastically.

"Yes, yes. No problem."

"Are you still free to come and see me?"

"Yeah, but I won't make it until about eleven p.m."

Is he kidding me? Eleven at night! That's one hour before midnight! I thought, internally offended. *He might as well say he doesn't want to see me at all! Or that all he wants is to get in my pants!* I was speechless. I didn't know what to say. If I agreed, I knew where this would end up. Although, it might help clear my head. Hearing only silence from me, Arnaud tried to convince me.

"That's really too bad, Scarlett, but I must have dinner with my client tonight. I'll try to get there earlier, though."

"Okay! Send me a text when you're done and I'll come meet you at the hotel. I'm at the Mercure on Promenade des Anglais. You know where that is?"

"Yes, sure do. See you tonight."

"See you tonight," I concluded, and hung up.

I couldn't believe he had dared suggest we meet up so late. Clearly, he didn't care about knowing how I had been doing. But above all, since I had spoken with that Samantha Brown, I, too, felt like having some fun. The upcoming nocturnal meeting with Arnaud-the-Greek-God, the womanizer, could only contribute to my detox. I grabbed the phone again and dialed Samantha's room number.

"Yesss!" she answered urgently.

"Sorry, Samantha, it's Scarlett. Were you sleeping?"

"No, no, love, what's going on?"

"I wanted to know if you guys were planning on meeting up for dinner tonight?" I asked.

"Yeah, we're meeting in the lobby at six. Wanna come?"

"Yes, I'll be there."

"Aren't you seeing your French stallion?" she asked, incredulous.

"Yeah but the stud wants to come around later . . . " I explained, insinuating the obvious.

"Hm, that's great for you because a stallion like that doesn't waste his energy, Scarlett. He saves it up in order to be highly efficient," she said in a tone that was meant to be reassuring, but had the opposite effect.

"Hm, see you later, Samantha!"

"Later, my love!"

Whoa! Now, that was far from reassuring. A stallion? No! I very well knew what stallions did to mares while mating. It was long, hard, straight to the point, no-frills. Not at all what I had in mind. I was even a bit scared of what was to come. *You're being paranoid, Scarlett! Arnaud is as gentle as a lamb!* I convinced myself and then went back to sleep to regain some more strength.

* * *

Quack-quack! Quack-quack! Quack-quack! announced the little duck from my phone.

It was already almost six. I immediately got up and got dressed to go meet up with Samantha and the others in the lobby. When I arrived, the rest of the crew was there waiting for me, so we left for the restaurant right away. We were walking toward Old

Nice, where Mary said she knew a place. We got there within ten minutes and went inside. I sat next to Samantha as, strangely, I very much enjoyed hearing her talk. Cecilia sat next to us. After a while and a few glasses of house wine later, the conversation stirred back in my direction.

"Scarlett has a date with her man tonight!" Samantha announced proudly to the rest of the group.

"That's great!" they exclaimed.

"Yeah," I said shyly.

"He couldn't have dinner with you?" asked Mary, curious.

"Nope! Completely unacceptable, isn't it?" I asked, conscious that had Arnaud truly wanted to see me, he would have come out for a meal with me.

"Well, it shows a lot about his intentions," indicated sweet Mary.

"So, who cares! The guy doesn't want anything else and won't beat around the bush to say it. That's all!" said Cecilia, cutting off Mary.

"Well, he could have at least played along," I said, disappointed.

"Scarlett! What were you thinking about when you saw him at the airport?" asked Cecilia.

"Well . . . "

"You were thinking about sex! There you go! That's what you were thinking," she said, taking the words right out of my mouth.

"Yeah," I confirmed, as if it was a crime to think as such.

"There's nothing wrong with that!" she exclaimed. "Sex is such a great thing!"

I was shocked, yet again. I knew Cecilia was mad about sexual pleasures but I was far from expecting her to confirm it in between two mouthfuls! No one was saying a word apart from Nate and George, who were having a completely different conversation at the other end of the table, to my relief. As for Mary, she had remained silent since she had been interrupted, and Michelle, on her end, appeared to agree with Cecilia. Samantha was getting ready to spice up the conversation.

"Yum! This is true, nothing better than good sex!" agreed Samantha, looking convincingly at me.

"That's not the issue, Samantha! It's just that Arnaud could have tried to, if only for a night, make me feel special."

"Ah! I see! You're a romantic," she concluded.

"Well, sort of."

"You need a man, then, not a stallion!" she declared.

"Yeah, maybe. But believe me, I also need a stallion," I stated, convinced that I needed to take my mind off things once and for all.

"Whoa! She's greedy and demanding, isn't she!" said Cecilia, impressed with my comment.

"All right, girls! Enough! Leave her alone," intervened Michelle and Mary, to my rescue.

"Okay! Okay! We're letting you off, Scarlett! But just one last piece of advice," begged Samantha.

"Yes, go!" they all commanded.

She ran her hand through her platinum blond hair, as if creating momentum before her big revelation. She then placed both her hands flat on the table, on either side of her plate, and softly whispered her advice in my ear.

"At every stage in life, we must make the most of what we have. When we're twenty, it's time to dance and flirt. When we're thirty, we must make the most of our beauty and absolute femininity. Five years from now, it'll be about babies. Your turn will have passed. My advice: It's your moment now, Scarlett! Seize it, as it won't come again. So what if you must meet a stallion in order to do so? Just go for it!"

What a wise piece of advice! Samantha was right. I had the chance to be free to have fun with a man however I liked. It was my turn, my moment. A few years from now, Extreme Flirts would be a thing of the past, so I might as well make the most of it while it lasted. As I was growing more and more convinced, I received a message on my phone.

Hi, Scarlett. On my way. Will be there in 15. Arnaud

Just in time, I thought. I paid my share and left the restaurant, hearing a *Good luck* chanted in unison.

* * *

When I got to the hotel, Arnaud was waiting. He kissed me on both cheeks and suggested we go for a drink in a pub he knew. I wholeheartedly accepted. We sat at a table in one of the establishment's dark corners. The waitress promptly showed up and asked what we wanted to drink. I opted for a glass of red wine and he a beer. We raised our glasses and as soon as we had taken our first sip, Arnaud went straight to the point.

"So, after our drinks, should we go to your room or my place?" he asked without a hint of hesitation.

My heart did a three-sixty. *No, really? He doesn't bother courting me at all!* I became somewhat frustrated.

"Hm. Arnaud, you could have been a bit more romantic . . . "

"Come on, Scarlett, you can't say that's not what you had in mind?"

I didn't answer right away. But let's be honest, that's exactly what I had been thinking! From now on, there were no more rules. Having temporarily put aside my principles, I was not allowed to get offended by anything. And, seeing the Greek god that he was, I decided to play the game.

"My room, then!" I officially declared.

"Hm, I love your lips" he replied right away, biting his own.

Oh! It looked as if I had turned on a blaze. I could feel Arnaud lighting up on his chair, examining me from all angles. I wondered what rank I would hold on his long list of conquests. Would I be number fifty? One hundred? Two hundred? I chose not to think about it too much. I admired his handsomeness and concluded that regardless of his frustrating attitude, I simply had to see him as a vital aspect of my evolution. Without hesitation, I suggested we go back to my room immediately. He looked at me, astonished, and kissed me without warning. My lips didn't even have time to welcome his.

"Delicious," he murmured, after a long kiss.

Indeed, it wasn't bad at all. And why should I be surprised? He must be talented. It was his specialty, after all. He enthusiastically kissed me again.

"Ouch! Ouch!" I exclaimed. "You're biting a bit hard!"

"Ah! Sorry! It's just that I really want you," he justified, biting his own lower lip.

"Yeah, I can tell . . . "

Arnaud was truly led by his sexual needs and when he kissed me he completely lost his bearings. I was no longer so sure I wanted him in my room. Although many women appreciated pain with their lovemaking, I wasn't a fan. Or maybe my lack of elation toward his personality ruined the rest? To make sure, I kissed him again.

"You see! No more biting!" he said slyly.

"Hm, true," I admitted.

Now that there was no more reason for me to revise my

decision, we made our way to the hotel. My doubts had subsided and just as they were close to having completely disappeared, Arnaud pushed me against the wall of some factory, next to a dark alley.

"Ah! Scarlett! I want you! Now! Like an animal!" he said, biting my ear this time.

"Come on, Arnaud! There are people passing by. We'll be at the hotel in ten minutes, calm down!" I begged, pushing him away.

"Grrr! You're so hot, Scarlett! Show me your boobs!" he commanded.

The stallion in him was about to jump on his mare. I could feel him very hard against my thigh. He was pretty much dry-humping it and looked like he would come at any moment. I didn't understand his reaction. Here I was thinking that having some experience would provide a minimum of self-control, but his urges were taking over. Damn! I wasn't dealing with a womanizer, I was dealing with a sex maniac. ARNAUD THE PERVERT! No way should that animal come have a mating session in my room. I pushed him violently.

"Arnaud! That's enough! I don't want this anymore!" I screamed.

"Come on, you've been begging for this."

"I said I don't feel like it anymore."

"Are you serious?" he asked, finally stopping.

"Yes!"

"I can't believe it! You're just a tease," he said spitefully.

"I don't care! I don't want this anymore!"

I moved away from him, toward the main road.

How could the situation have turned against me? I had been full of good intentions all night, but I wasn't going to let myself get ridden by a horse against my own will. After about a minute of walking, I turned around to see if Arnaud was following me. He wasn't very far behind. Still interested in reaching his goal, he quickly apologized.

"Sorry, Scarlett! I thought you were enjoying it!" he yelled from behind.

I didn't say a word.

"Come on, baby! Just a quickie!" he yelled louder.

I kept silent.

"Ah, fucking cock-teaser!" he howled at the top of his lungs.

I turned around, flashed a triumphing smile, and entered the hotel, convinced I had made the right decision.

Chapter 13

Orlando (MCO), Florida – Christmas Day

To help clear my mind, I had decided to put a hold on the Extreme Flirt Game for the holiday season. After my failed encounter with Arnaud, I had asked Becky and Rupert to not play matchmakers for a while, as I needed to get over my emotions. I shouldn't despair. Surely, somewhere in this world, there was someone for me. I was still determined to play my little game, but needed a short pause. I had decided to start it again in January. Had I known that bad encounters were going to continue, though, I would have forgotten about that stupid commitment right away.

It was my seventh consecutive day of flying since December nineteenth and I unfortunately couldn't make it to my parents' house for Christmas. My mother was pretty sad and so was I. However, I knew that getting reasonable days off during the holiday period was pretty much impossible, having still so little seniority. Before my flight, the morning of December twenty-fifth, I called her.

"Merry Christmas, Mom!"

"Scarlett! Merry Christmas to you too! Your father and I would have really liked you to be here. The whole family is coming! You're the only one missing."

"Yes, I know. I would have liked to be there too."

"You could call in sick, you know!" she suggested with authority.

"No, Mom, you know I don't like doing that."

"Not even for your family?"

"Mom! I didn't call you so that you could make me feel guilty for being responsible. I'm already exhausted and haven't made it to the airport yet. Please!" I answered, growing annoyed at the conversation.

"Ah! Sorry, kiddo. Where are you flying today, then?"

"Hm . . . I don't know. I didn't look at the destination, only the flight number."

"Well, I hope you have a good flight. Merry Christmas again! I love you," she said, full of kindness.

"Merry Christmas," I said, having already forgiven her, and hung up.

I couldn't blame her for being so directional. She wanted me close to her. How could I blame her? Mom had me curious, though. I searched through my handbag and unfolded my flight itinerary. For a few months now, I had been developing the bad habit of examining the names of the captains before each flight, hoping to see the name of the one I was so obsessed with appear. *Not today*, I thought, not seeing his name and having forgotten to even look at where I was flying to. Once in the car, I finally looked at the destination code written next to the flight number: MCO. And all of a sudden, I realized the mess I was in: Orlando, on Christmas day! Help!

* * *

There are many amusement parks around the world. One of the most famous, Disney World, is located close to the city of Orlando, in Florida. It's an enormous entertainment complex where we can meet all of the fictional characters from our younger years such as Mickey Mouse, Cinderella, and Sleeping Beauty. Disney World attracts everybody, including me. This makes Orlando the official dream destination for families and, more specifically, children.

I love Walt Disney and I'm even crazy about Minnie and Mickey. I'm not concerned about them, though. What worries me is the ride to Orlando. On the aircraft. In the air. On the ground. At deplaning. Everywhere! Operating a flight to Orlando is just like already being at Disney. It's seeing kids run around, scream, throw toys at their parents' faces; it's telling them off so they put their seatbelts on; it's constantly smiling because we obviously can't be rude to children. It's all of that at once, and more. As flight attendants, we must have lots of energy saved up, which, on this beautiful Christmas day, I seemed to be missing.

Nevertheless, I tried to remain positive. Maybe they would all be exhausted from the excitement, on their best behavior and happy to soon be meeting Pinocchio and Geppetto? I parked my car, grabbed my carry-on, breathed deeply, and headed for the airport.

Once past the security checks, I quickly went to one of the few coffee shops in the domestic terminal. I urgently needed a little pick-me-up. A double espresso latte should do the trick. Then I headed for the aircraft.

I got to the waiting area and walked decisively, aiming straight for the departure gate. Normally, I would rarely pay attention to the passengers seated in that area. I would simply board the aircraft, knowing I would see them all for hours on our flight anyway. However, that day, I discreetly glanced at the scene around me before setting foot on the bridge. And then I saw them. They were running around yelling, crying. Why weren't they sleeping? I was terrified. *Scarlett, they're just kids. They won't hurt you*, I thought.

Of course, I wasn't going to get killed or tortured by kids. They weren't life-threatening. What was going to get me, though, was everything else Orlando implied: spoiled children, impatient parents, endless requests. If we mixed all these ingredients together and released them into a short time-lapse, we ended up with a trailer suited for any action movie. Speaking of time, Orlando was a *touch and go*. Quickly touch down then go again, on two different runways. I would have time to fasten my seatbelt, unfasten it, drink a glass of water, run around the cabin, and sit back down for landing. I needed to calm down.

After the captain's briefing and the pre-flight checks, all flight attendants went to their respective positions, ready for boarding. Passengers started to come on board. I couldn't spot any baby in my section, which made me pretty happy. *At least I won't have to give my speech on baby safety*, I thought. We were off to a good start!

Boarding was going at a snail's pace. What was going on? I made my way to the middle of the aircraft to investigate. Ah! I could now see the problem. Children were walking down the aisle in front of their parents! How could a two-year-old make proper progress by pulling a mini Spider-Man suitcase down a narrow corridor while stopping at every row? It was impossible!

I approached the first child. I looked at his mother standing behind him and asked for her boarding pass so that I could help them to their seats as quickly as possible.

"May I see your boarding pass, ma'am? What is your seat number?" I asked.

She searched through the pocket of her jacket and handed me her ticket.

"Thirty-two D! It's toward the back. Follow me!" I said, internally exasperated.

Knowing that the kid would take ages to walk the long distance to the back, I lowered myself down to his level and gently asked if he could let me carry his mini-suitcase, which, according to me, was just as cumbersome as useless. Unfortunately, he didn't have much choice as I grabbed the suitcase as I asked for his permission. He looked at me with his big beautiful eyes and didn't flinch. *Perfect, one step closer!* I thought. Then, adopting a soft and friendly voice, I told him to follow me.

"Follow me, honey!" I ordered.

I turned around and positioned myself closer to the back of the aircraft. A few rows down, I turned back around. I looked at the kid. He was still a fair distance away. His family was following, still behind him, and so was a group of passengers, eager to reach their own seats. I crouched down, still holding on to his tiny Spider-Man luggage. With my knees bent, I clapped my hands on my thighs a couple times, encouraging him to continue coming my way. I felt like a crazy person calling out a dog to come running down the aisle of an airplane.

"Come on, sweetheart! Just a little bit more!" I urged him on.

He then stopped looking around and started off in my direction again. *We're gonna make it!* I thought. His mother was also encouraging him from behind.

"Go on, son! Go see the lady over there. Yes, that's it. A little further, my love," she hummed from her end.

Oh! I felt the strong urge to roll my eyes but held back. *Why didn't she simply pick up her child and sit in her seat as quickly as possible?* I wondered. I was still internally grumpy as she kept on encouraging her honorable son, determined to show him how to meander down the aisle of an airplane.

Trapped, I had no choice but to continue my little choreography. I went on. Side-steps forward for five rows, then STOP! A half pirouette and HOP!

"This way, sweetheart! A little bit more," I said again.

I continued. Side-steps forward for five rows and STOP! Half pirouette and HOP!

"Almost there!"

I had almost succeeded. Side-steps forward for five rows and STOP! Half pirouette and HOP!

"There we (finally) are!" I declared, relieved.

The mother settled in her seat. The father and the child did the same. I then gave the Spider-Man suitcase back and returned to my quarters at the back of the aircraft. The other passengers were finally moving along and my colleagues took over. I remained posted at the back for the rest of boarding, keeping a watchful eye on the cabin.

Shortly after, we were able to close the door. It was even surprising how quickly the kids had nicely taken their seats. Still, I could very well hear their piercing voices resonate from one end of the cabin to the other. *Everything will be all right, Scarlett. There's nothing shorter than a return trip to Orlando,* I encouraged myself.

* * *

We were on the runway and had just completed the last cabin

check. Seats were upright. Headphones were removed. Bags were put away under the seats. Seatbelts were fastened. I could now sit on my jump seat, ready for takeoff.

Next to me, there was another flight attendant sitting on her jump seat. Her name was Debbie. I had never met her before. She was a pretty woman, most likely in her mid-thirties, and seemed as quiet as a mouse. Her tone was soft, vulnerable, and soothing. She seemed discreet and benevolent, which pushed me to confide in her my current worries.

"I've never operated a flight to Orlando on Christmas Day. I wasn't expecting so many kids. I hope it'll go well."

"What do you mean?" she asked, unsure of how to read into my statement.

"With such a short flight, we normally don't have a lot of time to serve the passengers. And now, with all those kids . . . service might be twice as long if we're dealing with spoiled children," I explained.

"Ha! Ha!" she laughed. "You mean, if the parents allow their children to be spoiled, it'll take us an eternity to serve them?"

"Yeah, exactly!" I confirmed. "I hate waiting in the aisle like a fool while moms go through the whole menu with their little princes and princesses!" I added, amused.

Debbie seemed to share my opinion. Since my remarks appeared to perk her up, I got more off my chest.

"While we push our cart down one row at a time, parents could at least try to start thinking about what their kids will drink instead of waiting until the last minute. It's the same story every time. I ask them what they'd like and then the mother turns toward her kid and lists all the options. It drives me insane!" I confided.

My colleague, amused, developed further.

"True! She'll lean toward her son and suggest milk, apple juice, orange juice, water! And then, the poor little soul doesn't know. He hesitates. He looks at us, then at his mother and does . . . "

"Eeeeeuuuuuuhhhhh!" I pursued, laughing.

"Ha! Ha! Ha! Why not have coffee while we're at it!" she exclaimed.

We were laughing away for a few minutes and then suddenly, the announcement for takeoff came on.

"In preparation for takeoff, flight attendants to your jump seats," declared the captain.

The engines started humming. A loud noise traveled across the cabin. The aircraft was vibrating lightly, as if preparing to explode. I bent my head down, chin in toward my chest, and placed both hands on my knees. Prepared for takeoff, I was ready to get back home as quickly as possible.

The intensity of the muffled sound outside increased and we abruptly started moving forward. The scenery outside was passing before my eyes, little by little. We were speeding up. My body remained stiff, in case a *rejected takeoff* (RTO) happened. The horizon now appeared as a rectilinear green line, as if one of the kids on board had drawn it with a crayon. And then, quickly, within a millisecond, we were flying. *What a great feeling!* I thought, before hearing all the children scream with joy. *This Christmas Day might not be so bad after all!*

As soon as we were on our ascent, we continued our conversation.

"So, you must not have any children of your own, if you're that scared of them?" she asked me.

"No, not yet. But I'd love to one day. Maybe a few of them. When they're your kids, it's different," I answered. "And you, do you have any?"

"Yes, two," she said, her eyes glimmering.

"How old are they?"

"My oldest is seven and my youngest is five. We would have liked to have more, but after two miscarriages, we got our head around the idea of having just two. My sons are adorable. I love them so much and really try my best not to raise them as spoiled children, like you say," she confided.

"You won't be with them for Christmas. What a shame," I said with compassion.

"Well, I was there yesterday. And anyway, we won't get home too late tonight. Their father is looking after them. It's best I'm not there, I think."

Strange . . . how could she think that not being with her husband and kids on Christmas day was the better situation? I wanted to know more. She had brought it up, after all. Maybe she felt like opening up to someone.

"Why would you say that? Is your relationship okay?"

I suspected that her disappointment was a romantic one. Without any hesitation, she offered more explanation.

"My husband and I have been drifting apart for a while. It's as if we forgot about each other when we had our second child. And then we tried to conceive more and I had two miscarriages. I feel as though it affected our relationship. Maybe that's why we're feeling so distant now. I miss him but I don't know how to tell him. Sometimes I don't even know if I want to make it work, and he doesn't either, actually."

"I see," I said respectfully. "Do you still love him?" I asked.

"Yes, I love him. I just think that we're different now and I don't know if we can find each other again."

"Well, if you love him, you have to work on your relationship. You can't give up. You have children with him, that's a good enough reason. Talk to him," I advised.

I didn't really know what more to say. My experience in marital help was limited. I suggested she be honest with her husband and admit her concerns. It was the best thing she could do.

"We'll see. At least we look after the kids very well. I prefer to let things happen for now," she said, discouraged.

Suddenly, the seatbelt sign was switched off. It was time to get to work, as it was a very short flight. With a mere two hours and fifty-five minute flight time, we might not even be able to eat our own meals and would have to do so once on the ground. I got up and got at it, forgetting about Debbie's confidences.

* * *

The first part of the flight went relatively well. As soon as the seatbelt sign had been turned off, we had gotten up and swiftly started the passenger service.

I was working with a flight attendant named Todd. He was straight and very good-looking. *There's no chance that guy is gay,* I had thought. He had beautiful green eyes that made you weak in the knees. He was full of charisma and gallantry, which was, of course, much appreciated on an airplane.

During the first half of the flight, he hadn't stopped helping me with everything I was taking on. He was running to the back to get juice for the kids. He was lifting the drawers for the meals. He was urgently making the coffees I needed. He had even helped out the flight attendant who was alone in the back galley. He was everywhere at once, still always completing his own tasks with perfection. I couldn't have hoped for better company.

We had been highly efficient and had managed to finish our side of the aircraft way before our "rivals" in the left aisle. However, it wasn't because we had been extremely fast, but rather because they were a bit slow. I understood, once at the back, that my dear Debbie had been dragging her feet all throughout the service, truly aggravating her cart partner.

It was common for different flight attendants' rhythms to be off. The efficiency gap was sufficient to create some tension on board. A partner who chatted too much with the passengers got on our nerves. Another who was serving only two passengers while we served ten was annoying. And if one of them pushed the cart before their partner was ready, someone could have a fit. Each individual had their own personal blacklist of cabin crew. I had mine. I wondered if my name appeared on someone else's. *Debbie's name is most likely being written down on her cart partner's list at this very moment*, I thought.

Once the service was finally completed, we were lucky enough to get a quick ten minutes to eat our crew meals. I was hungry and was craving a real meal, not the breakfast served on the flight. Therefore, I decided to pick from the crew meals reserved for our return flight. Todd was by my side and as he saw me looking around the compartment tagged *Crew Meal Inbound*, he took part in my plan. I started reading the labels out loud so that he could make a choice.

"Curried chicken, beef stroganoff, vegetable lasagna, garden salad," I listed.

As we didn't have much time to heat up the meals, he opted for the salad. *Good choice!* I thought, and chose the same as him before closing the compartment door. We were about to start our descent so Todd and I quickly settled on the crew seats in order to wolf down our meals. That's when the unpredictable happened.

The other flight attendants had also finished their service and had arrived at the back for a bite. The ones who weren't hungry had gone to the front for a chat. As for the others, they were going through the meal container. I could hear them talk.

"I'm gonna have cereal and a hot meal. Can you pass me the omelet, please?" said one of them.

"I prefer Corn Flakes, are you happy with Raisin Bran?" said another.

I could hear them open and close the ovens. The compartment doors constantly slamming. Suddenly, a panic-stricken voice exclaimed:

"Where are the salads?"

I froze. Normally, there were only two salads on board and they were currently being devoured by two flight attendants, one of which was me. I looked at Todd with fear. He turned his head away, oblivious to the reason of my reaction. He was chewing away on a tomato and I understood that he was at ease with his meal choice. I realized I had the same right to eat my green leaves, so I continued to nibble on my salad. Again, I heard the same voice.

"Who took MY salad?" she asked, furious.

"I don't know," answered one of them.

"I told you to put it aside and now it's gone!"

Uh-oh! Someone had reserved one of the salads? I didn't remember seeing a name on either of them so I had a look at mine and Todd's lids. Nothing. No note nor name. The salads had been stowed away exactly where they normally were. The one responsible for the meals had failed to fulfill her task. Having other fish to fry, she had probably forgotten. The conversation went on.

"I completely forgot, Debbie. I'm so sorry," admitted the accused voice piteously.

Debbie? The same gentle Debbie? She was the accusing voice. No wonder I hadn't recognized her, camouflaged under a stern and threatening voice. Where had her soft and vulnerable tone gone? I heard heavy steps come my way. Again, not really knowing why, I got scared. I hurriedly swallowed my last bite and waited, as if to be persecuted by my executioner. A shadow appeared to my right. I lifted my gaze up toward it.

"You're the one eating my salad? I can't believe it! I had put it aside for later and you dared steal it away from me!" she reprimanded.

She was clearly trying to contain her anger to avoid alerting the whole plane. Still, the volume of her voice had gone up and could most definitely be heard a few rows away. I had to explain myself yet didn't know why I had to do so. Todd was also eating a salad but somehow, she hadn't asked him anything, completely ignoring him.

"I grabbed one of the salads that was in the same compartment as all the crew meals. Your name wasn't on it. It was simply with the others. I'm sorry, but next time you should warn everyone to avoid someone taking it," I declared with confidence and also sympathy.

I was proud of my answer. I didn't have anything to take the blame for. As if I had deliberately chosen to steal her salad! How dare she talk to me that way? She was telling me off the way we tell off a child, not even so much as glancing over at Todd, who had, by the way, his mouth full of garden salad. She didn't seem to appreciate my answer as she became beet-red and shouted at me again.

"You! To the galley now! We need to talk!"

The situation was getting ridiculous. I looked at Todd, hoping to find out his opinion. He shrugged to indicate his lack of understanding then suggested I follow her and try to calm her down. I still couldn't understand the reasons for this sudden attack against me. She had seemed so sweet at takeoff. Why me, why not Todd? I suspected this had something to do with my seniority. Todd had been cabin crew for seventeen years; she would have never dared to bother him with this nonsense. I breathed deeply, placed my now-eaten salad box on the table tray next to me, and got up to meet with Freaky Debbie at the back.

As soon as I crossed to the other side of the curtains, she verbally attacked me.

"How long have you been with the company, two years? Maybe three at the most? I've been here ten years, my dear! You're in no position to tell me what to do to put my lunch aside. Okay, you junior?"

I was petrified. I couldn't speak. I was indeed quite junior in the company but I still attended the same annual trainings she did. Her argument didn't hold water. Regardless, I was literally frozen in place, unable to reply anything. *Comebacks must come with experience!* I thought. I felt subdued. Tears were making their way up to my eyes. At all costs, I wanted to avoid further humiliation. I quickly brought the conversation to a close before running away.

"Listen, you have more experience than me, I agree. I'm sorry, Debbie, but my intention wasn't to steal your (freaking) salad," I curtly retorted.

I lowered my gaze to avoid further eye contact. That way I would avoid a second attack. Then I went to the lavatory, where

I allowed myself a few tears. I felt so stupid for crying over such a trivial situation but it was the first time I had an argument with a colleague. It had never happened before. Apparently, there's a first for everything.

Once my tears had dried, I came out to the main cabin. We were now on our descent and I had to check my assigned section before landing. I put the drama aside and proceeded with my safety checks. I was surprised at how well-behaved the children had been throughout the flight. *Next time*, I thought, *I'll be wary of my own kind, not of the little ones.*

* * *

Everyone had disembarked and I waited a little bit before making myself comfortable on one of the many empty seats. I wanted to be as far from Freaky Debbie as possible. So, as she had gone to business class to rest, I settled at the back of the aircraft, allowing some thirty rows or so to separate us. Todd spotted me in my isolated corner and came around to check if I was doing all right. I gave him every detail of what had happened. He advised me not to worry about it and assured me he'd look after me for the return flight. *Ah shit! The return flight!* I internally panicked. Debbie's jump seat was right next to mine. I knew that once all doors of an aircraft were closed, tensions on board could quickly amplify. My mind was set: I would not say a word and would hopefully avoid making the situation worse. I wouldn't say anything during taxi on the runway, nor during takeoff, and I would quietly keep to myself on my side of the aisle. *Everything will be fine*, I reassured myself.

* * *

New passengers boarded. Pure bliss could be seen in their eyes. No doubt, their vacation had been amazing. It is true, Disney World brings happiness to people. And plus, it was Christmas Day. For them, there was absolutely no reason to be sad. *If they're happy, I'm happy.* So I regained some energy.

The door was closed yet again. We checked our sections and sat on our jump seats. I looked to my right, out the window, and avoided turning my head toward Debbie. Our shoulders brushed. I could feel her body graze mine. There was an obvious tension between my shirt and her blazer. It was about time we took off.

All of a sudden, Debbie started talking. Her tone was back to the soft one she had used at our first takeoff. Freaky Debbie had disappeared. I leaned closer and continued to look straight ahead, into the cabin.

"I wanted to apologize for earlier. We still have to make it through the return flight and I don't want this tension between us to persist," she admitted.

I didn't like such a work environment either, so I agreed. However, it didn't mean I was ready to forget about that side of her personality; it only meant that I was ready to play along for everyone's benefit. Now, that was better. The tension from earlier vanished and I was relieved. I never liked having disagreements with colleagues.

The return flight literally flew by. It had only been two hours and forty-five minutes long and no one had had time to sit and relax. Once landed, passengers disembarked through the front of the aircraft. As the plane was slowly getting emptied, I grabbed my carry-on and put on my winter jacket. I was really looking forward to being home. I headed for the exit. I could hear the final *Happy Holidays* wished to the passengers.

Once the aircraft was officially empty, all cabin crew gathered. The chief purser thanked us for our spectacular work and wished us a merry Christmas. Impatient to get going, we wished her the same and left in no time. I was one of the first ones to set foot on the bridge. I was hungry for silence and briskly walked down the corridor. Still, I could hear the other flight attendants' voices behind me, including Debbie's.

"Looking forward to flying with you again! You have a good evening!" she said to a colleague.

"Oh! So am I! Don't forget to say hello to John for me!" answered the other.

What a coincidence, I thought. Apparently, Debbie and I had at least one thing in common. Her husband's name was John and my inaccessible crush was also called John. It amused me.

I continued on and finally exited the terminal. I got on the bus that would take me back to my car. Once seated, a sudden panic washed over me. Would it be possible that my John was also Freaky Debbie's John? Impossible! It couldn't be the case! I had to find out right away!

My heart was racing. I was sweating through my shirt. I was hot and cold all at once. What if John was indeed Debbie's husband? What if I had just had an argument with the one woman I had been envying for months? Freaky Debbie would officially become my worst enemy; the first flight attendant officially making it on my blacklist.

I opened the front pocket of my suitcase. I would possibly get my answer in the next few seconds. I slid my hand down to the bottom and grasped my flight itinerary. I unfolded it, holding it firmly in both hands. My radar was attentively going through each line of the document. This time, I couldn't care less about the captain's name on the fourth line. What I was looking for was of utmost importance. An important piece of information that could devastate my life, my heart.

And then, I saw the name. A name with four letters that hit me hard. My skin was sweating so much my white shirt was drenched. I wanted to unzip my jacket; to quickly cool myself down. One word, one short word was keeping me from breathing. *Breathe, Scarlett, breathe!* I commanded myself. Then, still seated on the bus, I read again: ROSS. DEBBIE RICHARD ROSS.

Chapter 14

Boston (BOS)

Well, well, well. What a nice Christmas present! I had received a lovely surprise wrapped in pretty pink paper, secured with a soft red velvet bow. When I had opened it, what I had discovered inside was a poisoned chalice. It had almost swallowed me whole on the plane, and had stabbed me through the heart while I was seated on the bus.

Freaky Debbie was John Ross's wife. She was my handsome captain's wife! The only man who had succeeded in making my heart beat strong. I now had all the reasons in the world to forget about John. I could never be with him. He hadn't had one, but two kids with her, and had even wanted more. Needless to say, they had obviously gone through careful family planning.

The only colleague I had ever had a dispute with was the mother of his children. Well, more than a dispute, she had actually told me off like a child. I did not wish to interfere with her life again in any way and have her scold me like she did on our flight. Moreover, she had demonstrated how much love she felt for John and her family. I was in complete shock the whole way home.

My head was in the clouds. How could I have had the slightest hope of winning over the heart of a man whose wife is a colleague of mine, and with whom he has two kids? Who was I to dare picture myself kissing (and even go a little further with) a married man? I could only be glad I hadn't gone knocking on his hotel door that night in Barcelona.

More than ever, I was determined to pick up the Extreme Flirt Game where I had left off. I vowed to myself that once the holiday rush was over, Miss Scarlett would go wild. Completely wild!

* * *

It's with that mindset that, a couple weeks into the year, I received an unexpected email.

From: Brian Burke <brianburke69@gmail.com>
To: Scarlett Lambert <scarlettlambert@gmail.com>
Date: January 22, 2017
Subject: News
Hi, Scarlett,
It's been a while! How are you?
I'm not sure if you're still single but I'd love to see you again. I'll be coming through Boston next week. Maybe we could go for a drink? Here's my number 323-387-4433.
I'll be waiting for your response
Brian

What a surprise! After almost two years without seeing each other, out of the blue, Brian wrote to me. He must have recently become single and gone through his contact list, looking for interesting prospects. From what I remembered, I had had a good time with him, so why decline his invitation? Plus, I still aimed to stay committed to the Extreme Flirt. I had to accept.

I had met Brian back in my first days working in aviation. He was one of the first pilots I flew with. He was based out of Los Angeles and I out of Boston. In my first few months as a flight attendant, I had gotten the chance to operate flights from California. As the western cities didn't necessarily fly to the same destinations as the ones on the East Coast, I had been lucky enough to go to Japan and Australia. As for the regular flights to Europe, they were much longer from there, so I got a few opportunities to enter the cockpit, have a chat with the pilots, and soak in the sunrays.

That's how I got to be friends with Brian, who had just been hired as a first officer. As we first had to cross the whole country to get to Europe, we had an exclusive view of the Rockies slicing through the middle of the United States. The scenery was breathtaking and Brian and I would marvel at the sight. While I was rarely exposed to such beauty at work, he was a constant witness to it from his glass office, but he was still always in awe along with me. He was very kind and after our first flight together, once we got to Munich, Germany, we had gone out for a meal with the crew.

When we met, he had a girlfriend, so nothing had ever happened between us. Back then, I hadn't mixed with enough pilots to find them pretentious, so had Brian made a move, I would have happily accepted.

Based on those fond memories, the idea of having a drink with him seemed rather pleasant. Therefore, we agreed that he would call me when he landed in Boston, which he did.

"Hi, Scarlett. I just landed. I'm staying at the Hilton close to the airport. I don't have a car so if you could come pick me up that'd be great. Then we could go for a drink near the hotel," he had shyly suggested.

I, of course, had accepted. He was only passing through Boston so I couldn't imagine declining his request. *I'll just have to call him once I'm at the hotel and he can meet me in the car*, I had thought. Before setting off, Becky had insisted I take a bottle of wine. She wanted everything to be perfect.

"Come on, Becky, we're going to a pub. I don't need wine," I had replied, convinced that I wouldn't drink it.

"You never know how the evening will unfold, Scarlett! Just take it in case you need it," she had recommended, over the moon for me. "It's been a while since you've had anything happen in your life; better be prepared. You wouldn't want to miss your chance."

Becky was right. I hadn't been touched by a man in so long. Too long. Not that I hadn't had any opportunity, but per usual, I had run away from them. I told myself that those days were over and that now, just like Becky, I would have fun with the opposite sex. I really hoped I'd find Brian attractive. Either way, if there were a couple things I didn't like too much about him, beer goggles would be there to save the day. My mind was set: I would go with the flow and have a good time.

* * *

On my way to the hotel, I made the mistake of picturing the

perfect scenario. I imagined I would get to the parking lot and would call Brian so that he could come down and meet me. He would open the door of the passenger seat and I would automatically be seduced by him. We would be comfortable with one another, just like we were two years ago. We would go to a nearby pub. We would have a beer and, not wanting to leave, would then order a pitcher. The evening would go by and, feeling an increasing desire for each other, we would ask for the bill. He would pay for our drinks and, once back at the hotel, would invite me up to his room. Before accepting the offer, I would kiss him to "test the goods." His lips would perfectly embrace mine and I wouldn't hesitate one moment about following him and continuing the evening on. We would open my bottle of wine and have more drinks. I would lose all feelings of modesty and awkwardness. I would finally be ready to have fun! The chemistry would be so intense I'd ask for more. And again, and again, until dawn. The perfect scenario. Everything would be spot-on. Now, I just had to hope that my wish would come true . . .

I finally arrived in the hotel parking lot. Feeling a bit timid, I decided to send him a text instead of calling.

I'm downstairs, waiting in the car. Coming? I wrote.

As soon as I pressed send, I realized the huge mistake I had just made. Why did I ask a question? I was a flight attendant and knew very well that we should never ask a question if we expected a specific answer. When I needed to move a passenger to another seat, I never, ever asked: "I'm sorry, ma'am, would you be so kind as to change seats since another passenger isn't feeling very well, blah blah blah?" Every time, the answer would be no!

Flight Attendant Rule # 1: One must never ask a question!

Instead, one must politely command the desired action:

"Ma'am, I'm very sorry but I need to move you to another seat in order to accommodate a family and their baby. Thank you so much. Can I help you with your luggage?"

Every time, I'd get the answer I wanted. Formulated that way, it simply left no space for arguing. The other way around, though, like the message I had just sent, opened the door to extensive discussion on the matter, which could easily affect the outcome of the evening. Impatient, I stared at my phone, waiting for Brian's reply. A second later, I got the answer I was obviously hoping I wouldn't get.

I'm not quite ready, come up. My room number is 1102.

I read it again. It was an affirmation; no question mark. It looked like Brian had outsmarted me. So, I was going to oblige and go up to his room. ARRRG! My perfect scenario was already being tweaked against my will. I grabbed my handbag, the wine bottle in it, and stepped out of the car, heading for the main door.

It was as if I no longer held any control over the situation, so I inevitably started stressing out. I suspected that by going up to his room now, we'd end up having dessert much sooner than anticipated. From what I remembered of Brian, though, that wasn't an issue with me at all. I would just have to chuck down half a bottle of wine first, then I'd be set. *Forget about the pub!* I told myself. My host most likely had the same idea I did . . . I would soon find out.

* * *

I got to the eleventh floor and found his room. I stood in front of the door marked 1102. I wasn't ready to go in yet. What would I discover on the other side? *So many things can happen in two years!* I thought. I shouldn't despair. I was here to have fun and would do so. Period. I breathed in deeply, my heart beating fast, and finally brought myself to knock on the door.

The door partially opened. I stopped breathing. I couldn't wait to see my old pilot friend. My throat became dry and my pulse sped up. I was really hoping it would all go well.

The door opened further and, gradually, the bottom brushed against the harsh beige carpet. Then I saw him. Brian was standing tall, right in front of me, truly happy to see me. His eyes were shimmering and I could even spot beads of sweat on his forehead. He already wanted me. As for me? Turns out that nope, not at all!

It was as if I was staring at a stranger. Gone were the mental pictures of the handsome pilot I had met two years earlier. Brian was short. Too short for me. He was wearing high-waist jeans, in which he had tucked his white T-shirt. This made him look even shorter. I might as well have been staring at a dwarf. Brian was a HOBBIT! The more I looked at him, the more I realized that I had been dreaming all along. Brian was the same he had always been. It is I who, in fact, had changed: the naïve and blind admiration I had felt toward pilots in my first year had long gone and I now found myself stuck!

"Hi, Miss Lambert!" he said. "Good-looking as always."

What was I supposed to answer to that? *Hi, Mr. Burke, quite the opposite for you?* I simply blushed and smiled instead. He gestured for me to come in and added:

"I looked online and couldn't find any interesting pub around except for a sports bar. I don't really feel like going to such a loud place. I'd prefer something more laid-back, so I thought we could stay here if that's fine with you."

I knew it! Brian was as sly as a fox. My plan was out the window. I wondered if I could stay true to the commitment I had made before coming in. I looked at my accomplice. I really wanted to have some fun, for me. It was of the utmost importance for my own well-being. There was my chance, so why hesitate? Brian wasn't *that* bad, was he? I looked at him closely in order to make an informed decision.

His gaze was deep. His jaw square, showing off a beard a couple days old. I liked beards, so that counted as a positive. His hair appeared to be a bit wet. He must have recently taken a shower and therefore was fresh and clean. I was relieved. His actual face wasn't bad. I could deal with that. As for his height, or lack of height, it was just a small detail that could be fixed once in a horizontal position. I had made up my mind! I was going to let myself be charmed by Brian-the-Hobbit's self-confidence. I announced the news.

"Yeah, you're right. There isn't much around. It may be for the best, too, as I happen to have a bottle of wine," I said timidly.

I was accepting the turn of events. I had to. After all, that's what I had wished for. *Own up to it, Scarlett! Own up to it!* I lectured myself.

Brian took out two wineglasses and I opened the bottle. He stretched out on one of the beds and I did the same on the other one. We talked about past events while drinking our magic potion. I was hoping that the alcohol would kick in and do its trick shortly. But sip after sip, my perception remained the same: I wasn't attracted to Brian. *Drink, Scarlett! Drink!* I commanded myself.

I downed a second glass in no time and suddenly became quite talkative. That was a start. *Either way, we're still on our respective beds,* I thought, *perhaps I can still run away if I need to.* That's what I was used to doing anyway, right?

"So, do you have a boyfriend, Scarlett?" he decided to ask.

Who did he think I was? Of course I was single! I wouldn't have gone through all that trouble if I had a man waiting for me at home.

"No, Brian, there's no one in my life. You? Are you still with that girl you were dating?" I asked.

I shouldn't have answered so quickly. And especially not have asked him if he was single as well. He was probably going to let his thoughts run wild now.

"Of course there's no one in my life, Scarlett. Why would I have invited you here if I was in a relationship?" he confirmed.

Hm . . . because you're a pilot! I thought. I could tell the conversation was about to be steered toward more intimate topics, in the direction I had initially hoped for. What would I do now? I no longer wanted to play along. I was a stupid single girl drinking too much wine in a guy's hotel room; a guy as single as myself who was inspecting me closely and hungrily. But I wasn't attracted at all. I needed a short break.

"Can I use the bathroom?" I quickly asked.

"Yes, of course," he said, a bit disappointed that I had diverted his plan.

"I won't be long," I assured him.

Running away to the bathroom was blissful! I was finally alone! I just had to gather my thoughts and forget about the huge pressure I had put on my shoulders. I tried to imagine what Rachel and Paige would say if they were here. They would probably laugh at the absurdity and tell me to close my eyes and just have fun with Brian-the-Hobbit. They were right. I was above all a woman who had physical needs that had to be attended to. I would go all the way.

I leaned in toward the mirror and stared at my reflection. My gaze beamed with strong will. I applied some of my raspberry lip balm in order to embody the seducer in me. I needed to get rid of the small creamy gloss excess in the corner of my mouth, so I grabbed a piece of toilet paper. That's when I got a clear view of the toilet and what was floating in it.

WARNING! PUKE ALERT! Crumbs! Many, many crumbs! Some big ones, some small ones! Dancing around the toilet bowl, *excremently* revolting. In his toilet! I was terrorized and completely disgusted by the brown floats which, I could safely assume, had only recently been expelled from Brian-the-Hobbit! Or should I say Brian-the-Turd? Actually, the latter was waiting on the other side of the bathroom door. I couldn't go through with it. No way! Not after what I had just seen.

I straightened myself up. I would, obviously, run away. Yet again. I breathed deeply and flushed the ugly remains. I didn't want to give him the opportunity to even question if the runaway crumbs belonged to me. Then I washed my hands and returned to the main room, ready for my quick escape.

When I got back, Brian was still comfortably laying on the bed. He shot me a piercing gaze, probably hoping I would be overtaken by desire. It was already too late, though.

"All right, Brian, it's getting late. I should go. I would have loved to stay longer but it'll have to be some other time," I hastily announced.

I moved toward the bed in order to grab my jacket but I should have known my host wouldn't let me off the hook so easily.

"Miss Lambert! Surely you haven't come all this way so that you could so easily slip away from me?" he asked smoothly.

He stood up and came up to me, in between the two beds. He

stood tall, as tall as he could, in front of me, smiling softly. *Maybe if I kiss him just a little bit he'll let me go?* I told myself. How naïve was I! How could I have had such a silly idea?

He then leaned his whole body toward me and, using his body weight, abruptly threw me onto the bed. His hands were on either side of my face and his legs were strongly trapping me close to him. He was staring at me tenderly yet emitting a strong and uncontrollable need to dominate.

I came here for this, I thought, *maybe I should give it a go? The more you have, the more you want, right?* I lifted my head toward his, indicating my agreement. I had just gently offered him my mouth, to try it out. But he, on the other hand, had completely taken over it.

My mouth was in shock. It felt as if I was being attacked by a sharp, pointy tongue that aimed for the back of my throat. Instead of getting closer to Brian, I backed away to avoid being cut open.

"Hm, you're such a good kisser," he confessed.

I didn't say a word. It was an abomination! None of it was pleasant. Nevertheless, I reluctantly allowed him another chance. After a couple more invasion attempts, he forgot about keeping up with a convenient rhythm and quite aggressively entered my mouth. Brian insisted on charming me with his non-existent skills. He was breathing weirdly and seemed to have lost control. Between each entry, he let out a jolted blast of air, making his lips vibrate, as if showing off his increasing excitement.

I was completely and utterly repulsed. Somehow, it was getting worse. The sound coming out of Brian was far from arousing. Instead, it gave me the impression I was on a National Geographic show, witnessing some sort of nasal snort sound coming out of a happy tiger.

"FFFFFFFEEEUUUUUHHHHH! FFFFFFFEEEUUUUFFFFF!"
He gritted his teeth.

Undoubtedly convinced I appreciated his performance, he lifted up my shirt to get a good feel of my breasts.

"FFFFEEEEUUUUUFFFFFF! FFFFFFEEEEUUUUUFFFFF!"
he went on.

The sound was driving me insane, and not in a good way! The more I tried to get into it, the more intense the FEUH became. All of sudden, my attention was brought to my hand. Brian was holding it firmly, guiding it toward his crouch. *NO WAY! I DON'T WANT THIS!* I screamed inside.

My subconscious then flashed the mental picture it had drawn of the inside of the toilet: brown crumbs happily splashing around cloudy water. That was enough! Brian-the-Turd wouldn't get any further with me. *He can grumble away with someone else!* I decided. Without further hesitation, I pushed the tiger away, got up, grabbed my jacket, and headed for the door. Before crossing the doorway, like a tigress having come to her senses, I decided to give him a quick advice.

"You know, next time you ask a girl to come up to your room, make sure your date doesn't see your big dump!"

Chapter 15

The Big Thirty

After my disappointing encounters with Arnaud and Brian, I finally decided to put an end to the Extreme Flirt Game. I would never force myself to date guys whom I didn't find interesting again. So I went back to my old and comfortable habits, hanging out with my friends, family, and colleagues. My life would then become much more pleasant and much less stressful. It was time I faced another fact: It was never worth forcing things. Life would look after me. Or so I hoped.

I had finally come to accept my status as a single lady and my birthday party couldn't have come at a better time. It's as if I was getting a fresh start in life, a chance to truly go with the flow.

That day, when I opened the door to my apartment, my friends were waiting for me.

"SURPRISE!" they all exclaimed at once.

"Hey!" I let out, startled and frozen in the middle of the doorway.

I did suspect that Becky had planned a little something for my thirtieth, but I had no idea she'd invite so many people. Rupert was there, along with all of his gay friends, which included a couple of old flames of his. Becky had chosen her rich French magnate, Damian, as her plus-one. I hadn't realized how much she liked him until then. There were also a few of my colleagues, and even Paige and Rachel had showed up. They were all there for me! Even my parents . . .

"Happy birthday, kiddo!" yelled my mother.

"Mom? Dad? You came all the way to the city just for me?" I asked, not believing what I was seeing.

"Thirty years old, Scarlett! It can't go unnoticed! But we won't stay long. You know how much your dad doesn't like leaving the suburbs."

"Oh yes! That I know! I'm so happy you guys are here," I said, thanking them for having driven so many miles for their daughter.

I knew how hard it must have been for my mom to convince my dad to come to the city, so it was important for me to mention how much I appreciated it. As for my mom, though, she missed me so much she probably had insisted on being here. As I was catching up with her, Paige and Rachel joined in the conversation.

"Happy birthday, Scarlett!" Paige wished me.

"Happy birthday, Scarlett!" said Rachel too.

"Thanks, girls. I'm glad you came," I added genuinely.

"Thirty is a big deal! Quite a big stepping stone in life!" exclaimed Rachel.

"Yeah, the infamous mid-life crisis for women. When we supposedly question everything in our lives, and when our maternal instincts sneak up to the surface," I added.

Curiously, though, it felt as if I had already gone through my whole life's reassessment not too long ago. Being twenty-nine was now behind me, but it had been a difficult year. In fact, I had desperately tried to find a suitable partner and had committed to meeting just about anyone. Unfortunately, my perfect life plan had gone out the window even though I had been more opened-minded than ever. Nothing had gone according to plan. Now that it was all behind me, it was time for a new chapter. I was ready, come what may. I would take it one day at a time and enjoy the journey.

Rachel had noticed my peaceful state of mind and so, once again, had elected herself as my appointed matchmaker.

"Hey, Scarlett, I haven't introduced you to my guest tonight. This is Mark. My boyfriend wanted to stay home with the little one so I invited him instead," she explained, most likely worried about my reaction.

The whole thing about her cousin is so annoying, I thought. She knew I wanted nothing to do with her Mark, yet here she was trying to introduce him to me. I didn't want to make her uncomfortable, so I reassured her and kindly greeted her companion.

"It's a surprise party, Rachel! The guests are part of the surprise!" I said, somewhat ironically, before turning toward Mark and offering one of my fake smiles.

"Hi, Mark," I said bluntly.

"Happy birthday, Scarlett!" he kindly responded.

My mom, who was still among us, decided to actively take part in the conversation.

"Who's this handsome young man?" she asked Rachel, while looking at Mark the way she'd look at a nice handbag in one of her favorite online stores.

"Mark is my cousin, Mrs. Lambert. He lives in your area, in Woodstock."

"Interesting," replied my mom, already falling in love with him. "What do you do for a living, my dear?"

"I work in the food service industry" he proudly answered. "I own a trendy café in Woodstock."

"Even more interesting!" she added, before turning to look at me. "Scarlett, we could go into town for a coffee next time you come home to see your mother!"

I couldn't believe it. Here was my mother trying to set me up with Mark-the-Cheater. As for Rachel, all smiles, she seemed pretty happy to think that she had done the right thing by introducing him to me. I knew my mother was worried about me being single but I didn't expect her to set me up on a date with the first man to come around. I had to put an end to the discussion as I had no intention of spending my thirtieth birthday with him. I told Mark and Rachel that I'd be right back and asked my mother to come to the kitchen with me, saying I had a surprise for her before she leaves with my father. She innocently followed me. Once the door was securely closed behind us, I spoke openly.

"Mom, it looks like you're pitying me because I'm single. But I'm fine with it, so stop trying to set me up with everybody. Okay?" I finally let out, almost screaming.

"I'm sorry, Scarlett, I'm not pitying you. I know that nowadays kids settle down when they're much older. It's just that I thought the young man looked interesting. Don't you agree?"

"No, he's not my type," I declared, not wanting to go into more detail.

"Ah! How come? You barely know him. He's very charming and I think you'd make a nice couple," she stated, disappointed that I didn't appreciate her suggestion.

Mom was stubborn. If I didn't mention the reason I wasn't into my friend's cousin Mark, she'd work at it all night long. It was my party and I wanted to enjoy it, so I presented her with the facts.

"He was married, he has a child, and he cheated on his wife many times. That's why!" I declared, tired of continuously hearing about that Mark guy.

"Oh! I didn't know that! I would never let you be with a guy like that. A guy with no honor, no values, no heart . . . "

Oh dear! What had I done? I knew very well that Mom was easily outraged by such infidelity stories. I had started a huge fire, which I now had to put out.

"All right, all right. They're not all the same. Mistakes happen. Mark is probably not a good guy, I agree, but still, I believe in getting a second chance in life."

How could I even say that? I, who was always fidelity's biggest advocate, was talking about second chances? Moreover, I wasn't putting out the fire, I was feeding it.

"Ah, Scarlett! Really? There is no second chance when we chose to marry a woman and have her children. We own up to our decision and take responsibility for our actions. A family isn't a disposable object with which we can have a little bit of fun. We can't get rid of it the way we get rid of an old sweater!"

Her arguments were strong. And mine, weak, boneless. I didn't know what to respond but didn't have to as my father came to the rescue. He burst through the door.

"Agatha! We can hear you from the other room. Enough! Leave Scarlett alone. It's her birthday, you know. We're leaving anyway," commanded my dad, sternly looking at my mother.

Dad often behaved that way. He would let my mother criticize me until the situation got out of control, then he would intervene. Yet, not too long ago, I adhered to my mother's philosophy. In fact, I didn't understand my sudden willingness to broaden my horizons . . . Come to think of it, I knew exactly where it came from, but I didn't want to admit it. Not now, anyway.

Once my parents were gone, I caught up with my friends and started drinking merrily. Mark tried his best, and in vain, to start another conversation. And then, a few drinks into the evening, I finally admitted to myself the reason of my contradicting opinion and of the argument with my mother. Deep inside of me, hidden away somewhere close to my heart, I knew the reason. And it had John Ross written all over it.

Chapter 16

Aboard the aircraft – Puerto Plata (POP), Dominican Republic

Sometimes, reality can be difficult to face. I often hear passengers complain once they're on board and returning home after their vacation. They curse the upcoming Monday and bless the all-inclusive hotels. For the majority of them, staying on one of the many beaches in the Caribbean all year long would be a dream come true. According to them, then and only then would they finally find happiness. But there's also a tiny minority of passengers who truly appreciate going back home. They're happy to get back to their little piece of heaven, which they wouldn't trade for the world. They look forward to seeing their dog, their children, and even to getting back to work on the following Monday. *Bring on Monday morning!* they say.

Among all of the different types of passengers, there are also the ones who manage to find excitement out of anything and everything. They are a surprising bunch, mostly because of their uniqueness, but above all because they really make you think and take a look at yourself. Some even succeed in awakening desires hidden deep inside yourself. And that's precisely what a peculiar passenger did on that day, flying back from Puerto Plata . . .

* * *

It was April, and we were flying toward the United States. The previous months had been extremely busy. Still without enough seniority to spend a few days down south, I had been operating return flights all winter. At least, though, I got to be home every night and didn't have to deal with jet lag. I knew that long-hauls were just around the corner, so I didn't fret over it too much.

I had even managed to maintain a pretty tan just by sitting on the steps outside the aircraft for a few minutes during the short breaks was had on the ground. Sometimes, on the return flights, my cheekbones would get a bit blushed, giving me a similar look to the one adorned by all the sunburned passengers.

On that day, a passenger caught my attention. Her complexion was black, red, brown, and white. All at once! I couldn't understand how I hadn't noticed her earlier.

I was busy serving drinks and, from my side of the cart, was facing passengers. Therefore, I had a panoramic view of the cabin and the hundreds of heads popping up from their seats. I often took that opportunity to get a feel of the mood my dear protected ones were in. I would observe the creases on their foreheads, their arched eyebrows, or the tilt of their heads. Were they reading a book or watching a movie? Did they appear anxious or relaxed? But above all, were they burned or completely carbonized?

I relished in observing my passengers' tans on their return

flights from down south. I honestly thought I had seen it all but I was wrong. When we believe we've seen it all, we find out there's always worse. Especially on an airplane. And on that day, that passenger was living proof.

I had just served the last passenger up to where my cart was located. I advised my colleague that we could move down, thus clearing a few more aisles for me to attend to. She moved backward and I forward. We stopped again and I turned to the passengers on my left, on the window side, in order to ask what they'd like to drink.

The passenger on the far end requested a glass of water. I then looked at the passenger in the aisle seat to find out what she wanted to drink. All of a sudden, I felt as if I was inside a horror movie.

"I'll have a Pepsi," she said.

I froze for a moment, taking in her request. How could this woman be asking for a Pepsi in such a calm manner? If I were in her shoes, I would have rushed onto the plane screaming for cold water, ice packs, dressings for my wounds, and loads of antibiotic cream. This passenger's skin wasn't just burned, it was "tanned," carbonized, peeled, overcooked. Poor thing! I had no choice but to offer my immediate assistance.

"Pardon, ma'am, are you feeling all right?" I instinctively asked.

The woman lifted her gaze up toward me. This caused her neck to stretch up, altering its original position. With each movement, I could spot shreds of dry skin falling all over her nice black top. *Like a snowstorm, but of dry skin*, I thought. She appeared to be in a trance. She looked at me and flashed a big smile, showing off all of her teeth, most of which appeared somewhat decayed. *How unlucky to have such bad teeth*, I thought. And so, I took pity on her. She then expressed herself.

"Yes, yes, I'm feeling well. I just forgot to put sunscreen on," she said, shrugging.

That last movement generated a new storm of dry skin, but this time the shreds were falling from her arms. I felt an urge of compassion for the man sitting next to her, by the window. Again, I made sure that my severely burned passenger didn't need anything.

"A cold-water compress on your sunburn might help to subside it," I recommended.

"Ah! Okay! Thanks!" she simply answered.

I immediately grabbed a small absorbing towel from my drawer and dropped a few ice cubes on it. I then sprayed a bit of water until it was damp and handed it to her. Amidst all the medical treatments, I was forgetting about her drink.

"What would you like to drink, ma'am?"

"Do you have Pepsi?" she asked, uncertain.

"Yes, of course we do," I confirmed.

I looked toward the top of my cart to grab an empty glass in order to fill it with Pepsi. It felt like I had taken an eternity to assist this one passenger. It was time to be efficient again. Just as I was about to open the drawer containing the sodas, my seriously burned passenger called out to me again.

"You really have Pepsi?" she asked.

"Yes, we do have Pepsi."

"Like, real Pepsi?" she said, growing increasingly excited.

"Yes, Pepsi, like real Pepsi." I reconfirmed.

What was so hard to understand? Was I speaking in tongues? In my cart, I had Pepsi. Real Pepsi by the official Pepsi brand. What could I have said differently so that she understood me right from the beginning? Actually, nothing. Absolutely nothing. The lady hadn't lost her hearing. Nope! She was simply in love with Pepsi and happy to finally be able to have it again.

"Yeeeee! I'm so happy to finally be drinking Pepsi! Yeeeee!" she started squirming in her seat.

Her legs were swarming around while her arms were in hysterics. Mrs. Pepsi was literally going crazy. I couldn't understand how a simple drink could make someone so thrilled. I had to investigate.

"Ah! I see that you like Pepsi. It's been a while since you've had it, right?" I innocently asked.

"That's right! I brought my Pepsi bottles to the hotel but ran out after a week. I had to drink the fake Pepsi at the hotel! Gross!"

Had I just heard the reason for her excitement correctly? I couldn't believe it. And I had taken pity on Mrs. Pepsi and her rotten teeth. I now knew the reason for the cavities. Still a bit shocked, I had to play along, at least while I was serving her the cherished beverage. I quickly grabbed a can and started filling up her glass. My burned passenger was getting into a frenzy.

"Yeeee! Yeeee! Yeeeee!"

I had to say something. A kind word, so as not to appear to be judging her.

"Ah! This is true! Pepsi sure is tasty! Yum!"

It gave me the impression that someone was playing a dirty trick on me. But I quickly realized that it had nothing to do with a trick. I had just served a woman who had genuinely forgotten to apply sunscreen on her body, just like many others before her. Now that she was well roasted and relaxed, she was on her way back from an all-inclusive in the Dominican Republic, and she had just humbly admitted her love for Pepsi. As simple as that.

I was startled but strangely, her reaction gave birth to a revelation in me. My Pepsi, the one that I wanted to quench my thirst with, had already crossed my path. His name was John Ross. And so right there, standing in the aisle while serving Mrs. Pepsi, I swore to myself that one day I would at least try to get a taste of my own cherished beverage. If only for one night, so that I could finally be satisfied.

Chapter 17

Boston (BOS) – Madrid (MAD) – New York (JFK) – Dublin (DUB)

Transatlantic long-hauls had now started and I had already flown a few times to Paris and Barcelona. However, on this early June evening, I would be operating a six-day-long pairing. First, I'd be going to Madrid for one night, then would spend the following night in New York. The next day, I'd be flying to Dublin, Ireland, where I'd also spend just one night, in order to get back to Boston the following morning. It was a nice pairing as I would only be operating direct flights. I had been a flight attendant for four years now and had finally started to see nicer flights on my schedule. So I was pretty happy to go to work, and my new work conditions shot my energy levels through the roof.

Once in the crew room, I leaned my suitcase against the wall and proceeded to print my *routing*. I now knew how important it was to have a paper copy, as it included valuable details for each flight. That's where I could find, among other things, exact departure and arrival times, flight numbers, names of the hotels we were staying in, as well as the names of each crew member operating one or many of the same flights. As soon as I had printed it, I quickly scanned through it. Suddenly, a particular piece of information startled me. So much so that I dropped the piece of paper. I was speechless. I had to inhale deeply, which is what I did. I picked up my flight itinerary from the ground, folded it in four, and put it safely inside my handbag.

I then made my way to the security checkpoint reserved for crew members. Strangely, while walking through the airport, it felt as if I had lost a few calories. My energy went missing. Shaky, I could barely set one foot in front of the other. After a whole minute, I finally made it to the two men dressed in navy uniforms who were keeping an eye on the people passing through. As if in slow motion, they both looked at me and uttered two simple words.

"GOOOOODDDD EEEEVVVEEENIIIING!" they said.

I was getting weak, ready to faint any minute. Had I been bitten by a poisonous snake somewhere in between the crew room and security? I knew very well that wasn't the case. I barely managed to respond to the two men and then put my index finger down on the fingerprint reader. The green light switched on and I moved to the other side, to the international terminal.

I was only about ten minutes away from the aircraft. Not knowing how to get my energy back, I made my way to the ladies' room. I needed to splash some cold water on my face. *I couldn't care less about runny mascara right now*, I thought, and dipped my face in the icy water contained within my two hands.

A couple of purifications later, my fever had passed. I erased the black lines covering my cheeks, dried my skin, and reapplied whatever was necessary to regain some radiance. I made it to the gate at the appointed time.

When I got there, every other crew member was already on the plane. I was happy to see that I knew them all and wouldn't have to make an effort to remember their names. My head was already high enough in the clouds. I took out my white binder, the one containing the passenger announcements. As we were flying toward Madrid, Spain, I was the designated flight attendant qualified in the country's official language. Therefore, throughout the whole flight, I had to translate every announcement into Spanish. Normally, I enjoyed the task as it allowed me to put into practice the many Spanish classes I had attended in college as part of my International Studies diploma. However, that evening, the task seemed to me to be a huge chore. Hopefully I would snap out of it soon.

Boarding was launched and passengers slowly started to progress through the cabin. I was standing close to my designated door and had one hand on the jump seat's headrest to avoid falling over. Still, I was staggering while welcoming my passengers. Suddenly, Megan, my colleague on the right-hand side of the plane, gestured for me to come assist her in the middle of the cabin. She was helping an old lady to her seat. I moved toward her, forgetting for a moment my obsessing uneasiness.

"Scarlett, I can't understand a word she's saying! She talks too fast! Can you please help me?" she asked, already on edge.

"Yes, yes, no worries," I said, taking over.

I looked at the old Spanish woman hunched over in the aisle. She was wearing a knit cap, which she had probably knitted herself. She had a strong grip on her brown leather purse in one hand and a walking stick in the other.

"*Disculpe, señora, se necesita ayuda?*" I kindly asked.

"*Sí! Claro que sí! Mi marido está enfermo y no estamos sentados juntos! No se puede!*" she snubbed, angry that she wasn't seated next to her ill husband.

The issue wasn't really hard to resolve. I would wait for all passengers to be seated and would then make the necessary modifications to accommodate the lady. I just had to explain it to her.

"Well! *No hay ninguno problema. Yo voy a . . .* UH! *Voy a . . .* UH!" I hesitated.

What was happening to me? I couldn't speak anymore! Impossible! I knew perfectly well how to speak the language! I made another attempt.

"*Lo que queria decir es que...* UH! And UH!" I repeated, embarrassed.

My uneasiness had caused me to forget my Spanish skills. I was appalled! One minute from now I'd have to speak over the public announcement system and dictate the safety procedures to all the passengers. *I just need to read one word at a time and it'll be fine,* I thought.

I sighed and got a grip of myself. After a couple more attempts, I managed to explain to the lady how I would deal with her problem and suggested she take her assigned seat in the meantime. She thanked me and positioned herself, hunched over, in the corner of the aisle. Then I heard the chief purser's boarding announcement spoken over the speakers, in English. A sudden and uncontrollable stress swarmed over me and the back of my neck was drenched with cold sweat.

I ran to my jump seat and grabbed my announcements binder, ready to speak into the microphone. Barry, the chief purser, finally finished his speech. It was now my turn to speak. I took hold of the intercom and pressed the red button that would scatter my voice throughout the whole cabin. I was scared to talk. *If I end up stammering like a novice, what am I gonna look like?*

I thought. There was no more time to think, it was my duty and I had to deliver. I went for it.

"Señoras y señores, les damos la bienvenida a bordo de este vuelo de Americair con destino a Madrid. En preparación para..." I stopped.

I was suddenly lost in thought. Once again, my mind was somewhere else. *This is not a good time to think things through, Scarlett! Go on! Speak!* I ordered myself.

"... el despegue, les pedimos que pongan su..." I stopped once more.

What a horrible announcement! I was most likely the worst reader my company had ever made the mistake of hiring. Moreover, the cabin was filled with Spanish people who seemed, for the very first time in my life, to be paying attention to me. I had to rectify the situation.

"... equipaje de cabina debajo del asiento delantero o dentro de los compartimientos superiores. No está permitido fumar durante el vuelo y las botellas deben colocarse debajo del asiento. Gracias!"

I was relieved. One of the announcements was completed at last! Now, I really had to snap out of it as to not make the matter worse and make a fool of myself. I went on to close the overhead bins and make the necessary moves to reunite my Spanish lady with her ill husband.

Things seemed to be looking up and I went to the back of the plane for a glass of water before takeoff. At the back, Megan was talking to Edith about a trip to Peru. Normally I would have been the first to jump into such a conversation, but this time I didn't feel like it. I had other matters to worry about. So I drank my glass of water and went to sit on my jump seat.

Once seated, I tried my best not to make eye contact with the passengers in front of me. I could feel them staring but I simply didn't feel like striking up a conversation. I had to stay silent to review not only my emergency security procedures, but also my own concerns. This short moment was mine and I didn't intend on letting a bunch of curious souls invade it. I blankly stared at the far corner of the ceiling. Then I looked at the back of the cabin and directed my gaze at the carpet in the aisle. Then I turned my head toward the window to take a look at the runway. Bottom line, I was looking everywhere but in front of me.

We were still moving on the runway but the captain hadn't yet made his takeoff announcement. I'd probably have to feign indifference for a few more minutes. I continued blankly staring at my surroundings, expressionless. From the corner of my eye, I could see the lady seated in front of me observing me. She had already been staring at me for at least three whole minutes. I could feel her indecisiveness and knew she wouldn't control herself much longer.

Just like I predicted, she rested both her hands on her knees and leaned forward as an attempt to catch my attention. Seeing her leaned at a forty-five-degree angle, I had no choice but to politely look at her. She called out to me.

"So yeah . . . Do you sometimes stay in other countries?" she asked, happy to finally be able to ask me her question.

"Yes, when we fly to Europe, we always stay over for at least one night," I explained with a gentle smile.

"Yeah, must not be an easy job, huh?" she added.

"It depends on the flight and the passengers," I answered, not offering any more detail.

"And . . . you're not scared of turbulence? Did you ever get a big air pocket?" she continued on.

My ears suddenly started ringing. The infamous air pocket myth! If only I had a dollar every time I got asked that silly question. I suddenly got the urge to explain to the woman how silly her question was. Air pockets don't exist! An aircraft doesn't move forward in the air and then suddenly cross a hole with no air in it! Air is everywhere. The Earth is surrounded by it. There are only warm and cool air currents, just like in the ocean and its many swirls. I settled on simply reassuring her.

"No, ma'am, I've never encountered severe turbulence, only light, which is absolutely normal," I assured her.

"Ah!" she finally concluded, and looked out the window.

I then heard the captain's announcement and we took off flying.

* * *

Two minutes into our ascent, Barry started the endless announcements again. I grabbed my white binder and looked for the section called *After Takeoff*. With my eyes locked on the few lines I had to read, I started stressing out again. I could see the lady in front of me carefully watching. This time, I hoped I would sound professional and unravel the safety instructions in an impeccable Spanish. Barry finished his part. It was my turn.

"*...les pedimos que permanescan sentados con el cinturón de seguridad abrochado hasta que la...*" I stopped abruptly.

What was going on? Never had I hesitated to pronounce this word in the past. It was very simple to say. *SEÑAL!* I repeated internally. *S-E-Ñ-A-L!* I practiced it again, before pronouncing it out loud. By that time, I was beet-red out of embarrassment. I sounded like a student attending her first language class. Something was truly affecting me, more than I could have imagined. I finished my speech, stuttering, and swore to myself that I would make sure to put an end to this humiliation as soon as the seatbelt sign was switched off.

A few minutes later, I was allowed to get up. I had to go to the back to get started on my duties but instead, I walked up to the front to speak with the chief purser. Barry was still seated on his jump seat and was going through his stack of documents. Seeing the look on my face, he immediately jumped up, worried about me.

"Poor Scarlett! You're white as a ghost. You're not feeling well, are you?" he asked, concerned.

"No, Barry, not at all!" I confided in a panic.

"Is it because of all the damned announcements? Are they stressing you out?"

"No, it's something else. But it affects everything else. I can't keep on making a fool of myself like that in front of the passengers. It's as if I have forgotten how to talk!"

"Listen, I must admit that your announcements today aren't quite up to standard, so don't do them anymore. I won't write it in the flight report," advised my savior.

"Oh! Thank you! You're taking a huge weight off my shoulders! I promise tomorrow will be better," I confirmed, relieved, and then immediately returned to my duties.

I was truly unsettled. Seeing how confused and clumsy I was, Megan had taken it upon herself to work twice as hard. During meal service, she made sure to be working on the side of the cart with her back to the passengers, allowing her to serve ten passengers while I served only three. I didn't recognize myself. Why was this flight putting me in such a state? I had to speak with Becky as soon as possible. Only she could help me with my sickness.

After landing, I absentmindedly waved good-bye to my passengers. I was really looking forward to talking things through with my best friend. My mind was set on calling her, wherever she may be. Once the aircraft was empty, I grabbed my suitcase and dragged myself outside. Megan, out of support or perhaps out of pity, waited for me and stayed with me all the way to the crew bus, making sure I made it all right.

"You'll see, a good nap will make you feel better. Then we can meet up for a pre-drink. Sangria will sort you out!" she encouraged.

"Ah! Thanks, Megan. That's so kind of you but, honestly, I think it's best I stay alone tonight," I graciously answered.

I couldn't believe what I had just said. To spend the night alone in Madrid? I normally always wanted to share delicious tapas with my crew. This city was meant for partying. Strangely, though, I no longer felt like it. I wanted to think about things and speak to Becky as soon as I could.

When we arrived at the meeting point, the rest of the crew was grouped up behind the van. One at a time, they handed their suitcases over to the driver so that he could strategically place them in the back compartment. I, in turn, gave him my suitcase and entered our means of transportation. Once seated, I inserted my headphones into my ears and let my mind drift away with the melody. I finally had time to think. *What a great pleasure it is to finally set my thoughts free!* I told myself. Looking out to the stony mountains along the way, my uneasiness finally subsided. My little heart was feeling better. Hope was filling it and it was beating strong again.

I opened my handbag and reached for my flight itinerary. I unfolded it and read the overwhelming inscriptions again.

AMERICAIR 144 New York (JFK) – Dublin (DUB) - captain: JOHN ROSS

AMERICAIR 419 Dublin (DUB) – Boston (BOS) - captain:

JOHN ROSS

Chapter 18

Madrid (MAD)

I had just gotten out of the shower and had put on my gray comfy sweatpants. Fatigue was making me shiver. I opened the door to the balcony to let some warm air into my room. I could hear the Madrid life getting busy outside. I loved the sound. It wasn't quite *siesta* time but some storekeepers were already shutting their doors. I could make out the grinding sound of the panels sliding down in front of the stores' windows. A few friendly conversations made their way to my ears. These echoes were priceless and I had arrived at the hotel just in time, as the Spanish *siesta* was about to begin. I could then follow the city's rhythm. I would call Becky when I woke up. As for the rest, the city would take care of giving me back the energy I needed.

When I opened my eyes, it was already six p.m. Sleep was trying to pull me back in and was very tempting, but I had to get up. Actually, hunger had woken me up and I felt like going for a walk. But first, I wanted to talk to Becky. I sat on the edge of the bed, took my cell phone out, and opened Skype. I called her on her cell. A European ringtone was heard. Becky didn't answer . . . I thought she was back at home. I had to talk to her.

I looked through my documents in case I had taken note of her schedule at the beginning of the month. I thought I had. I finally found a hardcopy in the front pocket of my suitcase. I looked at it and noticed that she was in fact going back to Boston tomorrow. She had landed in Toulouse just as I had landed in Madrid. Maybe she was at the hotel, getting ready to go out for a meal with her crew. I found the phone number of the hotel she was staying at and dialed it.

"Le Novotel Toulouse, *bonsoir!*" answered the receptionist in French.

"Hi, yes, *bonjour*, I'd like to speak with Becky Henson, please."

"Yes, *bonsoir*, madam! Who would you like to speak to?" she asked, somewhat confused.

It must have been due to my English, which she didn't fully understand. I repeated my request.

"I'd like to speak with Becky Henson, please. She is part of Americair's crew," I said, carefully pronouncing every word.

"Okay. Just a moment, madam, I'll transfer your call. Good-bye!" she answered.

The phone started ringing again. No one answered. It kept ringing. Maybe she was in the shower? Still ringing. After a while, I gave up and hung up. She must have gone out. I'd try calling again later.

I quickly got dressed and stepped out onto the balcony. The narrow streets were packed with people. The city was awakening again and the sun hadn't even set. It was still considered early; restaurants hadn't reopened. Therefore, I had plenty of time to go for a walk through the city before finding a cozy spot.

I started by heading toward Puerta del Sol, which is Madrid's equivalent of Times Square, where everyone meets up to celebrate the new year. Each street in the area is more vibrant than the next. I then went across, toward Plaza Mayor. I was trying to stay focused while walking, to avoid getting lost. I was also firmly holding on to my handbag, aware of the many pickpockets in the area.

I crossed the grand square and made my way to the La Latina neighborhood. When I finally arrived where I wanted to be, my mind was still cloudy. I entered a charming café-bar and ordered an ice-cream flavored mojito. The server nicely put it in a take-out container for me and I went back outside to sit on a bench for a good dose of people-watching. My first sip was one of the most delicious taste experiences I had ever had in my life. Mint ice cream was mixed with two or three ounces of dark rum. Surprisingly, with every sip my head was getting clearer.

What are you gonna do two days from now, when you see John again, huh, Scarlett? I wondered. I had dreamed of that day hundreds of times, imagining myself softly kissing him. And then, the image of his face had slowly faded away. I had even been convinced that my handsome pilot had been nothing more than a fleeting fantasy, a thing of the past. But, lies! Seeing how much his name had troubled me on the last flight, he had definitely gotten under my skin. Why me? I couldn't fall for a married man!

I was now halfway through my mojito. Hunger could be heard in my stomach. I got up and headed back to the street I had taken to get here. I had noticed many tapas bars on the way. As I made myself comfortable on one of the six wooden benches close to a *taberna* counter, I was still thinking about him.

Scarlett, you said that if you were to see him again, you'd definitely make a move, and now you no longer want to? I questioned myself. True. After Barcelona, I had started to forget about John. However, I had sworn that if we were to cross paths again and he still made me feel the same way, I'd act on it, even if it meant betraying some of my principles.

Scarlett, things have changed since then! You can't put yourself first. You've met his wife! said the angelic voice in my subconscious, reprimanding me.

Who cares about her! She pretty much jumped down your throat on the plane. Follow your heart, Scarlett. Think about your needs! commanded a more evil-sounding voice in my subconscious.

The voices kept spinning around in my head. They were in complete disagreement. My tiny angelic voice wanted me to be reasonable and fair, asking me to ignore my emotions. As for my evil voice, it was directing me to jump at the opportunity and finally be selfish; that my personal pleasure was important. I didn't know which was right.

Do you think John will want me? I asked.

He didn't do anything last time, in Barcelona, even though he had the chance to in the elevator. He won't do anything this time either, Scarlett. You're fooling yourself! stated the angelic voice.

Wake up, Scarlett! John was dreaming about having you in his bed. He was devouring you with his eyes in Paris, and in Barcelona. If he looks at you the same way again, that'll be your sign and you'll have to seize the opportunity, commanded my evil voice.

I was confused. None of it was helping me think clearer. I ordered a glass of red wine and a couple of tapas before continuing my examination.

But why isn't it up to him to make a move? If he wants to cheat on his wife then he should come on to me! I stated to the voices in my head.

Scarlett, that man has good values that he simply doesn't want to steer away from. He has children and is a responsible father. He will never make the first move. He hasn't even thought about it, explained the angelic voice.

What?! John has definitely thought about it! Look at you, you're gorgeous! Make the move, my dear Scarlett, and you'll see, you won't be disappointed. That man is just waiting for it! And that way, he won't be able to blame himself, as he will not have deliberately provoked anything, explained the little devil inside my head.

The evil voice was starting to truly win me over. It was pulling me into debauchery. Very real images of John and I laying together in bed were suddenly appearing in my head. I took a big sip of red wine, gobbled up a piece of ham and cheese, and continued my analysis.

But, if I decide to come on to him and he welcomes my advances, I will have encouraged a married man to cheat on his wife! I thought, outraged.

Exactly, Scarlett. And you don't want to live with that for the rest of your life. There are enough men in the world to avoid stealing one from another woman, pointed out my protecting angel.

Excuse me! If something ever happens between John and you, well, it'll only be because your captain will have given you free rein. You won't have twisted his arm. So, you won't have to deal with any guilt! then pointed out my little demon, winning the argument.

I had my answer. I wanted to live through the strong emotions that the simple thought of him gave me. All my worries and fake anticipations were pointlessly messing with my head. My mind was now set. My heart would tell me what is best for me. I got up, paid my bill, and returned to the hotel.

* * *

As soon as I entered my room, I jumped on my phone and opened Skype again. I needed a pep talk and knew that Becky was the best person to give me one. She must be back in her room by now, and I was risking waking her up. I dialed the number to her hotel again. A man answered.

"Le Novotel Toulouse, *bonsoir!*" he said.

"*Bonsoir*, monsieur, may I please speak with Madam Becky Henson?" I politely asked, pronouncing very clearly as to not be asked to repeat myself again.

"Yes, certainly. I'll transfer your call now, madam!" the man confirmed.

"Well, *merci*, monsieur! Good-bye!"

I was looking forward to speaking with Becky and getting her blessing. This time, she picked up the phone.

"Hello?" she said sleepily.

"Ah! Sorry, Becky! Did I wake you?" I asked, genuinely sorry to have interrupted her sleep.

"Who's this?" she asked, still unaware of who was calling her.

"It's Scarlett! You know, your roomie!" I let out.

"Scarlett? Why are you calling me here? Is everything okay?" she asked, with a hint of concern.

"Yes, yes, all good. I'm calling from Madrid. I'm worried about something and would like your opinion. But if you're too sleepy we can talk tomorrow when you get back," I stated, not wanting to disturb her night.

"No, no! I had just gone to bed. The flight is leaving late tomorrow. I have all the time in the world. What's going on?"

"Well, tomorrow I'm flying to New York and the day after I'm operating a flight to Dublin, and then back to Boston," I said, pausing to gather my thoughts.

Just thinking about it made my earlier uneasiness reappear. Perhaps it was due to the large, *too large*, amount of alcohol I had ingested? Becky wanted to know what I was getting at.

"Yeah, so what's the issue with your schedule? It's nice. Direct flights, that's great," she assured me.

"No, no, the flights are nice. That's not what I'm worried about," I clarified, so I wouldn't mislead her.

"So, what's the problem?" she persisted.

"Actually, my handsome captain is going to be on my flight from New York to Dublin and will be spending the night in the hotel with me."

"No way! So, you've agreed to see each other again and he'll sleep in your room? Wow, Scarlett, that's awesome!" she exclaimed, overjoyed.

"No, Becky! Let me start over. John will be the captain on my flight and the whole crew will be staying at the same hotel. He will have his room and I will have mine," I explained to avoid further confusion.

"Okay! Well, it's still great news, don't you think? You're finally gonna get your chance, Scarlett! Go for it!" she advised with vigor and confidence.

"You think?" I asked, still hesitating.

"Yes! Scarlett, it would be ridiculous to let a man who rocks your world that much slip away! No matter where he's from, what his life or his past consist of. You must follow your heart!" urged Becky, as if she was holding life's secret to happiness.

"Will he want me?" I wondered again.

"You'll see it in his eyes. And I think that yes, he will," she assured me.

I was relieved. I now had her blessing. I could sleep peacefully. At least, until tomorrow. Just as I was about to hang up, I heard a man's voice in the background. Naughty Becky! She had brought someone back to her room. I immediately checked with her.

"You're not alone, you naughty girl!" I asked curiously.

"No, I'm with Damien," she answered, without a hint of embarrassment. "He came to visit for the night."

"Damien? The French guy with the yacht?"

"Yes," she answered, a bit more shyly.

"Ah! Why didn't you tell me!" I exclaimed, feeling silly for having discussed my meaningless pilot stories so openly.

"He didn't hear a thing, Scarlett. I would have said something if it was an issue. Sleep tight and don't let yourself worry anymore," she assured me.

Her voice was so calming that as soon as it made it to my ears, I felt better. My eyelids felt heavy. It was time for bed.

"Thanks, Becky. Say hi to Damien for me! Have a good night!" I kindly ended.

"Good night, Scarlett and good luck in Dublin!" she said before hanging up.

I closed Skype and set my alarm for the next day. I turned the light off and slipped under the covers. Just before falling asleep, one last thought flashed through my mind: *The next two days are going to feel like an eternity!*

Chapter 19

New York (JFK) – Dublin (DUB)

I t felt like a whole century had gone by since I had landed in New York. I had counted the hours, the minutes, the seconds, the milliseconds, and had even gone as far as counting the nanoseconds. My impatience had kept me from getting a proper rest during my pre-flight nap. I couldn't stay still. As soon I sat on the corner of my hotel bed, my right leg would start acting up, jolting up and down.

That morning, when I went out to get a latte close to the hotel, I was victim of hallucinations. In the line at Starbucks, a man with a very similar shape to John's almost gave me a heart attack. I quickly realized it couldn't be him, regained composure, grabbed my coffee, and headed to the mall. I tried on a gorgeous sweater in my favorite store and, coming out of the fitting room, I almost blacked out again thinking I had seen John in a store nearby.

My heart was sick of being stimulated for no reason and it urged me to hurry back to the hotel, for its own sake. I obeyed. Soon, my hallucinations would become reality.

* * *

When the crew transportation dropped us off in front of the airport, my heart started racing again. *Poor little heart! It'll have to get used to it as this is just the beginning,* I thought. After passing through security, Barry, our chief purser, announced that he needed to go to the crew room to grab some paperwork. Therefore, he advised us what time we needed to be on the aircraft and then set us free.

The crew split up. Some flight attendants went for a quick stop at the duty-free and others, to Starbucks. Megan and I didn't feel like anything in particular so we decided to make our way to the aircraft right away.

"Apparently Dublin is a very cool city. I've never been. Have you?" she asked excitedly.

"Once," I simply answered.

"And so? Do you know where to go for dinner? Where to go out? A traditional pub maybe?"

Then, silence. I wasn't answering. I obviously understood her questions but I couldn't process the information. I could only hear words spoken one after the other. Pub. Out. Traditional. And then, as a background noise, the sound of her stilettos pounding the floor. Megan called out to me again.

"Hello! Scarlett! Were you listening?"

"Sorry, Megan, my mind was elsewhere. What were you saying?"

"Ah! Forget it! We'll have plenty of time to talk during the flight. Looks like whatever was troubling you on our flight to Madrid hasn't been sorted out, huh?" she asked out of curiosity and sympathy.

"No, not completely," I admitted, without adding any detail, and we continued to walk in silence.

I liked a lot Megan. She was charming, always smiling, and

above all, she minded her own business. She respected her colleagues, always waiting for them to confide in her if they felt the need to. She got hired not long after me and was about twenty-four years old. She was very feminine and always applied her makeup with perfection. Her high black leather stilettos suited her very well. Seeing her meander down through the gate, toward the aircraft, I wished I also had such a strong presence.

Damn! The gate! We were already here. Would I have the strength to go on board? I was getting hot flashes. *This is no longer the time to be a coward*, I decided, and stepped one foot inside the aircraft. I followed Megan toward the front of the cabin. From the first couple rows, we could hear men talking inside the flight deck. *John is already here!* Megan continued walking to the front galley and I heard her talk to the two pilots.

"Hi, my name is Megan. The crew isn't here yet but they shouldn't be long."

There was a pause. Then a man spoke. I couldn't make out what he was saying. Megan concluded the conversation in her oh-so-radiant manner.

"Yes, okay! Perfect! See you soon!"

Then she came to sit next to me. Now that she had introduced herself to the pilots, I thought I might as well do the same. Anyway, I couldn't wait any longer. I got up and approached the cockpit.

I could hear voices. I didn't recognize John's. It had been a whole year, so I had probably forgotten what it sounded like. Like a spy, I stayed hidden with my back to the metallic ovens. *I am being completely ridiculous! I'm thirty, after all!* I decided to act like a grown-up and entered.

"Hello!" I said, smiling in a very laid-back way.

The two pilots turned their heads in my direction. I quickly looked at the first officer, then hurriedly set my gaze on the captain. As soon as I saw him, I stopped breathing. John was in front of me.

"Hi!" they both replied in perfect unison.

The first officer greeted me and flashed a discreet smile but I totally ignored him. As for the captain, he gave me the nicest smile I had ever seen in my life. That smile was, by far, more charming and enchanting than the ones in Paris. Even more electrifying than the last one he gave me, before opening the door to his room in Barcelona. I was hit by cold sweats. I got weak in the knees. I had to make sure I didn't blow my cover. I quickly added a meaningless sentence so that I could swiftly leave:

"You've arrived soon?" I stammered.

What had I just said? I was praying for my question to go unnoticed. John would see right through me and my clumsiness. To my dismay, my handsome captain grasped the opportunity to tease me a little.

"Soon?"

I had to answer his question and take control back over the situation. John's smile was hypnotizing. And so was his face. And his eyes. His smell was driving me insane. I stammered again.

"Erm! I mean, have you been on the plane soon?"

What had happened to my vocabulary?! Soon? I meant to say LONG! Nothing complicated with that! L-O-N-G! My face turned red; Scarlett red. John must have been happy to see me lose my composure that way, in front of him. Seeing the two pilots kindly laughing at me, I had to laugh as well. I lifted a hand up toward them to indicate that they wouldn't get any further explanation from me and headed back to one of the passenger seats to wait for the rest of the crew.

I was pretty embarrassed to have acted in such a confused way but, oh well, I had to live with it. *Surely, one day I'll get used to his presence*, I assured myself. I would have to since I'd be spending two days with him. The flight there. And the flight back. Just thinking about it made me feel terrified, yet privileged.

Once the crew was on board, Barry advised the pilots. John stood in front of the first row and started his briefing.

"Hi, everyone! This is Sebastian Collins, the first officer," he said, lifting a hand toward the pilot. "And I'm John Ross," he added confidently.

The crew greeted both of them and he went on.

"Today we are operating flight 144 to Dublin, with an estimated flight time of six hours, thirty minutes. No turbulence in the forecast."

As he finished his sentence, he quickly glanced at me. I was hooked on his every word. After giving us a few more details, he looked at me again and wished us a nice flight, then returned to the cockpit. Barry continued with some additional information.

Per usual, he asked us to choose our positions on the aircraft. When it got to my turn, I had to choose between three positions, one of which consisted of working at the front, in first class. Although I wasn't crazy about preparing gin and tonics or offering freshly ground pepper to my passengers, I chose that position, for a reason only I knew.

In fact, since it involved spending the whole flight in the front, consequently being close to the cockpit, one of my additional duties was to look after the pilots' comfort. I would get them their meals, prepare their coffees, and make sure they had everything they needed.

I had rarely chosen that position in the past, obviously never wanting to attend to pretentious pilots. Megan, who knew me, had been surprised by my selection and had pulled a disappointed face. I understood that she would have liked to work with me, so I suggested she come visit during the flight.

Once the briefing was finally over, Barry launched boarding. I was in my galley, preparing a few champagne glasses for my precious guests. I was so eager to see them! *Who would I be serving?* I wondered. A Lady Coco? I prayed it wouldn't be the case. I then made my way to the aisle to assist one of the passengers. When I returned, I got an unobstructed view of the flight deck, and of my captain. I discreetly spied on him, hoping not to get caught.

Just as I turned away to look at the boarding door, I heard John call after me. He must have sensed my desire to talk to him. I was walking on air. I floated toward him and placed myself in front of the door. What would he say? *Ah! My lovely Scarlett, I'm so happy to see you,* or maybe, *I've been waiting for this moment for a whole year, Scarlett, I hope the feeling is mutual.* Yes! Yes! It's totally mutual! I'm obsessed with you!

"Can you please ask the chief purser to come and see me? I need to speak with him," he said, expressionless.

How disappointing! I knew it! I had been dreaming all along. Here I was, thinking about him and only him. I had to get a grip and get to work. Of course his priority wouldn't be to mess around with one of his flight attendants. He had a plane to fly. Maybe he'd be a bit more open once in Dublin? I was hoping he would, and passed the message on to Barry.

Boarding was completed. I had started serving champagne flutes and offering newspapers to my passengers. The door had just been closed. Then, I saw my colleague Diane come toward me with a piece of paper.

"Barry says the singer Helena Hanks is seating in economy at 9K. He'd like you to go over and welcome her on board, assure her we'll be looking after her during the flight," she said.

"Erm! Isn't it his job?"

"Yeah, but he says he doesn't have time right now," she explained, before returning to her own duties.

ARRRGGG! I hate when someone does that. When someone delegates! Barry was too busy. Really? Just like me, he probably simply didn't want to suck up to a "celebrity" so had passed his dirty work on to me. He was the chief purser but somehow now I was the one who had to act as the master of ceremonies? I looked at the piece of paper Diane had given me.

Helena Hanks! I hated that Californian singer. Above all, I hated having to put on a show for an artist just because their name was Mr. This or Mrs. That. I just had to get on with my task and get it over with. I headed for seat 9K.

When I arrived at the given seat number, I found it empty. Nobody there! *Yeah!* I thought. *She isn't here, there's been an error!* I went looking for Barry to let him know he had received the wrong information.

"Hey! Barry!" I called out. "Your Helena Hanks isn't here. Seat 9K is empty."

"Impossible! I saw her earlier. I'm the one who checked her boarding pass."

"Okay... She must be in the lavatory. I'll wait for her to get back, then," I said, convinced that must be the case.

"Okay great! Thanks!" he replied before advising the cabin crew to arm their doors in preparation for takeoff.

I executed the requested task and stood in the aisle while the safety video was being played. I stood up straight and attempted to smile politely. Many were looking at me instead of looking at their screens. In my head, I was having fun dictating the safety procedures at the same time as the narrator.

"In the unlikely event of loss of cabin pressure, an oxygen mask will automatically fall in front of you. To start the flow of oxygen, pull the mask toward you and place it firmly over your nose and mouth. Breathe normally . . . "

I congratulated myself for every word I got right. Ah, the things I do to entertain myself! I continued my little game while observing each and every one of the passengers in my section.

"Even if the bag does not inflate, oxygen will be flowing. Please put your own mask on before assisting others . . . "

Another point for me! I thought, still observing my passengers. The woman in 2B looked very familiar. She was wearing a massive beige hat. She was very pretty and was chatting with her neighbor. She must have been around thirty-five years old and I really felt like I knew her from somewhere. Intrigued, I checked her name on the passenger manifest.

I went through the document and quickly spotted the first class section. There was no name under the seat 2B. I counted the number of names on my list. Fifteen. I returned to my position in the aisle to count the exact number of passengers seated in my section. The result: seventeen. Obviously, it wasn't adding up. As the manifest ruled over all else, I came to the conclusion that two passengers had taken the wrong seats. Surely, one of them was that fake movie star and her hat. *No wonder she's hiding behind a sombrero!* Just as I was about to inform Barry of the situation, it dawned on me!

That woman who looked familiar was in fact Helena Hanks! I didn't know her per se, but I had seen her on TV, which is why she looked so familiar. But how could she have gotten mistaken? 9K was in economy! Far from 2B, which was in first class. Seeing her chatting away with her neighbor, I assumed that he, too, had inadvertently made it into my section. I immediately advised my chief purser.

"Barry! I found where Helena Hanks is sitting."

"Great! Did you go see her?" he asked, relieved.

"No, no yet. Actually, it looks like she is seated in my section, in 2B," I admitted, a bit irritated.

"Hm, weird. I definitely saw her boarding pass and she was sitting with her partner in 9J and K."

Lady Sombrero was traveling with her lover! Were they both complete idiots or were they blinded by love, not realizing that 2B and C were completely different from 9J and K? Apparently, two heads were not better than one! I was eager to find out the reason for the seat change. Determined, Barry got up and headed toward her.

"Hello, Mrs. Hanks. I don't want to sound rude but I can't find your name on my list of first class passengers. Can I please see your boarding pass?" he asked, extremely politely.

Hearing how much he was sugarcoating it with that semi-celebrity was infuriating. I was looking forward to knowing what her retort would be as instead of getting her ticket out, she put on a very sorry face. With exaggerated kindness, she explained herself.

"Well, actually, the girl at check-in told us there were a few empty seats in first class and suggested we take them. I followed her advice."

Barry was hesitant. I could tell he didn't know what to say. Helena-the-Star was using her charm. My chief purser was completely taken aback. Lady Sombrero was surrounded by bright, harp-playing angels singing for her liberation. So, Barry gave in:

"Well, all right for this time, Mrs. Hanks. But I'd like to say that we do not usually allow people to grab such seats," he clarified, making sure a similar scenario didn't happen again.

He came back to the galley, where I was waiting resolutely.

"You've got to be kidding me!" I exploded, offended.

"No, it's fine, I'm letting her sit in first, Scarlett. I don't want any problem with the media," he explained.

"Uh! Come on, Barry! It's not just because she's popular that we have to let her use her fake celebrity status! It's not fair! I'm sure whatever she said about the girl at check-in isn't even true!" I went on, outraged at the unjustified favoritism.

"I understand, Scarlett, but I've made the decision so we're just gonna deal with it, okay? I'll put all the event's details in the flight report. At least the company will know what she's done."

His statement reassured me a little bit and I left to do my final cabin check before taking place on my jump seat for takeoff. *Anyway, it's going to be Barry serving her, not me!* I thought, somehow boycotting her. Suddenly, my thoughts went my back to my obsession: John was talking to me. I could hear his voice in my ears. He was speaking to me. Well, sort of.

"In preparation for takeoff, flight attendants to your jump seats. Have a good flight!"

We took off right away. I lowered my chin toward my chest, rested my hands on my knees, and let my handsome captain fly me away.

* * *

We were three and a half hours into the flight. I had to enter the flight deck to grab the meal trays I had given John and Sebastian a little while ago. At the same time, I would also bring them their coffees. I advised Barry I was about to enter the flight deck and closed the galley's curtains. Then I dialed the entry code and waited for one of the pilots to electronically unlock the door. I gave the door a strong push to enter and closed it behind me.

"Did you enjoy your meal?"

"Yum, you know how tasty airplane food is!" said Sebastian, somewhat disgusted.

"Yeah, well at least it fills you up!" I answered, then grabbed the two trays.

I didn't feel like talking with the first officer. I would have preferred to hear John's voice but he simply smiled at the short conversation. I looked through the spyhole to ensure nobody was waiting on the other side ready to intrude the cockpit, and came out with the trays. Then, I grabbed the two coffees and re-entered, closing the door again behind me.

I gave the first coffee to Sebastian, carefully handing it over to him on his right-hand side, to avoid the horrible mess that would affect the dashboard in the event of a sudden turbulence. I did the same for John, on his left-hand side. He thanked me by saying, "Thanks, missy," which made me blush. He didn't notice a thing as it was still nighttime and the only light around was the faint glow of the hundreds of buttons in the flight deck. In order to stay close to him a little longer, I asked Sebastian if the sun was rising soon. I had, obviously, spoken to the first officer solely to avoid appearing over-interested. I was doing everything I could to appear independent, so I barely looked at John. A stupid game, I'll admit, but I couldn't help it. Just as I was waiting for Sebastian's answer, John cut in.

"About thirty minutes from now, you'll see the sun rise right in front of us. I'll call you, if you'd like to come in for some pictures," he kindly offered.

"Ah! Yes, I'd love that. If I'm not too busy," I answered, hoping I wouldn't be.

As ten minutes had already gone by, I asked John to call Barry so that he could keep an eye on the door, allowing me to exit the cockpit. The security procedures started off again.

Exhausting? Absolutely! Procedure #1: Call the captain to advise we're coming into the flight deck. Procedure #2: Make sure no nutcase is trying to hijack the plane. Procedure #3: Dial the entry code. Procedure #4: Call again in order to exit the flight deck. Procedure #5: Look into the spyhole to make sure no one can come in. Procedure #6: Quickly exit. Procedure #7: Kick the damn door closed. Procedure #8: Shoot, I forgot to bring the captain's coffee! So, there we go again! It's a never-ending ordeal.

When I got back to the galley, Barry and Megan were chatting. She was asking him the same questions she had asked me previously.

"It'd be cool to go out for dinner with the whole crew. It's my first time in Dublin. Apparently, it's THE spot to go out to a pub. Do you know any restaurants?"

"Yeah, I know a couple. I'm up for going out somewhere. Let's have a look when we get to the hotel," he enthusiastically answered.

Well, that was perfect. There were already a few crew members planning to go out for dinner together. The evening looked like it'd be a lively one. I was hoping John and his first officer would join us. *I'll investigate when the time comes*, I thought.

I wondered how Lady Sombrero was going. I asked Barry.

"Ah! Don't get me started! I can't put up with her anymore! She's such a princess!" he whispered.

"I told you she thinks she can get away with anything! Is her boyfriend as bad as her?" I was curious to know who she was traveling with.

"No, he's fine. He lives in Dublin and seems to think very highly of American stars."

"Ah, really? Our local celebrity making it in the big world, huh? He must think we're all worshiping her here, letting them sit in first!"

"I know! He seemed quite impressed."

"Ah! Ridiculous! Do you still find her as charming now?" I teased him.

"I hate her! I'm never buying one of her albums again."

"You should have known, Barry. How can you not have read through her *I'm a famous singer with a sombrero on my head, so obey me* kind of attitude?"

"Yeah . . . Well, I fell for her blond hair."

"Of course! You should always be wary of blondes," I concluded, laughing and getting up to go pick up the garbage in my section.

There were only two and a half hours left to the flight. The sun would soon be rising. There was an incoming call from the flight deck. I immediately picked up:

"Hello, Scarlett speaking."

"Hi, Scarlett, it's your captain, John, speaking."

Was he teasing me? I couldn't tell. Maybe he was a pretentious pilot after all? No way! I settled on replying with as much attitude.

"Yes, John . . . I know who you are," I confirmed, carefully pronouncing every word.

"I'm kidding, Scarlett" he said, amused. "I just wanted to tell you that the sun is rising, so if you still want to take pictures, you're more than welcome to."

I looked at the time and turned the ovens on to warm up the meals. I then advised Barry that I was going into the cockpit to take a couple pictures before the breakfast service. I dialed the code, pushed the door open with my hip, and entered.

"Wow, how beautiful!" I exclaimed, as if I was witnessing the sunrise from the flight deck for the very first time.

"Yeah, amazing!" confirmed the first officer.

"The clouds make all the difference, don't you think?" John asked me.

"Yes, you're right. They're so fluffy!"

So far, I quite liked our little interaction. He had teased me and hadn't ignored my comments. Who knows, maybe I stood a chance? I sat on one of the jump seats inside the cockpit and silently started taking photos. After a couple shots, Sebastian contacted the air traffic controller and I decided to flatter John's ego.

"Who is he talking to?" I whispered, as to not disturb the first officer.

"To Ireland's air traffic controller."

"Ah, really? Why is he talking to him?" I asked, as if I knew nothing about aviation.

"To advise him of our position."

"Hm, the air traffic controller is there so that we don't fly into anyone else, right?"

"Yeah, among other things. He also, for example, gives us authorization to change our altitude."

"Wow! So many things to know, huh?"

"Funny you should say that. I was just talking to a flight attendant the other day who gave me the usual speech: *You pilots, you're all overpaid for the work you do.* It really made me laugh."

"What do you mean?"

"I don't get paid for what I do, but for what I know."

"Well, you're right!"

I obviously knew how to make men feel like a big deal. It was working like a charm and John's words were flowing much more smoothly. I thanked him for the valuable information about aviation, without letting him know that I already knew the answer to all of my questions.

The sun was now high in front of us, and I had to return to work. Once I was standing next to the armored door, John called out to me one last time.

"Sebastian and I were just talking about a good restaurant he knows in Dublin. You guys are welcome to join us if you'd like," he said.

"I already know that a couple people want to go out so it should work out. I'll mention it to them," I said, over the moon about going out to dinner with him.

"Great!"

Then he picked up the phone to advise Barry of my exit from the flight deck.

"Thanks! See you soon!"

Barry and I started the breakfast meal service as there were only two hours left to the flight. He made an announcement to wake the passengers up.

"Ladies and gentlemen, good morning. We are now two hours away from our arrival in Dublin, where the local time is nine a.m. A few minutes from now, we will come down the aisle with a continental breakfast . . . "

I hated that announcement! It sounded like a military wakeup call! One minute earlier, the cabin was as calm as a millpond, and then, action! Passengers still half asleep were yawning away, letting out quite unpleasant smells into the cabin. Some, on the other hand, were furious and made sure that I, the trumpeter, knew it. *Sorry! We have no choice!* I thought. We had to start the service right away because, compared to the economy class, first class's service was a lot more elaborate.

Once the meal trays had been distributed, we served hot buns, marmalade, and coffee. Lady Sombrero, who had just woken up, lifted her colossal hat up to see me and requested a cup of coffee.

"May I please ask you to put your cup on my tray?" I asked.

She obliged and I filled her cup with the liquid. Once it was full, I moved my tray towards her so that she could grab her cup and I advised her to be careful.

"Watch out, the coffee is very hot."

She rolled her eyes and immediately took a sip.

"Ouch! Ouch!" she screamed, waking up the rest of the cabin. "It's burning hot!"

"Are you all right, ma'am?" I quickly asked.

"No! I burned my tongue! You served me boiling coffee!"

If I could have poured the whole pot on her head, I would have done so. I really wanted to! *Her beige hat would look so much better in brown.* I had to calm her down.

"Sorry, Ms. Hanks. I didn't know it was that hot. Would you like a glass of ice water to ease the burn?" I suggested, not knowing what else to say.

"No! Nothing at all! My vocal cords are ruined! Thanks to you!" she accused.

How rude! Her vocal cords? If you asked me, she already sang like an amateur anyway. The little incident just happened to be a great opportunity for her to consider a career move. How about theater? She already looked like an actress, making a scene for her audience in first class.

Hearing her accusations suddenly gave me some courage. I had to go on with my service and whatever I did would never satisfy such a passenger. *Might as well give her her money's worth!*

"Again, I'm sorry, Ms. Hanks" I said, in an extremely compassionate manner.

I pretended to move down the aisle to serve the passenger behind her but stopped in my tracks. I took a step backward and, still holding my coffee pot in one hand and the tray with creamers in the other, I slowly leaned toward her and whispered in her ear:

"Anyway, ma'am, whether it's hot or cold, it won't help you sing any better."

I didn't even look at her reaction. But I knew she was speechless. Her boyfriend, sitting next to her, wouldn't have heard a thing, and I'm sure she wouldn't provide him with the details. She probably didn't want to make a fool of herself any more than she already had. Throughout the rest of the flight, I ignored her and only offered what she dared to asked for.

Finishing my work in the galley, I was overtaken by a triumphant pride. I had finally shut Lady Sombrero up, without making the situation worse. I started quietly humming while cleaning the dirty counter. Hearing me sing, Barry inquired:

"You seem happy. May I know the reason why?"

"Thirty minutes from now, 2B will finally be out of my life!" I explained, dramatically gesticulating. "Isn't it a good reason to sing?"

"Oh yes! It sure is! A delicious Guinness and she won't be more than a fleeting memory!"

"For me, a Bulmers cider!" I added before I continued

humming.

Lost in thought, I dedicated the melody to the evening I had been dreaming of. Would it end the way I hoped? Would John show me a noticeable sign of interest?

Chapter 20

Dublin (DUB), Ireland

"Everyone who wanted to come out for dinner is here?" Barry asked the group.

"Diane is missing," I said.

"She's coming," mentioned Megan. "She just called me before I came down to say she wasn't ready yet."

"Okay! Let's wait for her," said Barry.

Some flight attendants are always late, no matter what. Diane is one of them. On the plane, we would look for her to start the services. At the hotel, she would check out at the last minute. The crew would already have been on the bus for ten minutes when she would finally arrive, with her hair still wet. It was always the same reason: insomnia. What could one say to that? That tragedy had affected every one of us at one point or another. We all had suffered from sleep problems before and knowing how grueling counting sheep in the middle of the night could be, we couldn't hold it against her. This time, however, I wondered what her reason would be. She finally appeared, jogging toward us.

"Sorry, everyone! I fell asleep when we arrived and the alarm didn't go off when it was supposed to," she explained, out of breath.

"That's okay!" we all responded in unison.

"So, where are we going for dinner?" asked Barry.

"Sebastian knows a restaurant close by, if you'd like," answered John.

"Yeah, and it's located just across from a small traditional pub. We could go there after," he suggested, selling everyone on the idea.

"Perfect! We'll follow you," said Barry, speaking for everyone.

When we came out of the hotel, we crossed the street and entered the large park where I had gone jogging earlier, after my nap. It was called St Stephen's Green and was one of the city's biggest parks. We followed the central path. In front of me, I noticed that Megan was talking with the first officer. They seemed to be hitting it off. I was hoping the evening would be one to remember.

A few yards farther along, we arrived at the center of the park. Children were splashing around a beautiful water fountain. John was on my right-hand side and we hadn't said a word since we had left the hotel.

"Children are so lovely! No malice. They only think about playing," he said, charged with emotions.

"They remind you of yours?" I asked, curious to know what his kids were like.

"Of course! It's hard not to think about them, being so far away," he confided.

"Do you feel guilty for leaving?"

"Always! If anything were to happen to me . . . "

"You mean a plane crash?"

"Yes, among other things. I know, it's silly to think that way since I'm in the best position to know just how safe my aircraft is."

"Precisely, John! Flying is the safest means of transportation there is! I think we both have a higher risk of getting hit by an Irish car by forgetting to look in the right direction than crashing on the runaway!" I vividly explained, pointing to the street near us.

John smiled at my remark and made sure we crossed safely. He rested his hand on my back and let me go in front of him. I could feel him paying attention to my every step. *What a gentleman! I thought.*

"Anyway, seeing how you landed that aircraft, I'd never worry about my own safety!" I teased.

"If I understand correctly, you feel safe around me?" he asked smoothly.

Whoa! He was putting words in my mouth. Was he trying to seduce me? Did he really want to know if I felt safe around him or was he being sarcastic? He was most likely playing the same game I was, so I shouldn't let the cat out of the bag. I would not let him know my deepest thoughts unless he gave me a very clear sign first. There was no way I was going to make a fool of myself by answering his question seriously. I continued with the teasing.

"Oh! Absolutely, John! You're the only one I trust on a plane! Without you in the front, I'm lost! I can't work and my passengers suffer the consequences! Come fly with me, John! Fly!" I sang on the sidewalk of Merrion Row.

My little scene grasped his undivided attention. He looked as if he was admiring me. The more I was gesticulating, the more he was smiling. Therefore, I was far from wanting to end the show but as I ran out of ideas, I finally stopped. John stopped in his tracks as if to lecture me.

"Nice one, Scarlett! But completely unrealistic. I don't believe you!" he said, faking disappointment.

We were both laughing loudly when we arrived at the restaurant. Going in, we immediately felt the very cool vibe, which confirmed we had made a great choice. A young woman greeted us from the counter.

"Good evening!"

"Hello! We'd like to know if you have availability for a party of six?" asked the first officer.

"Hm! Let me check what I can do," answered the woman, and then went inside the restaurant to investigate.

She came back a minute later.

"Please follow me!" she enthusiastically announced, guiding us to our table.

We followed her, happy to have gotten a table in such a crowded restaurant. I wanted to sit close to John but also didn't want to seem too interested. I decided to take a seat in the middle of the table and have him inevitably end up near me. On my left, there was Megan, and on my right, Diane. Sebastian sat in front of Megan, and Barry in front of Diane. As for John, he sat in front of me. *Yeah!* Nothing could have made me happier. Megan, amused by our arrangement, took the floor.

"Well, we couldn't have been more organized than this!"

"This layout suits me just fine," said Sebastian, smiling at her.

His comment made her blush and made us laugh. Hearing his remark, I wondered if John had thought the same as Sebastian, having me in front of him. I looked up and our eyes met. His gaze was as sparkling as ever and I couldn't figure out if his eyes naturally gleamed or if they did so only when looking at me. I was intimidated. He looked so self-confident. I couldn't hold his gaze for long. I looked down at the menu.

* * *

Three bottles of wine later, having finished dessert, none of us felt like going to bed. The night was still young, so we crossed over to O'Donoghue's pub. Upon entering, we could see two men playing traditional Irish music at the very back. Right away, we went up to the bar to order some drinks. John leaned in to speak to me.

"What would you like to drink?" he softly asked in my ear.

His proximity made my pulse speed up. Luckily, the folk music was intense, otherwise John would have heard my heart racing. I leaned in as well, to communicate my drink selection.

"A cider," I said, then looked away, self-conscious.

He got closer to the counter and yelled our order to the barman. He returned with two pints, a Guinness in one hand and a cider in the other. I thanked him and let him know our friends had gone across to a quieter corner. We caught up to them.

Once we were all seated on our respective benches, I remembered Becky's words: *You're gonna see it in his eyes.* She must have been right as I could gradually sense that, with his eyes, John was revealing his attraction toward me. I couldn't explain how, but I could feel it. The way he laid his eyes on me was strangely similar to that in Paris and Barcelona, only different in one way: it was much deeper.

With every blink, his amazing black pearls shot right through my heart and they were increasingly sparkling with every minute that passed, from one conversation to another. However, I was still waiting for a green light. Without a clear sign, I wouldn't be ready to admit my feelings for him. *Come on, give it to me, just a little , John! Just one!* I mentally commanded him. I took a sip of cider and spoke to him:

"How did your parents meet?"

"Hm, funny question" he said, surprised. "Why do you want to know that?"

"Out of curiosity. I was wondering why your dad was Irish and had chosen to leave this lovely music behind to settle in the States."

"Out of love, Scarlett. Only love can push us to make such huge decisions."

John smiled at me and continued.

"When she was eighteen, my mother came to Ireland with a friend. That's when she met my father. Once summer was over, she brought him back with her and they got married the following winter."

"Wow! Love at first sight!" I exclaimed dreamily.

"Yes! That's right! The best part of their story is that they both died together on their wedding anniversary, just before Christmas," he confided, in a surprisingly serene manner.

"Oh dear! John! That's so sad. You lost both your parents at once! How old were you?"

"They passed when I was fifteen, in a car accident," he added, still calmly.

The story deeply saddened me. What a cruel destiny! Poor John! At that moment, I liked him even more. I would have wanted to softly kiss him, comfort him. But it must have been me who had a long face, since he started trying to make me feel better.

"Come on, Scarlett! You should see your face right now! Don't worry, the beautiful memories will never die and I'm holding on to the best ones."

"Yes, for sure . . . But what happened to you after?"

Dammit, Scarlett, stop it with all your questions! I scolded myself. I couldn't help it. My handsome pilot! Such a sad story! I wanted to know.

"I was put under my mother's sister and her husband's care."

"That's why you didn't go back to Ireland?" I asked.

"That's right. After my father's death, I lost contact with his Irish family. I only ever come here when I have to for work."

Wow! That was the most profound conversation I had ever had with a colleague. He spoke with so much honesty . . . I now felt true admiration for the man, and I also felt privileged. John had opened up to me, seated on an uncomfortable bench in an Irish pub. He must have trusted me. His presence and his words were fascinating. I wondered if someone had noticed our obvious closeness. What if someone had? How would Freaky Debbie react if she knew? No one could find out about my crush. I quickly glanced around the table.

Megan was still talking to Sebastian, which didn't surprise me. They didn't seem to care about my presence, nor John's. Barry and Diane had disappeared. Everything was under control. To create a diversion, I worried about my two colleagues' absence:

"Do you know where the others have gone?"

"They went out for a smoke," answered Megan. "I think that after the pub, they want to get some fresh air in the park in front of the hotel."

"Oh really?" I asked, a bit disappointed to see the evening ending so soon.

"It's already eleven p.m., but it could be cool to go for a walk before going to sleep. What do you think?" Megan asked.

Already eleven p.m.! Time had gone so quickly! Megan was

waiting for our answer. I didn't want to leave, even if my bum was hurting from the lack of comfort on the wooden bench. If we were to leave, maybe John would take the opportunity to go back to the hotel, just like he did in Paris . . . I needed more time. Maybe with another beer he would demonstrate his interest? Not wanting to blow my cover, I let him decide.

"Hm, I'll get another Guinness. Then we can see about the park," he said, looking at me for approval.

"Yes, I agree."

I offered to pay for the next round. He accepted and came to grab the drinks with me. Once back in position, I decided to express my gratitude:

"Well, thanks for telling me your parents' story. It's a truly beautiful love story."

"Happy you liked it. Do you believe in love at first sight, Scarlett?" he whispered, not letting anyone else hear.

What kind of question is this! Of course I believe in it! I experienced it with you! I thought. But instead, I simply answered:

"Yes, I do. And you?"

"Of course, that's how my parents met."

"Have you ever experienced it?" I continued.

"Yes."

"With your wife, I guess?"

Why had I asked that? Obviously, it was with his wife, otherwise he wouldn't be married to her right now! I didn't feel like hearing about Freaky Debbie. Especially not from John. I had to rectify the situation.

"Ah! Sorry, John, that was a stupid question. Of course, it's with her," I said, rolling my eyes.

"Hm, if you say so," he said, sighing.

What? *If you say so?* Nothing else? No details? How could

he keep me in the dark like that? A true psychological torture! Should I conclude that Freaky Debbie and John had not fallen in love at first sight? And if she wasn't the lucky one, who was? Me? There I was again, hallucinating. And what about my clear sign? It was nowhere to be seen! Arg! I quickly chugged my cider and saw Barry and Diane walk toward us.

"We're gonna continue the evening in the park. Are you guys coming?" asked Diane.

"Yes! We're ready!" confirmed Megan, also speaking for Sebastian.

As I had just finished my pint, I no longer had any excuse to stay. I needed air anyway. I was hoping that my handsome pilot did as well.

"Yeah, I'm also ready. Some fresh air will be good," I said, hoping to convince John.

"Okay! Let's go!" he said decisively, and jumped to his feet.

We exited the pub. I walked in front of him, alone behind Megan. I was disappointed with the outcome of the evening and no longer felt like talking. Regardless of the deep conversation about love at first sight and of the other intimate subjects we had talked about, nothing confirmed that he was attracted to me. *You're gonna see it in his eyes!* Yeah, right, Becky! His eyes were just sumptuous. Nothing more! I had no point of reference. *Why go to the park? Why continue investigating the matter again and again? I give up!* I decided, following the group on the way back.

* * *

Lost in thought, I snapped back to reality when I felt a sudden warmth wrapping around my hand. I looked down and saw that strong fingers had weaved their way through mine. John was holding my hand! I was shocked and could barely keep putting one foot in front of the other. He slowed down, making me follow suit. Then he stopped altogether. I did the same. My heart was about to explode. What would he do? Kiss me? Here, in front of everyone? We couldn't expose ourselves to the group. *Ah! Whatever!* I thought. *Do it, John! Kiss me!*

He stared into my eyes to fully get my attention, even though I had been paying attention to his every move for a very long time. For an eternity even. I was waiting for him to move in close to me so that I could reciprocate. *His mouth will be mine any moment now*, I dreamed. Then, he delicately moved his lips. *This is it, Scarlett! You finally did it!* Fireworks were illuminating my insides. My body was warming up, literally getting the hots for him. John opened his mouth:

"I'm very happy that you're here, Scarlett," he whispered, then let go of my hand and continued to walk.

What? That's it? No tongue twisting? Not even a little smooch? What a disappointment! What kind of message did he think I'd get from that? He was very happy . . . So, was that a *go* sign for me? I wasn't entirely convinced. I started walking again, my head low. When we finally arrived at the St Stephen's Green's entrance, the gate was closed.

"Ah! Damn! We're too late," exclaimed Diane.

"There's light inside, maybe the entrance by the hotel is still open," suggested Barry.

"Yeah, I hope so," added Megan.

We walked along the park's fence, heading for the other entrance. John was walking close to me. Neither of us was talking. His last words echoed through my head. *I'm very happy that you're here, Scarlett.* I analyzed each word, one syllable, one letter at a time. What was I supposed to surmise from that? And then, all of a sudden, it hit me: The verdict was in! I had had my sign! John had just given it to me. I no longer had any choice; I had to act on it.

My heart started going crazy. Beating harder and harder, it was trying to burst out of my chest. Fear was giving me cold sweats. The clue I had just gotten helped me evaluate my chances. Failure was conceivable, and I dreaded it. A few minutes later, we arrived at another closed gate.

"Well then, what should we do now?" asked Diane, settled on not going to bed.

"We could go to the pub next door. It's not even midnight," suggested Sebastian.

I looked at Barry and Megan and gathered that they agreed with the proposal. I didn't know what to say as John had yet to speak his mind. Again, I wanted to wait for him to make a decision.

"I'm gonna head back," he said. "You guys have a good night."

He waved good-bye to everyone, looked at me, and crossed the street to the hotel. *Whoah I did not see that one coming!* John was slipping through my fingers and I couldn't do anything about it! It looked like I had, once again, hallucinated. There hadn't been a sign at all. I was devastated.

I started walking along with the rest of the group. From the hotel's main window, I could see John going up the stairs. I reminded myself of all the things that came between us, and decided this outcome was probably for the best. I walked past the building and continued toward its back alley. In between each footstep, clear images were coming back to me. Paris. Barcelona. The way he confided in me. His gaze. His hand holding mine.

The indescribable chemistry between us. Suddenly, I heard a voice. It was clearly calling out to me.

Scarlett! You weren't dreaming. John wants you. Seize the opportunity! It's now or never! Go!

All my doubts vanished. I had to get back to the hotel.

I abruptly stopped walking.

"Hey, guys! I'm tired. I'm not gonna go with you actually. I'll see you all tomorrow! G'night!"

As soon as I had said bye, without even waiting for their reply, I turned around. I walked briskly, trying to avoid breaking into a run and blowing my cover. I reached the front door in no time.

It's as if I had transformed into a dangerous predator. And my prey was nearby. I could pick up its smell. I, too, went up the stairs. On the way up, I skipped over a couple steps, which quickly put me out of breath. I went past floor one. I could hear footsteps in front of me but still couldn't see John. I jumped over a couple more steps. The sound seemed close. I was completely out of breath. I had to slow down. I didn't want to look like some hungry animal out on a hunt.

I breathed deeply, barely catching my breath. I continued going up and as I saw the stairs to floor two, I finally spotted him. John also saw me. He seemed surprised.

"I decided to go to bed too," I said, panting.

I climbed up to him. I was hoping he'd say, *Scarlett, I'd love to hold you in my arms, kiss you and make love to you all night long!* but obviously, he didn't say any of that. He simply smiled instead. I remained silent. We went through a first door, then a second, and another one. My heart couldn't take it anymore. My arteries were pumping as hard as they could. Any moment now, one of them would explode and provoke internal bleeding. John stopped in front of his room.

"Good night, Scarlett, see you tomorrow," he said kindly.

It's now or never! repeated the soft voice. I had to listen to it. *Surely, my instinct can't be wrong,* I thought, and positioned myself between him and the door to his room.

"John! You can't leave like this! There's something going on between us. I don't know how to explain it, but I just know. Please tell me I'm not crazy!"

There it was! The cat was out of the bag. I had laid myself bare right there, in the middle of the hotel's hallway. What would he say to me? Surprisingly, I didn't look away like so many times before. My hunting instincts took over. From then on, my shyness gave way to a boldness that dared face his charismatic presence.

He looked down and sighed. Out of relief? Out of joy? Exasperation?

"Good night, Scarlett," he repeated.

Arg! Arg! Arg! *Good night?* Why not punch me in the face while you're at it?! How humiliating! I, in turn, sighed. All I needed to be completely knocked out was a childish kiss on the cheek. And that's exactly what he set about to do. Arg!

John leaned in, his face close to mine, to give my left cheek a friendly kiss. I was staring at the ground. He moved back to make his way to my second cheek. But en route, he made an unsuspected stop. Curious, I looked up. Then, I felt his delicious mouth parting my lips. John was kissing me! FINALLY! Our first kiss! The best kiss of all! And perhaps the last? No! I wanted more!

"John! Let's go inside your room, we wouldn't want to be seen," I whispered.

He looked at me with fiery eyes. His manliness was dominating him. And all the better, because I felt like being dominated.

There was no more doubt. Not that night. He slipped the magnetic key inside the lock. I heard the clicking sound and we swiftly crossed to the other side.

The hunter I had been earlier no longer existed. The roles had switched. I was now delighted to have become the prey.

"Scarlett! Do you have any idea how long I've been waiting for this?" he roared, passionately pushing me against the wall.

"Since a moment ago?" I answered, puzzled.

He smiled.

"Since Paris," he said, making my mouth his again.

"Me too," I let out, before being pulled toward the bed. Had I heard him right? John had wanted me all along? Well, if tonight was the only night we could allow ourselves to have, I'd definitely make the most of it. I admired my trophy, pulled his head between my hands, and, looking right at my target, commanded my desires.

"I want you so bad," I said, then found myself undressed like I had wanted to be for so long.

* * *

John was bare-chested when he pulled me against the hard erection in his pants. He turned me on so much, he drove me crazy. I had been aroused and completely naked for a while now. My patience was reaching its limit. I wanted him inside me; it was the only thing that would satiate me. However, it looked like he wasn't quite ready as he was pushing my hand away anytime I tried to unzip his pants. The captain in him wanted to stay in control.

His piercing eyes were observing my reactions. They didn't

miss a thing. He strongly held on to my chin so that I would stop moving. I could no longer think.

Intrigued with my body, he moved his mouth toward my throat, then my chest. I could feel his beard softly grazing my skin. He was savoring me, sensually yet forcefully lifting me toward him. Seeing him devour me that way, I had an uncontrollable urge to dig my fingernails into his back.

"Take me now, John."

As soon as I had expressed my wish, John stopped and stared at me. A second passed. Maybe two. He softly smiled, moved his handsome face closer to mine, and kissed me. He was making me wait but I knew very well what was coming. His lips were hypnotizing and while I was letting my imagination run wild, he moved away and stood up next to the bed. He was admiring me. I did the same. I could feel his desire grow more and more intense. He then undid his jeans, letting them fall to the ground. He moved his body closer to mine, his mouth closer to mine, and finally fulfilled me. Hallelujah!

* * *

The sun had just risen and a soft pink light glimmered through the room. I hadn't been dreaming. John was there, next to me, gently holding me. I had no desire to leave, but I had to. The longer I stayed with him, the more intense the feeling of being his mistress would become. I turned and watched him sleep. I knew that this privileged moment between us would probably be the last. I tenderly placed my lips on his as a good-bye and silently slipped out of bed. I put my clothes on and tiptoed to my room.

I would have liked to know what was going to happen next but had preferred leaving on the sly to avoid asking him. I had been his lover for a night; I had no right to ask for more. I felt no regret. Not yet. And I hoped John wouldn't feel any remorse. The softness of his kiss didn't lie, but still, I wanted his confirmation. I had a flight to operate with him; all I needed was to wait for the right moment to talk to him about it . . . that is, of course, as long as he showed up.

Chapter 21

Dublin (DUB) – Boston (BOS)

We had started our last drinks service before landing in Boston. I had been walking on air the whole flight through. That morning, when we had arrived in the lobby, John had asked if I had slept well. When he heard me respond "marvelously well," he had smiled and answered that so had he. His eyes were glimmering, so were mine. I felt triumphant, but conscious that I hadn't won in any way, and wouldn't ever win.

Nevertheless, I wanted to make the most of the happiness the night had provided me with and to avoid any awkwardness between us, I had chosen another position on the plane and had worked in economy with Megan. My passengers were spoiled with my extreme joy as I was smiling and laughing away with them, and was attending to their every need. I was on the verge of frenzy. That fact was confirmed when I had to serve them what irritated me the most: tomato juice.

"What would you like to drink?" I asked the man in seat 18A, by the window.

"What do you have?"

Normally, that question would have really annoyed me. *Seriously? This is the third time I've been down the aisle in six hours. I still have the same selection as the time before, and the time before that, and the time before the time before that!* Then, I would have exasperatedly smiled at the man, rapidly listing some of the items: "Water, juices, sodas, coffee, and tea." However, that day, it was different.

"I have a few juices, some sodas, water, coffee, and tea" I slowly said.

"What kind of sodas do you have?" he pressed on.

"7UP, Pepsi, Ginger Ale, Diet Pepsi."

"And what kind of juice?"

Normally, I would have hastily presented him with two choices: apple and orange. I would have, obviously, omitted to mention the tomato juice, knowing very well the inevitable aftermath. Strangely, that day was different.

"I have apple, orange, and tomato juice."

"Ah! I'll have a tomato juice, then," declared Mr. A.

"Very well." I smiled.

I served the chosen liquid without a word and offered it to him. I continued on to his neighbors.

"And for you?" I asked the couple seated in B and C.

"Hm, why not have some tomato juice? One each!"

Still on cloud nine, I served them two glasses of tomato juice, spattering a bit on my white shirt. I wiped the couple drops with a cloth without worrying too much about it and handed the glasses over to Mrs. B and Mr. C. Then, I moved on to the passenger seated across, in the middle section of the cabin.

"What would you like to drink?"

"A tomato juice," said the young lady at 18D.

"All right, one tomato juice coming right up!" I said, officially announcing that we had tomato juice on board the aircraft.

I poured some more tomato juice and handed it to Miss D. I then attended to the old man seated behind her.

"What would you like to drink?"

"A tomato juice," he answered.

Still unfazed, I started pouring the liquid. Suddenly, my tomato juice carton was empty, leaving me with a glass half full. Normally, I would have sighed and advised the passenger that I was out of tomato juice in my cart, offering him an apple juice instead. This time, though, I chose the hard-work option.

"Megan, do you have tomato juice?" I asked my colleague.

"No, I just finished it."

It was most likely due to my public announcement. I still had time, without even having to lie, to advise Mr. 19 that I was out of tomato juice. But no! I had decided to overcome all obstacles. I called out to my colleague in the other aisle:

"Diane!"

No reaction.

"Diane! Diane! Diane!"

She was not hearing me at all. I should have known. She was always lost, that one. I called out to her colleague:

"Erik!"

He turned toward me. I quietly mouthed my request: *tomato juice*. I had finally gotten a reality check and had realized that those words should not be pronounced out loud. Erik understood my request and discreetly passed a carton of the precious liquid over. I served Mr. 19 and came back down to Earth.

How will I talk to John? What am I gonna say to him? I couldn't ask anything of him, nothing he hadn't already given me. I finished the service and decided not to attempt anything. I had already done enough anyway. *And, if John wants me, he can just tell me.*

* * *

"What did you buy for fifty dollars?" asked the customs officer.

"Olive oil and a sweater."

"That's all?" she insisted, with an investigatory tone implying, *I don't believe you, you air hostess traveling all around the world!*

"Yes," I confirmed.

She wrote a cryptic code on my declaration card and handed it back to me. I had never successfully deciphered the meaning of all the fateful codes. I went down to the baggage area and then out the exit. Luckily, I didn't get searched. I was walking quickly since John had gone through customs before me. We still hadn't said a word to each other. Only smiles, which probably didn't mean anything. He was just a few yards ahead of me and walked slowly. Perhaps he was waiting for me? Either way, I was on his heels.

When we got to the employee bus, we were alone. *What a fortunate coincidence!* I thought. We would have time to talk. We sat across from each other. I was nervous. What would I say to him? *John, I want more . . . ?* And then what? *I want to be your mistress and always come second?* Was that what I really wanted? No! Of course not!

Just as the door was about to close, I saw Sebastian, the first officer, come on board. *Ah, dammit! He's gonna ruin everything!* He sat next to John and started chatting with him.

"Wow! What a nice flight! Not a hint of turbulence! We even managed to land early."

"Yeah," John answered simply, looking at me.

"When are you working again?" asked Sebastian.

"A week from now," he answered, without throwing the question back at him.

Ah! That Sebastian guy is annoying! I shrugged at John to indicate my indifference toward his first officer's words. He inconspicuously smiled at me.

"Yeah, you're lucky to have a week off. I work again tomorrow," went on Sebastian.

"Oh, yeah, that's too bad," said John, impartial.

"And, above all, I'm going back to Dublin!"

"Hm."

Quite evidently, my captain's mind was elsewhere. And seeing him stare at me, I knew very well where it was. Sebastian, not noticing a thing, continued with his monologue. I was just hoping that John would get off at the same stop as me so that we could finally talk.

When we arrived in the parking area, he was still intensely staring at me. He took advantage of his work partner's short moment of distraction to flash one last smile. A smile full of hopelessness. And then, ever so discreetly, he moved his lips to say something. *You're beautiful*, he mouthed. From that, I understood that he didn't regret a thing. I sealed my lips to indicate there wasn't anything more to say. He had his life, and I couldn't be part of it. I didn't want to be. Not that way.

The bus made a first stop. The door opened but no one got out. Then I realized that sooner rather than later it would be my stop, or his. Who knew when I'd see him again? In a month, six months, a year, maybe two? I had no idea. And it saddened me.

The bus abruptly halted at the second stop. It was mine. John remained seated. I wanted to stay on the bus and accompany him to his car but I was already standing. I didn't want to raise any suspicion. Sebastian also got up. He waved to us both and quickly got off. I then realized my opportunity to sit back down. I hesitated. It was no longer up to me to trigger anything. I had done my part.

I said bye to John the way a simple colleague does and made my way to the exit. But before I could make it, the door closed in front of me. The driver hadn't seen me and was getting ready to drive off again. *Go back to your seat, Scarlett! It's a sign!* said the little voice. *Scarlett, it's up to him to make a move now. Leave!* advised the other voice. I was still hesitating. *Get out!* commanded the last voice.

"Excuse me! Sir! I'd like to get off! Open the door!" I yelled from the middle of the bus.

John was still observing me silently. He smiled at me one more time and watched me get off the bus, my head low.

As I set foot outside, I felt an extreme emptiness wash over me. The one and only man I had been obsessed with for so long was, again, getting far away from me. I didn't know when I would see him again. I wasn't ready to count the days or the months before seeing my handsome captain again. Neither was I ready to go through another detox to try and get over him. I had to face the facts: I was hungry for John's love. I wanted to taste every inch of his body, drink his every thought, his every word. I had just left him, yet his absence seemed unbearable. I had had enough of waiting around. I had to find a cure to my pain. From then on, only my own well-being mattered. Living another year without him was out of the question. No thanks!

* * *

When I came through the door, Becky was waiting impatiently. She had left me two voicemails, begging me to call her as soon as I landed so that I could tell her everything that had happened. I had promised to tell her everything once I got home, which is what I did. After many long and detailed explanations, Becky gave me a big hug, pretty much congratulating me for having broken my convictions and having followed my heart. She was proud of me. As for me, I didn't really know what to think. I only knew that I still had John under my skin and was determined to quench my thirst. I asked my best friend for advice:

"Becky, what should I do now?"

"Do you think he wants to see you again?"

"I don't know. For now, the only thing I'm certain of is that I want more."

"You have to talk to him and tell him how you feel."

"What is that gonna change in this whole situation?"

"Well, Scarlett! You just told me you wanted more. He's married and will probably stay married. But if you want more, you have to find out if he does as well. And then, I don't know . . . you'll see when you get there, right?"

"You're right," I conceded.

"Do you have his phone number?"

"Nope."

Becky considered my options.

"Well, there's always his work email," she informed me.

"Yes! How do I find out what it is?"

"Nothing easier! It's our full name, separated by a dot, and followed by @americair.com."

"Great! You're awesome, Becky!" I exclaimed, sitting down in front of my laptop.

Where would I start? *I miss you, John? I'm considering becoming your mistress? I'm throwing my principles and my code of conduct out the window for you?* I decided to let my heart speak. It often provided the best results. Once I had finished drafting the email, I read it to Becky.

To: John Ross <john.ross@americair.com>
From: Scarlett Lambert <scarlettlambert@gmail.com>
Date: July 7, 2017
Subject: . . .
Hi John,
I'm not sure if I'm crossing the line in writing you this email. I tried not to do it but, really, I couldn't help it. I waited a whole year to see you again and frankly, I don't want to wait another one. I'm shaken in the same way I was after seeing you in Paris and Barcelona. But this time feels worse because I know what I'm missing.
I think of you and wonder: Will we ever live a night together like that again?
Scarlett

I immediately looked at Becky, hoping to get her approval.
"Excellent! It's moving, yet straight to the point," she assured me.
"Ah, really?"
"Yes! Go, send it!" she ordered.
"Are you sure?" I still hesitated.
"YES! A hundred percent sure! Send!"
I hovered the mouse over the send button. I closed my eyes, hoped I wasn't making a huge mistake, and clicked the fateful button.

Chapter 22

Lyon (LYS)

C rying. It is just so exhausting! Especially when one cries many times a day, for a month. And that's exactly what I had just done: cried my eyes out for a man. For that John Ross who didn't even bother kindly replying to my message. *Bastard! Men... they're all the same!* I had thought a thousand times. *As soon as they get what they want, they just ditch you* . . . I was completely destroyed but didn't really have the right to be. Regardless of having spent only one night with him, I was going through a heartbreak. And, my sad state had bad timing since I had been flying non-stop for a month, to destinations that weren't the best, which made the matter worse every day. I hit rock bottom a month after having sent my unreplied-to email.

We had just landed in Lyon, France. I hated that destination and had tried everything I could to avoid seeing the letters LYS appear on my schedule. I hadn't succeeded. The reason for my hatred had nothing to do with the city itself. Not at all. The food in Lyon was delicious and so were the Rhône wines. My disdain was actually rooted in the hotel we slept in: the Château

Perrache.

To be honest, I thought it was haunted. Many spooky stories were being told about it around the airline. Some colleagues said they had seen a woman watching them in the middle of the night, some had caught a glimpse of a shadow in the television screen, while others had woken up to find that objects weren't where they had been left. All I knew was that the hotel terrified me so much I was never able to fall asleep.

My urge to cry surfaced again when I entered the hotel's main hall that day. Half of my sadness was caused by a man and the other half was due to the horrifying hotel itself. The place scared the shit out of me. And with reason! It had been requisitioned by German authorities during World War II for its Gestapo siege. According to history, the room in which I was going to sleep might have witnessed many interrogations of Hitler's opposing party members. Worse, a Jew may have been tortured or even killed in that room. My imagination was playing up again.

I got into the shower. I smelled like aircraft and had to purify myself. Under the water, I could think, or rather, scold myself again: *Scarlett, you should have known that John wasn't going to reply. Why would he? He can't. Never could. He only let himself be tempted that evening in Dublin because you were physically there. And a little bit of alcohol had contributed to your success. That's all. You have to forget him now. He's a thing of the past. At least you had a little taste.*

That's what the problem was! I had had a taste. I had touched his lips, his body. I had felt a passion that had made me feel so good I couldn't stop thinking about it. My desire had only grown since. I was far from satiated like I had imagined I would be. I knew that one could be addicted to Pepsi but I hadn't realized that I would be even more obsessed with John, my own Pepsi, as soon as I had consumed him. I was madly enamored. As I turned the water off, I started crying for the thousandth time.

When I set my foot down on the bathmat, my attention was immediately drawn to the steamed mirror facing me. Typical of any horror movie. Suddenly, I hallucinated an invisible finger tracing a heart on the water vapor. More tears came rushing out. Why me? At that moment, I wished I had never met John. Ever!

Night came, I tried to sleep, but in vain. I couldn't manage to fall asleep. Perhaps it was because I had left the light on? I didn't want to turn it off, fearing the darkness. The hot August air was suffocating and the air conditioning wasn't cooling the room down. I decided to get up and wander down to the main hall in my pajamas.

The hallways' ancient wooden floors were cracking under my steps. I had the impression of being followed by someone. I accelerated the pace and reached the front desk in no time. Not really knowing how to kill time, and since the hotel's Wi-Fi wasn't complimentary, I decided to use their free Internet.

"Good evening, monsieur, is it still possible to use the computers at this time?" I asked the man at reception.

"Of course, madam," he answered, before showing me to the minuscule business center.

I thought I would browse travel blogs and daydream a little to take my mind off things, but first I decided to check my emails. I most likely wouldn't have any new messages since I had just checked my mailbox before leaving the airport, but it had become a habit to check any time I was in front of a screen.

I logged in to my email account. To my biggest surprise, it showed two new messages. I stopped breathing. At last, a message from John! Even better: two! My heart started pumping excessively fast and I started sweating. I hadn't even read anything yet and I was already happy. I finally had an answer! No matter what it was, I would accept it. I opened the first message.

From: John Ross <john.ross@americair.com>
To: Scarlett Lambert <scarlettlambert@gmail.com>
Date: August 14, 2017
Subject: Re: . . .
Scarlett,
I read your email just as I'm about to get on a flight.
Apologies for the delay, I only look at my work emails once a month. To answer your message, yes, I am still deeply moved by our evening together, and yes, I do think of you. I hadn't planned what happened between us and the last thing I want is to hurt you, or give you false hopes that would hurt you even more. My children are my priority and I should have controlled myself to avoid all of this.
Easy, you might say, but it wasn't the case. You showed up in my life out of the blue, for a reason I still ignore. But believe me, I had a lot to lose in this story and I am taking full responsibility.
Scarlett, I hope to see you again soon to tell you all of this in person. I'm thinking of you and wish you all the happiness you deserve.
John

I was relieved. His answer wasn't what I had hoped for but I had to accept it. I appreciated that John had mentioned his concerns about our impossible situation. He couldn't give me more. I didn't blame him. At the very least, I knew he was thinking about me and had taken the time to respond. In fact, he had done so as soon as he had read my message, as opposed to what I had previously assumed. I read his email three times. And then I suddenly remembered I had another one. How could I have forgotten? With no further ado, I read it carefully.

From: John Ross <j.ross.dublin@gmail.com>
To: Scarlett Lambert <scarlettlambert@gmail.com>
Date: August 15, 2017
Subject: Thoughts
Scarlett,
All through my flight across the ocean, I thought of you. I want to know your every thought. I imagine we'll probably be seeing each other within a year.
John

He wanted to know *my every thought?* We would *probably* see each other within a year? I had been waiting for this moment for a month and now that I finally had what I had asked for, I didn't know what to say. Actually, all I had to do was answer his request. Simply.

From: Scarlett Lambert <scarlettlambert@gmail.com>
To: John Ross < j.ross.dublin@gmail.com >
Date: August 15, 2017
Subject: Re: Thoughts
Hi John,
You wanted to know my every thought, so here we go . . .
Since we spent the night together, I have not stopped thinking about you. A month later, I hear back from you. I had come to terms with the fact that that night with you would be the only one and that it was best that way. Even though I know it's best not to take things further, I am convinced that next time I see

you, it'll be the same all over again. We will want each just other as much.

I completely agree with the fact that you have everything to lose in this situation and wouldn't want to ruin your life, nor your family's.

You are speaking in code so I'm not entirely sure of what you really want from me. Your first message is clear: You will not leave your wife for me. I know that and wouldn't want it anyway. So, the real question is: What do YOU want? Your second message implies that you still want me. I want you too . .
.

I will be waiting for your reply.

Scarlett

As I pressed send, my heart filled with happiness. I had no idea what his reply would be but I knew that John sincerely wanted to see me again. And I wanted to see him too. I was looking forward to seeing him and kissing him. But only time would tell. That night, I went back to bed feeling at peace and finally slept like a baby. Upon my return to Boston, I found another message from John in my mailbox. That message was the first of many that would succeed in making me even crazier about him. And maybe him crazy about me?

From: John Ross <j.ross.dublin@gmail.com>
To: Scarlett Lambert <scarlettlambert@gmail.com>
Date: August 16, 2017
Subject: Re: Re: Thoughts
Scarlett,
I realize that you are not happy in this situation and must apologize again for having made you wait a whole month to find

out. Please know that the whole story upsets me as much as it upsets you and that all I know right now is that I want you and I have fun with you. It's the first time I've cheated on my wife and I have to deal with that fact. I have always avoided putting myself in complicated situations. I really don't want to hurt you but I want to see you again because I know it'll be even better than last time. Am I making myself clear now?

John

From: Scarlett Lambert <scarlettlambert@gmail.com>
To: John Ross < j.ross.dublin@gmail.com >
Date: August 17, 2017
Subject: Crystal Clear
Hi John,
Thank you for apologizing for having made me wait a whole month. :) It is now much clearer.
When shall I see you again?
Scarlett

From: John Ross <j.ross.dublin@gmail.com>
To: Scarlett Lambert <scarlettlambert@gmail.com>
Date: August 16, 2017
Subject: Chat?
I'd like to hear your voice . . . Can we talk?
If that's okay with you, I'd like to give you a call tonight. What's your number?
John

Oh, hold on! Weren't we supposed to fix a date just to have some fun in bed? And now John was admitting to wanting to hear my voice! I was confused. I was dying to talk to him but felt a bit too fragile to venture into such intimacy. If we started exchanging daily emails and phone calls, would I still be able to content myself with a simple physical relationship? I doubted it. Nevertheless, as I also wanted to hear his voice, I gave him my phone number. As planned, I received his call that night.

"Hi, Scarlett."

"Hi, John," I answered shyly, my heart beating like crazy.

"How was your day?"

"Pretty good. I went down to the Charles River to hang out in the sun with my friend Becky. And you?"

"I went swimming with the kids."

"Ah, I see. And your wife?" I blurted out, not thinking.

"She's away for work. Can we talk about something else?"

"Of course!"

I didn't know why I had brought up the subject right at the beginning of our conversation. What a horrible mistake! I had made up my mind. Sex for sex. Nothing more. Doubts and guilt had no reason to be. It was too late now anyway. I changed the subject.

"When do you think we can see each other again?"

"Well, I had a look at your schedule and I don't see how it could work out with mine in the next week. You're working a lot and so am I," he said, disappointed.

"Yeah, I know."

"I think it's best we ask for the same flights for next month . . . "

"Good idea! Let's do that," I confirmed, happy that such an option was possible.

"Let's keep in touch, then, beautiful Scarlett."

"You know the right thing to say to make me blush, huh?"

"It wasn't my intention. I truly believe you are beautiful. I have an exquisite image of you in my head. Of you in my bed in Dublin," he continued, his voice deep and powerful.

"Oh! And you think I don't have one of you?"

"I hope you do. It'll keep your mind busy until our next encounter."

"Don't you worry about that."

"And mine will stay busy thinking about you."

His last statement provided me with a real sense of comfort. But what about his relationship with his wife? What was going to happen in their bed? I was jealous. I tried not to show it. As we finished our conversation, my desire to see him had gone up a notch. It was a bad sign.

* * *

The day after our phone conversation, I received a new message. John was so charming and caring. Without realizing it, he was getting closer and closer to my ideal man. Yet the situation was far from ideal. It felt like I had fallen into quicksand and couldn't pull myself out even if, for the time being, I was only ankle-deep. I was already unable to come to my senses and stop communication with him. I wanted more.

From: John Ross <j.ross.dublin@gmail.com>
To: Scarlett Lambert <scarlettlambert@gmail.com>
Date: August 18, 2017
Subject: Paris
Good morning,
Happy to have spoken to you last night. I had lovely dreams thinking about you . . .

Try to ask for Paris for the month of September. With your seniority, you should be able to get it. Otherwise, Lyon.

John

From: Scarlett Lambert <scarlettlambert@gmail.com>
To: John Ross < j.ross.dublin@gmail.com >
Date: August 19, 2017
Subject: Not Lyon!
Hi John,
I asked for Paris but not Lyon. I hate the hotel there! It's too hot, the air conditioning doesn't work, and it's full of ghosts . . .
I hope Paris will work out.
Speak soon,
Scarlett

From: John Ross <j.ross.dublin@gmail.com>
To: Scarlett Lambert <scarlettlambert@gmail.com>
Date: August 20, 2017
Subject: Oh! Oh!
I'll protect you, beautiful Scarlett. But if you don't like Lyon, that's fine. Paris it shall be. I'm leaving for Istanbul tonight. I will write you from Turkey. :)
Take care,
John

From: Scarlett Lambert <scarlettlambert@gmail.com>
To: John Ross < j.ross.dublin@gmail.com >
Date: August 23, 2017
Subject: Schedule
I got my schedule and have two Paris but you aren't on my flights. We'll have to find another solution. You didn't write

since you've left. I don't like it . . .
Scarlett

From: John Ross <j.ross.dublin@gmail.com>
To: Scarlett Lambert <scarlettlambert@gmail.com>
Date: August 24, 2017
Subject: News
Hi,
I see that you're waiting to hear from me on a daily basis . . .
and so am I! The cost of Wi-Fi at the hotel was horrendous so I
decided to do without it for a day and make you wait. :)
That's too bad about Paris. Are you free on the 28th?
Sleep tight and take care,
John

From: Scarlett Lambert <scarlettlambert@gmail.com>
To: John Ross < j.ross.dublin@gmail.com >
Date: August 25, 2017
Subject: :)
Hi,
I forgive you for making me wait. I'm used to it now.
I hope your flight went well. Istanbul is so nice, isn't it?
I'm also disappointed about Paris and am not free on the 28th.
Maybe it's for the best . . .
Scarlett

From: John Ross <j.ross.dublin@gmail.com>
To: Scarlett Lambert <scarlettlambert@gmail.com>
Date: August 25, 2017
Subject: For the best?
Do you really think what you've just written? I don't.

Let me suggest something else then. I'm flying to Rome for 72 hours in the middle of the month. Come with me? I saw that you had the days off . . .

John

What an interesting offer! Rome, my favorite city! And so romantic . . . I was indeed free to go with him. However, I was hesitant. Leaving with him would also mean lying the whole way there and hiding the truth from the rest of the crew. Once in Rome, we would have to be careful so that nobody saw us. Not to mention that I'd be spending three full days with him. What if he couldn't stand me anymore after two hours? Worse, what if those three days made me fall even deeper in love with him? I had to take time and consider the situation before making an informed decision. Therefore, I stayed quiet for a few days which, curiously, drove John crazier than I could have imagined.

From: John Ross <j.ross.dublin@gmail.com>
To: Scarlett Lambert <scarlettlambert@gmail.com>
Date: August 30, 2017
Subject: My turn to wait
Scarlett,
You're running through my mind way more than you know. Although we haven't seen each other again, I think about you every day, honestly. Do you think being in this situation is easy for me? Hell no! You're really making me pay for that first month by not responding and making me wait. You should know that I'm not playing games with you. I want to see you and am trying my best to do so.
I'm still waiting for your answer about Rome.
John xxx

From: Scarlett Lambert <scarlettlambert@gmail.com>
To: John Ross < j.ross.dublin@gmail.com >
Date: August 30, 2017
Subject: Rome
Hi John,
You're on my mind as well, in case you were wondering.
No, I'm not trying to make you pay for anything. I'm not
playing games either, but let's not forget that our first encounter
was all about a physical connection, nothing more. And now it
looks like it's heading into a different direction. I don't want
to be part of it. I thought you were the one who had made that
clear from the beginning.
I haven't made up my mind about Rome yet. I looked at your
crew and I know pretty much everyone on it. We'd have to be
careful not to arouse any suspicion.
On the other hand, if I go, it'll be perfect for us to make the
most of each other, as much as we want . . .
I'll get back to you . . .
Scarlett xxx

For days, I wasn't able to give him a definitive answer. And then
Becky successfully reasoned with me:
"Scarlett, you've been dreaming about John for too long. Go to
Rome, otherwise you'll always wonder *what if* and you'll regret
it," she advised.
"I know, Becky, but I'm scared."
"Of what?"
"Of coming back even crazier about him. I don't want to be
his mistress or a stepmom or a homewrecker."
"Nobody wants that, Scarlett, but don't you want to be
spending three dreamy days with the one who's been haunting

you for a whole year?"

"Yes . . . "

"So go! Go with him. Let him treat you like a princess and enjoy it. Then, if you don't want to embark on a roller coaster, you'll have to break it off. Because if you go any further, you're gonna be the one getting hurt," she recommended.

"You're right. Break ties, that's what I'll do! But only after Rome," I answered, convinced I'd be strong enough to do so when the time came.

I picked up the phone and called John. I had made up my mind. I would go to Rome with him!

Chapter 23

Boston (BOS)

"Ladies and gentlemen, this is a general boarding announcement for Americair flight 762 to Rome. We now invite all passengers to please make their way to gate C14."

It seems early to start boarding . . . departure is scheduled for ten p.m. I look at my watch. Oh! Actually, it is time. I hadn't noticed the minutes ticking away. Obviously distracted.

If we stick to the plan, I will be flying to Italy on this warm, starry September night with my handsome captain. I'm nervous and, honestly, I'm no longer sure of what to do. When I got to the airport earlier, I immediately proceeded to terminal A. John was waiting for me on a bench. It was unlikely that we'd run into our colleagues as Americair doesn't operate from that area.

I had been excited to see him again. Upon spotting him, I got weak in the knees for the thousandth time.

"Hi, John."

"Ah! Beautiful Scarlett" he sighed.

I sat next to him, our bodies not touching. He rested a hand onto mine, smiling. I blushed.

"You're gonna have to get used to it. You'll be seeing me for the next three days," he gently teased.

"I know, I'm just nervous, that's all."

"Don't worry, everything will be fine," he assured me, squeezing my hand.

"You really believe that? John, we barely know each other. What if this doesn't go down the way we think and you end up hating me after an hour?"

"Impossible!" he exclaimed, without a hint of doubt.

John gives off such confidence that all my worries disappear when I talk to him. Close to him, I feel reassured. Far from him, it's the opposite: I panic. I'm scared to give him my heart only to see him refuse to give me his. I didn't want to vocalize my fears and so had simply smiled. He had moved his face close to mine and we had kissed tenderly.

"I have to get to the aircraft, Scarlett. I'll see you in Rome. The next seven hours will be the longest of my whole career as a pilot!" he said before leaving.

I had briefly remained seated on that bench, lost in thought. Seeing John had provided me with such overwhelming happiness, but as physical distance grew between us, I had started to feel the polar opposite. His departure had reminded me of the brutal reality. Four days from now, I would suffer from his absence the same way I had for a year and during the month I was waiting for his reply. Would I return from Rome shattered or finally satiated? I shouldn't speculate too much.

After our brief encounter, I had made my way to the crew room in order to pick up my standby ticket. When I pushed open the door, a few crew members were still there. I knew them and it proved quite difficult to go unnoticed.

"Hi, Scarlett!" called out Diane, the insomniac flight attendant.

"Hi!"

"Hey! Hello!" added Todd, the handsome green-eyed cabin crew, grabbing his carry-on.

"Hello, Todd!" I greeted, happy to see him yet remembering that our last flight together had been back when I had met a particular Freaky-Debbie.

"Where are you going?" asked Diane, curious as ever.

"Rome. I'm going to visit a friend for three days," I lied.

Once again, I had betrayed my principles as I, Scarlett Lambert, never lie. It looked like John had unwittingly messed with my personal value system, since coming up with a reason for my trip happened quite naturally. I was almost convinced that I actually was going to Italy to visit a friend. After grabbing my ticket, I wished my colleagues a great flight and went down to Americair's check-in counter.

With my boarding pass in hand, I then went through security. While walking down terminal C, I started doubting again, scolding myself, feeling guilty. *Scarlett, do you realize that you're going away with a colleague's husband? Normally you're a reasonably good person but now, well, you're not being good at all.*

I don't want to feel bad for following my heart, which I have the right to do. But the situation is still very hard for me to accept. What if I really fall in love with John in Rome? Because, let's admit it, the probabilities are incredibly high. Would I then be able to cut off all ties like Becky recommended? I didn't dare answer that question.

I am now seated in gate C14's waiting area and refuse to budge. I settled in on a seat far from the other passengers. This way, I can ponder away: Do I board the plane or not? With my legs shaking, I observe my surroundings. Among the crowd I find Italians. So many Italians. They talk loudly, are agitated, and seem unable to sit still even for a moment. What a surprise! For an instant, at the very least, they amuse me and allow me to forget about my concerns.

I turn my head toward the aircraft. My gaze quickly finds the flight deck. From my uncomfortable seat, I catch a glimpse of the open window on the pilot's side. A light beam emerges from it, outlining a man's profile. My captain is there, a few meters away from me. There are only hundreds of passengers, a desk, a ground agent, a bridge, and ten years of our lives separating us. I don't know what to do. I won't be over him after Rome. I can feel it. I'm absolutely convinced of it.

Boarding was just announced. A line of people makes its way down to where I'm sitting. I remain where I am. I'm not ready. I need more time to think this through. I've always dreamed of starting a family, having kids, and being with the same man for my whole life. Getting on that airplane tonight won't give me any of that. How could I have thought I'd be happy in such a situation? Of course, I could go to Rome and make the most of John for three days. But then I'd come back a wreck. If I love him as much as I think I do, I'm going to ask for more. I will want him to be all mine and mine only. Yet being with him would also mean becoming a stepmother to the two children he conceived with another woman. I am obviously way ahead of myself. John, on his end, must only be thinking about getting in bed with me. Why can't I, just for once in my life, think like a man and simply live, one step at a time? The ground agent is talking into her microphone.

"Ladies and gentlemen, this is the final boarding call for all passengers traveling to Rome on Americair flight 762. Please make your way to gate C14 immediately. Final call!"

I must hurry: What do I do? There's no way I'm setting foot

on that plane with this much hesitation. Knowing myself, if I'm not absolutely convinced of having made the right decision, I will end up ruining our adventure in Rome. *Breathe, Scarlett, and close your eyes.* Now I'm in the dark. *Concentrate!*

I am picturing our story. The story of John and Scarlett. I remember the first time I saw him in Costa Rica. He appeared so out of reach. I have wanted him since that very first day. A year and a half later, sitting in this airport, I can finally get what I wished for. I just have to board that plane to find out where destiny will take us. It's time for me to trust in life. There's no point in wanting to control everything, in knowing everything ahead of time just to try and protect myself. I have to live this story through to the end, otherwise I will regret it for the rest of my life. A woman's voice is being heard again.

"We are asking Ms. Scarlett Lambert to please proceed to gate C14 immediately. Thank you."

I open my eyes and look at the woman behind the desk. The waiting area is now empty. I jump up. My legs have become as strong as steel. My mind is clear. I am boarding this plane and no one can stop me. Nobody. I hand my boarding pass over.

"Ms. Lambert?" asks the ground agent, grabbing my ticket.

"Yes, it's me, sorry for the delay," I say, smiling.

"No problem, Ms. Lambert. The captain just advised me that he wasn't leaving without you. Do you know him?"

"Yes, I do. We're going to Rome together."

About the Author

ELIZABETH LANDRY is a French Canadian writer, a blogger and a flight attendant. In 2010, she created the blog www.lhotessedelair.com to write about her job at 36 000 feet in the air. It quickly led to a publishing contract with a major Canadian editor. Her work has since been presented in various TV and radio shows across Canada and France. CALL ME STEWARDESS is the English translation of the first volume of her successful trilogy.

To follow the author:
WWW.LHOTESSEDELAIR.COM
Instagram: @LHOTESSEDELAIR
Her shop: WWW.BOUTIQUEFLYWITHME.COM

Made in the USA
Columbia, SC
13 November 2021

48881417R00162